Margaret Elphinstone has worked as a writer and a gardener in various parts of Scotland. She is the author of two novels, *The Incomer* (The Women's Press 1987) and *A Sparrow's Flight* (Polygon 1989). She has also published two gardening books, *The Green Gardener's Handbook* (Thorsons 1987, co-author Julia Langley), and *Organic Gardening* (Greenprint 1990), as well as editing an anthology of garden poetry. She has published poetry and short stories, including *Spinning the Green*, in *Despatches from the Frontiers of the Female Mind* (The Women's Press 1986), and her first poetry collection, *Outside Eden* (Sundial Press 1990). She is currently working on her third novel, and teaches English Studies at Strathclyde University. She has two daughters and lives in Edinburgh.

MARGARET ELPHINSTONE

An Apple from a Tree

and Other Visions

The Women's Press

First published by The Women's Press Limited, 1991
A member of the Namara Group
34 Great Sutton Street,
London, EC1V 0DX.

An earlier version of *Conditions of Employment* appeared in
Chapman (Edinburgh, 1989).

British Library Cataloguing in Publication Data
Elphinstone, Margaret
   An apple from a tree
   I. Title
   823.914 [F]

   ISBN 0–7043–4281–2

Typeset by M.C Typeset Ltd, Gillingham, Kent.
Printed and bound in Great Britain by Cox & Wyman,
Reading, Berks

For Katy

Contents

Green Man

1

The most human feature of the valley was the railway. It emerged from a cutting between the hills and swept out above the bogland on a narrow embankment, the loch lying to the north of it. All that was left of the halt was a rusted shed, ramshackle and crazily tilted, by the solid little bridge that spanned the burn. A smaller burn flowed out of the loch, and the two, conjoined, wound their way through heather-tufted marshland, round the long green curve of Airie Hill. Drifts of trees fell across the northern slopes like blown leaves, winnowed away from the bare bones of the hills. There seemed no reason why anyone should have stopped here. Forgotten passengers on the ghost of a departed railway, shooting-parties in tweeds and brogues, solitary salmon fishers in season, shepherds who dropped off here to cover the grazings on these hills which no farm or cottage overlooked. There was nothing else here, nor ever had been. Lochskerrow Halt. A name on a map which lent it meaning only by the dotted line where there was once a railway. The cuttings remained, the long embankments, the grey shingle that crunched under feet that followed the tracks of the departed trains. People once looked out on these hills, incurious eyes strayed over the blank marshland, travellers munching sandwiches glanced out of carriage windows, yawning, and perhaps read a sign that gave a label and a meaning to this place – Lochskerrow Halt. An incident on a journey, a milestone, marking time between Dumfries and Stranraer, a short pause between a beginning and an end.

The only traveller today was a young woman. She walked

steadily along the track of the railway, hiking boots scrunching on the clinkers. She had joined the railway at Mossdale, after it crossed the viaduct, and now she walked purposefully westwards towards Gatehouse of Fleet, Creetown, Newton Stewart, Stranraer and Portpatrick. She wore a capacious green anorak with a turned-down velveteen collar of the kind they sell in agricultural stores. In her pockets she carried a map and compass, and in the grey rucksack on her back she had brought food, chocolate, a spare jumper. An efficient and determined person, a person with a destination in view, who had not strayed into this territory idly; a woman who had a day to herself, and who had already decided where she was going.

After Mossdale the railway crossed a small loch by way of another viaduct and then took the traveller by a straight, elevated route over stretches of marshland. Then it enclosed her within a deep cutting, where briars and broom and elder bowed over her from steep banks. The railway emerged again, skirted the long slopes of the hill, with quiet vistas of hillsides to the north blanketed with spruce trees. She passed a track on the left, a last house, but the railway went on regardless and she followed. For a foot-passenger the hill was long, and the curve of the railway, seeking always its own level, described an arc so slow as to be almost imperceptible. The stones were hard underfoot, but here and there other walkers had made little paths on the banks, or the grass was flat and wide enough to walk along beside the tracks. She trudged on and finally the bend was achieved, the hill passed, and the track straightened again, preparatory to crossing over the marsh beside Skerrow Loch. The old railway shed loomed ahead of her. She stopped and consulted the map. Lochskerrow Halt. As remote a station as one could find in Britain, apparently quite pointless. Only a loch, fringed by brown reeds, and hillsides mottled with the browns of autumn and the dark green of the everlasting spruce.

And a tent. A peculiar tent, a round brown tent, like an upturned pot. And a trickle of smoke that curled away into

blue autumn air. She stared at it. Someone come for the
fishing, or the quiet. Somebody who had a strong desire to be
nowhere, and chose here. But the tent was an odd shape, an
attractive shape, like a breast. She scowled at the thought
which was not one that she had chosen to think, and crossed
the track so that she could see better. The person had camped
right down by the loch. Whoever it was must be stupid, or
immune to midges. She turned to go on.

It was something about the tent, the shape of it, or the
colour. It was not quite like anything that she had seen before.
It certainly didn't come out of any camping catalogue. She
stopped again and stood hesitating on the edge of the railway
track. The fire was on the far side of the tent. It must have
been hard to make a fire; after the rain everything was
soaking. But at least it was safe. There was a gap in the
smoke, a hesitation, then it curled up thickly again, like a
question mark. Someone had laid more fuel on the fire.

She fingered the map in her pocket. Next stop Gatehouse.
She had decided to follow the track. Though the tent was
intriguing, demanding her attention, she never spoke to
strangers. She was confident but not foolhardy. She had
learned self-defence in evening classes last winter. She didn't
want to see any campers, they destroyed the illusion of
perfect loneliness. But campers had orange tents and neat gas
stoves and this tent was neither orange, nor red, nor brown,
though it was almost all of them. The smoke rose steadily
beyond it. The hills lay bare and autumnal under a gentle
September sky. The loch was silent at her feet. It was like a
landscape out of a window, magical, for ever out of reach, a
place glimpsed once and destined never to be named. But it
has a name, and I am standing here, she thought. There is no
roof over my head, I breathe the air that belongs to this place.
She stood there for another minute, then she stepped off the
railway and climbed carefully down the bank.

The tent was pitched on a small green hummock of dry
land, a few feet above the edge of the loch. To reach it she had
to jump from tussock to tussock of lumpy grass, and brown

water oozed and squelched where she had passed. Standing on the shore, she heard no sound but the harsh shiver of a breeze among the dying reed stems and the lap of water on the shore, rippled by a small wind. The tent was big, bigger than it had seemed from above. She felt a pang of sudden anticipation, or fear. All she saw was a tent and smoke, but her stomach registered something alien, another world. She pushed the thought away, and walked quietly round the tent.

The person tending the fire had its back to her; a crouched-down person in what was apparently a cloak of coarse wool, woven into strange intricate patterns of whorls and circles and spirals in curious russet shades, like a maze in autumn. A person – and here she shrank back, with that same pang of anticipation – a person with green hair. She must have moved suddenly, or made some small sound, or possibly the person had been aware of her all the time for, when he looked round, he did not seem at all startled but regarded her with grave interest. Her hands flew to cover her mouth, and her whole body reacted to that sudden fulfilment of fear that seems close to fainting, as if the quiet hills had risen from their foundations and were spinning madly round her. She stood aghast, feeling the blood drain from her cheeks and her heart thud painfully.

He was green.

Completely, uncompromisingly green. The vivid, vibrant green of fresh spinach plants, or bogland grass, or young hawthorn. His hair was thick and green, and hung over his forehead in a green fringe. His skin was green, his eyes were green, even his lips were green. Under the russet cloak he wore strange loose garments of dark green, but his feet were bare – and green. He watched her with gentle interest, and stretched out a green hand to her. She recoiled.

"Sarah," he said.

I am going to faint, she thought, and even in her terror dismissed the idea as soon as she had found words for it. This was not the moment to faint. She took a deep breath and looked at him. The hills subsided, breathless from their crazy spinning, and relapsed into their comfortable places with the familiarity of a million unmoving years. The water still lapped at the shores of the loch behind her, and across the northern hills a curlew called. Only the man in front of her remained unquestionably green. She stared at him, and slowly her brain adjusted to this new reality. Chlorophyll? she wondered, but the question that came out was different.

"How did you know I was Sarah?"

"When I realised you were on your way."

Words failed her, an unusual experience for her. His accent was hard to place, a touch of the local softness, laid over clipped English vowels. Just like hers. Perhaps it was hers. Her brain threatened to start reeling again, and she checked it sharply.

"Who? How . . .? What are you doing here?"

"I am meeting you. It's a great pleasure," he said with maddening formality.

"But you weren't expecting me?"

"Not in so many words, no."

She couldn't take her eyes off him. It was such an exuberant green, not a pale, subdued green that might by some stretch of the imagination verge on sickly white or pink, nor a very dark green that in a certain light might pass for black or brown. It was the greenest of greens, proclaiming itself almost insultingly as a colour in its own right, a living colour that bore no resemblance whatsoever to any colour that human skin was supposed to be. A green man. Sarah shook her head slowly, and stared at him as if she could never encompass what she saw.

"Who are you?" she asked at last, and was annoyed to hear her voice sounded frail and squeaky.

"Not yet," he said. "I hope so, by the end of my journey."

"Hope to what?"

"Who I am," he said. "But perhaps in this country you are already who you are."

"What?"

"Who."

"How," she heard herself say before she could stop, and giggled.

He smiled at her sympathetically. At least his teeth were white. If he were not green, she found herself thinking, he would be extremely attractive. She decided to ask something very simple and specific. "Is this your tent?"

"Yes. Come in."

"Not yet," she said, jumpily. "I was just interested. It looks different."

"It would, naturally."

"Where did you come from?"

"It was the nearest place to here."

"I don't understand."

He seemed puzzled. "It couldn't be otherwise. When you came, you must have come from the nearest place too. There was no other way to pass."

"When I came," said Sarah, slowly and thoughtfully, "I started from my home, which is near Mossdale. Where did you start from?"

"I also started from my home."

"And how near Mossdale is that?"

"Only a thought."

"You live a thought away from Mossdale?"

"As we all do."

"Excuse me," she said. "Don't think me rude, but are you being irritating on purpose?"

"I am trying hard," he said humbly. "Come and eat and drink with me."

"I brought my lunch. We can share it if you like."

"And mine also. It's always the best way to begin."

Begin what? She didn't bother to ask. She was beginning to feel that it would be pointless. He got up, like a cat uncurling itself, and surprised her again. He was tall, over six feet certainly, but his movements were quite unmanlike, feline and graceful, lacking only a certain power or energy that she had subconsciously expected. He drew back the tent flap and disappeared inside. Sarah came a little closer to the fire. It was very neatly made, and had been packed over with turfs like a charcoal burner's oven, with only the thin spiral of smoke curling out at the top. She gazed down at the uncoiling smoke as if it held an answer.

When he reappeared he held a round pot in one hand, and a plate in the other, both reddish and covered with more of the swirling designs in autumn colours. He laid them down, and spread his cloak on the grass in front of the tent.

"Please sit down."

She sat down self-consciously, feeling that she was taking her part in some ceremony which had not previously been explained to her, and wondering if her part held any clues of which she was unaware. He spread food out before her, and poured drink into two cups. She watched the liquid as it glugged out of the round pot. It was vivid green. He nodded to her, and offered her a cup. She looked down into it, watching the green stuff still swirling around, frothing a little at the edges. "It won't turn me . . . It won't have any effect on me, will it?" she asked nervously.

"You are already as you are." It could have been a compliment.

"But this won't . . . change me?" she asked delicately, not wishing to be more blunt about it.

"Everything changes. But for one to seek to change another, that would be presumptuous." He sounded almost angry.

"I'm sorry," she said quickly. "I didn't mean to insult you. But this is quite a surprise. It's like walking into a different world."

"Of course," he said. "For you as for me. We each bring a little of our own world with us."

She swallowed, and took the plunge. "Have you come from another world?"

"Just as you have."

"But this is my world."

He looked around, puzzled. "Then you belong here."

"No, this is Lochskerrow Halt. But it's my planet."

"Lochskerrow Halt. Just as on my planet. But we call it something different."

"No, wait," said Sarah, putting down her drink and pressing her hands to her head. "Do you mean that Lochskerrow Halt is on another planet?"

"It depends which is another."

"Another from Earth," said Sarah. "My planet."

"I thought you said you lived at Mossdale."

"Yes. Mossdale, Earth. It's still all one planet."

"That's certainly true," he said. "It's all one."

"Please," she said. "Could you be a little more specific? Did you come from Earth or from somewhere else?"

"Yes."

"Yes what?"

"Please."

"I can't bear it," she said, torn between tears and anger. "Do you do it on purpose?"

"Drink with me," he said. "It will make it much easier."

Spurred by frustration, Sarah drank. The drink tasted green, like new peas, or the pale hearts of lettuces.

Then she said, "Will you answer me one straight question?"

"I answer all your questions," he pointed out. "Though it's not what I'm accustomed to."

She thought about that. "Do you find it rude?"

"Only pointless," he said. "But that was in another world. Ask as you please."

"Do you have a name?"

"Of course."

He seemed surprised. He'll never answer this, she thought. In no good fairytale or folktale would they ever answer this, but why not try? "What is your name?"

"I thought you knew," he said, smiling at her with the utmost friendliness. "I find it very odd that you don't. My name is Lin."

"Say that again."

"Lin."

10

"Lin?"

"That's it, more or less. Sarah, will you eat?"

The dish held curious flat loaves which would have appeared more bread-like if they had not been green, and assorted nuts, or berries, or sweets. Whatever they were, Sarah didn't recognise them. She reached for her rucksack and laid out her own food: two cheese and Marmite sandwiches, a tomato, a bar of chocolate and an apple. Lin added her offering to the plate and sat down on the cloak, the dish of food between them. "Let's eat."

Cautiously she took one of the green loaves, feeling it would be churlish to stick to her own cheese sandwiches. It was strong and yeasty, as if it were more alive than ordinary food. Lin took a sandwich and chewed it with a puzzled expression. He asked nothing, however, and she resisted the impulse to ask if it were all right. That would merely make another question. The problem was that every sensible re- mark she could think of was a question. If questions were pointless, then what kind of conversation was left with someone of whom she knew absolutely nothing? Sarah ate in unaccustomed silence, but her companion seemed content. He ate very slowly, and he watched her with an interest which, though disconcerting, was not uncivil or frightening. He looked at her as he might look at the scenery, or a pot plant on the table. She had never, in the presence of a strange man, worried less about being a woman.

"If you never ask questions," she asked eventually, and realised as she spoke that she was asking a question, "then how do you find out what you want to know?"

"It depends what I want to know."

"What do you want to know, Lin?" There was urgency in her voice, as if by supplying him with some motive, or reason for his presence, all would be made explicable.

He appeared to give her question serious consideration. While she waited she unwrapped the chocolate and handed him a piece. "Nothing," he said at last. "The idea is not so much to know as to follow the thought."

"Which thought?"

"You called it Lochskerrow Halt."

"I did what? Have some chocolate."

"The place we have reached," he seemed to be seeking for words, "where your thought crossed mine. It's not easy to describe in this language, which travels only in straight lines . . . Ugh!"

"What's the matter?"

Lin jumped to his feet and ran down to the loch, where he spat vigorously, washed his mouth out, and spat again.

"Was it the chocolate?"

"I'm very sorry," he said, wiping his mouth, and coming to sit down again. "That was extremely uncivil of me. Chocolate, you say. I shall remember that."

"It's supposed to be sweet. You don't find it so?"

"It tastes like shit," he said. And then added at once, "I'm sorry. I forgot. You don't like to have that mentioned."

"I don't?"

"Taboo," he said. "We don't have them. I forgot."

He seemed absurdly put out. "Really," said Sarah, "it's not important. Who told you about our taboos, anyway?"

"You, of course."

"Me? I didn't say a thing. And it isn't a taboo with me, particularly." It seemed important that he should realise she was a fairly liberated person.

"But it is you. There isn't anyone else."

"But there must be. Where did you learn English?"

He seemed quite at a loss, like a parent trying to find out what a baby wants, wishing the child could only talk and make itself understood. "Of course I speak your language when I speak to you," he said patiently. "How else would you understand what I say?"

"What language do you speak at home?"

"Very little." She sighed, and he explained with the same air of apology. "I'm not accustomed you see. That must be why I don't do it to your satisfaction."

She didn't know whether it was the drink, or the strange

12

food, or his greenness, or the whole incomprehensible situation, but she was beginning to feel ridiculously emotional, as if she were about to experience an earthquake, or a period. He appeared to have come from another planet. An alien from outer space. She looked at him and her face quivered. At that moment he was extraordinarily desirable. The realisation of it swept over her like a wave, leaving her shaken and breathless. Nothing he said made the least sense, and no man on earth had ever treated her with such dispassionate clarity before. He had done nothing, asked her nothing, shown no interest in her whatsoever, unless he knew her perfectly already, as he had known her name. Like an angel. A stupid thought – she pushed it away from her, disgusted. This was not the clean, white, milk-and-water disguise of angels in her child's picture Bible, this was a creature definitely male, attractive, and dynamically green. A fertility god – no, not that either. If he were thinking about sex he would have frightened her by now.

He was still looking at her, his green eyes large with concern or kindliness. Sarah didn't need kindliness from men. Not in her world she didn't. Rebellious emotion surged into her chest so that she could hardly breathe. She felt hot and confused. Something must happen to relieve this tension. Still he said nothing. Despising herself, she burst into tears.

He neither fussed nor spoke, nor even offered her a handkerchief. While he waited for her to stop he poured out two more cupfuls from the round pot and sipped his drink, gazing out over the grey water. A hawk hovered over the forest beyond, hanging motionless in the fine air. As he watched, it dived, dropping like a stone until its shape was lost against the background of spruce.

Sarah sniffed and swallowed, and wiped her nose on her sleeve. "I'm very sorry," she said. "I never usually do that. It was the shock."

He frowned at her, as if he were trying to bring some new idea into focus. A question hung in the air between them. She stared at him, and caught his meaning. "Many things," she

13

said slowly. "We are ashamed of far too many things."

"You don't have to answer," he said. "Not with words. They change everything."

She would have liked to touch him. If she did that, it seemed, things would become much clearer. She dared not, the act would have far too many implications, on her planet, anyway. She changed the subject.

"On earth," she remarked, "the plants are all green. Nearly all green. That's because they take energy from the sun and make sugar. It's called photosynthesis. Plants can do that because they have chlorophyll which is what makes them green. Animals get energy from the sun by eating plants. They can't get it directly because they don't have any chlorophyll."

"Where I come from," he answered her, "energy is a gift."

"Energy," said Sarah, "comes from heat and light and movement and electricity. You can't have any energy unless you get it from somewhere else."

"A gift," he replied, "is something given."

"On Earth," she went on, "everything depends on everything else. Plants depend on light, and animals eat plants, and people consume just about everything. Children are fed by their parents, and men depend on women, without whom they would not exist."

"Without one another," he echoed her, "we would not exist."

"If you came here to see what the Earth was like, you'll get a very false picture of it if you stay at Lochskerrow Halt."

"Sarah," said Lin slowly, "I would like to learn something from you."

"From me? What?"

"To ask a question."

"Go on then."

"It's not so easy. You have to tell me if I do it right. This is the question."

"Yes?"

He seemed to be struggling for words. "Where . . .?" he

14

began.

"That's it. Where . . .?" she encouraged him.

"Where . . .? On which part of it . . . is the Earth more like itself, than here at Lochskerrow Halt? Which place on it will tell me the thing that Lochskerrow Halt is not telling?"

I asked for that, thought Sarah. Where? London, Belfast, Athens, Babylon, Hiroshima, the Garden of Eden? "It depends," she said cautiously.

"But there is a place?"

"It varies. It depends on who you are. It wasn't what I meant to say, Lin. I only meant that this world is very large. I was thinking about the sort of thing you hear on the news. Where we are . . . this isn't the sort of place where anything happens. It's not the centre of the universe."

"That can't be true," said Lin.

"No?"

"We are here."

"But that's insufferably conceited! Who do you think you are? No, no, don't answer. It'll only make me cross. Lin, tell me this, even if it's a question. What are you thinking about?"

"I was wondering where that stuff came from."

"What stuff?"

"You called it chocolate. It felt very bad."

"In what way bad?" asked Sarah curiously, wondering whether he were sensitive to saccharine, the processed food industry or the political implications.

Lin looked at her, his mouth turned up and his shoulders shook. He began to laugh, and he went on laughing until the tears sparkled on his green cheeks like drops of water on spring leaves.

"What's so funny?" Sarah was put out.

He rolled over, gasping for breath, laughing like a child overwhelmed by hilarity, so she felt a sudden urge to join him, to dissolve into fits of giggles as she would have done unquestioningly were she ten years younger. She resisted. "I said what's so funny?"

"Again," he said breathlessly. "You just did it again."

15

"Did what?"

He lay on his front, so his face was hidden by his thick green hair, and laughed into his hands, wriggling like a baby. Sarah watched him rigidly, with mounting disapproval. He showed no signs of stopping, and finally she could stand it no longer, and screamed at him, "What's the joke? I said what's the bloody joke?"

He rolled over and sat up, and took her hands in his before she could pull them away. "Hush," he said. "Listen!"

She listened. A slight wind stirred the rushes, and they bent before it, sibilant. Wind over water, the surface of the loch ruffled into patterns, gleaming where the pale sunlight caught it, black lines of shadows. The burn sounded faint, a gurgling of water over rock. Curlews were still calling from far across Airie Hill. His hands were warm, human hands, strong capable hands that held hers delicately, not restraining her, imparting an intense desire, but not desire as she associated it with men. It was merely the desire to communicate. There was an innocence about him, and an urgency. She looked down on the green hands laid over her hands, small, practical hands burned pale brown by the summer that had flown. Then she looked at his face. Growing accustomed to the greenness, she could see beyond that now, and saw how he really looked, alert and listening, straining to catch something that eluded him, a thought, or a question. He seemed to give it up; his eyes came back to her face, and he looked at her with the vulnerability of someone who has just been woken from a dream.

Again, that wave of emotion. She took her hands from his and moved back so that she was sitting on the very edge of the cloak, away from him.

"I have been hurt enough by men." She wasn't sure if she said it aloud, even, but she registered that he heard her. Whether he had the knowledge to understand her was another matter. "It's very difficult," she said, reverting to her ordinary conversational manner, "if I can't ask you questions. I don't know another way of finding out about people."

"But you can. You do it very well."

"Lin," said Sarah. "What did you come here for?"

"For the same purpose as you. I followed the thought."

"And how did you come?"

"By the same thought."

"But the chances are, if you came from another planet, that you travelled several million light years to get here. You had the whole of space to choose from, and you ended up at Lochskerrow Halt. How did you know where to come?"

He looked at her helplessly. "It's very hard for me to follow you," he said. "How could I not have come?"

"What were you thinking about just now, when you were holding my hands?"

"What were you thinking about?" he countered. Again the question came without difficulty and he looked triumphant.

"I heard the curlew, and the ripples on the loch."

"So did I," said Lin.

"Lin?"

"Yes."

"Where you come from, are there women as well as men?"

"Oh yes," said Lin, but he seemed as if he were not listening.

"Do people get married?"

"I don't understand."

She tried to put it another way. "Have you children of your own?"

He turned to look at her. "How could I own a child?"

"I meant, are you the father of many children?"

"Oh yes, a great many."

"But you can't be! Not the physical father."

"Oh that," said Lin, as if he had suddenly seen what she meant. "Oh no."

"Then who are the many children?"

"They are themselves, of course."

"I give up," said Sarah, lying back and closing her eyes. "What's the answer?"

"I can't believe it," said Lin. She opened one eye and

squinted up at him.

"Can't believe what?"

"That there should ever be such a question, Sarah."

"Yes?"

"The words are difficult. You want to know where I come from, but I am not there any more. Perhaps you want to find out who I have been. But that isn't true any more. Do you understand me?"

"No, frankly."

"It must be important to you then, what you were before you came here, before you walked round the corner of the tent and saw me."

"Well, of course it is. It's only about an hour ago. I only left home this morning."

"Yes. So did I."

"And travelled several million light years?"

"No, that was your idea. If I had thought of it, I probably wouldn't have come."

"I have travelled five miles," said Sarah ironically, lying on her back with her eyes shut. "I left after breakfast this morning. At breakfast, I was an art teacher who had slept in late because it was Saturday morning, who had decided that because it was a nice day I'd go for a long walk, maybe as far as Gatehouse, then I'd hitch back. I thought I might even cross the viaduct and go right through to Creetown. I was wrong."

"Never wrong."

"Don't interrupt. I had two pieces of brown bread and marmalade for breakfast, and a mug of decaffeinated coffee. The big problems in my life are third-year boys, the clutch on my car, and a man called John Macgregor who has just gone to Australia. The best thing in my life is that I had a fairly successful exhibition in Dumfries in the summer holidays. I sold several pictures. I don't always want to teach schoolkids. I want to be a painter. I'm hopeless at maths, I never read science-fiction, and I didn't do anything to deserve this."

"Your nose," observed Lin, "is covered with small brown

18

spots, or blotches. Not unhealthy. In fact they look like something good. I've never seen anything like it before."

"Freckles," said Sarah, without opening her eyes. "The reason I'm vulnerable is because I'm lonely. A man called James Jenkins asked me out to lunch on Friday. I said no. It would have been much too complicated. But a part of me wanted to say yes, yes to anything."

"Your eyes, when they are open," said Lin, "are blue. I have never seen blue eyes before."

"Brown is the dominant colour on this planet." Sarah opened her eyes and sat up. "Does anything I say tell you anything you didn't already know?"

"I'm not omniscient. I understand the facts you tell me but there are things lying on the edges of them that I can't bring into focus. It frightens me a little."

"Frightens you? Don't say that," said Sarah sharply. "I didn't think I could frighten you. I certainly don't want to."

"You're not responsible," he said. "You understand, of course, there is the reason why I came. I knew it would be difficult; I even intended that it should be."

"Why did you come?"

"Sarah," he said. "It's very hard to perceive what you know and what you don't know. Some things are more obvious to you than to me. It's you, not me, who know why I came. I thought we were both quite clear about that."

"But I haven't the faintest idea. I wasn't expecting you."

"But it's your world. The reason is in your world. Otherwise you'd think you were in mine."

Sarah pressed her hands to her head. "It's too much," she said. "I never thought I was stupid before. I don't think we're speaking the same language."

"It's very difficult to translate, certainly."

"Are you translating, or am I?"

"Everything is translated."

"I give up," she said. "I don't see how we can go on talking like this. It just goes round in circles. I know what you're going to say next. You're going to say, 'Of course'."

"Of course."

"It frustrates me." She was gazing out over the loch. The water was still now. The small breeze had died to nothing. The afternoon was turning golden, long autumn shadows lying over the brown hills. It was warm as summer, but the sky was washed pale with recent rain, and the burn sounded loud and swollen by stormwater. "There is so much I would like to understand. If you come from another world, another planet or a different kind of reality, I don't know which, – there is so much I want to know, so much to find out, but I seem to ask all the wrong questions. Or maybe asking any questions is impossible. Don't you feel curious about anything? Do I look strange to you? Do I seem to be different?"

"Everything is different. I don't feel curious, no. I feel passionate."

"Passionate?" she repeated, amazed, and retreated to the far end of the cloak.

"Is that the wrong word? I care very much what happens. That's what I meant."

"Oh. I suppose you do have the right word," said Sarah, moving back. "We tend to invest it with other meanings. You know, I think this conversation is getting more and more useless."

"You expect a great deal of words."

"I suppose so. It's peculiar, I thought until I met you I was more interested in painting pictures. I see myself as fairly inarticulate."

"Perhaps it would be better then, to concentrate on the picture."

"I'll need to think about it."

"You decide how long."

"Until tomorrow?"

"As it pleases you."

"Do I have time to think about it? You're not going to go away, are you?"

"Time is yours. You'll find me here as long as necessary. I won't go until you have given me my reason."

20

"The reason why you came?"

"When you're ready."

"I don't understand that bit. Lin?"

"Yes."

"Tomorrow is Sunday. I'll come back in the morning and I'll bring the things for the picture. Would that suit you?"

"Yes. I think that will give me long enough."

She didn't ask what for. If there is to be no asking, she thought, then all I can do is think about the picture. And if nothing makes any sense, I can make a picture out of that. She stood up.

"Goodbye, Lin."

"Sarah, you must take care." He seemed quite agitated, and he stretched out his hand to her as he had done when he first saw her. This time, she let him take her hand.

"Why?"

"Because of course you'll find everything different. But I can see you're very strong. Only, please take care."

She squeezed his hand. "I'll be all right. Take care yourself. See you tomorrow."

2

Sunday morning brought the mist down. The air lay thick with it, weighted with undissolved water, so that droplets seemed to form in front of her eyes, only to melt away when she tried to focus her gaze upon them. Briars and bracken bent low under their burden of shimmering water, soaked grass brushed her boots, disseminating seed across her damp trousers. The railway had lost its beginning and its end, nothing was visible except a few yards of track before her and behind, no hill, no curve, no destination. The moorland sounds were muffled, so that the curlews' cry came distorted like a call from another world. Sarah recognised Lochskerrow by the wooden bridge and, having crossed it, she found her trail of yesterday, now dew-bedaubed, as if her tracks had become illuminated in the night. She scrambled down the bank, her rucksack, heavier today, bumping on her back.

The tent loomed out of the drizzle, domed and pinkish, and she saw that, in the night, spiders had made webs all over it, so that it was adorned with patterns like a maze, streaked with dark where water had soaked into the material. When she walked around it she found nothing. The smooth surface of the tent was blank and shut, and the spiders' webs, undisturbed, winked and glimmered in the hazy light. She stood, irresolute, then walked around again. She was standing where Lin had laid his cloak down yesterday. Looking down, she saw the grass was slightly flattened. With absurd relief she walked around the tent a third time, and still perceiving no entrance she called softly, "Lin?"

The entrance opened up before her, a dark slit appearing

between the webs. He stood waiting for her, the tent flap held back in his hand. His greenness still came as a shock to her. The first thing she had thought when she remembered in the morning what had happened, was how extraordinarily familiar he had been. Even if they had talked nonsense, it had a sense to it she had recognised. It had been easy to be with him, and the touch of his hands had been warm and comfortable. But she had forgotten, when she thought about him, how very green he was. In the grey, undefined drizzle of a September day, his colour seemed to impinge almost violently upon her senses. A green man, she thought, should turn red and gold in autumn, his cheeks should reflect the russet of falling leaves, and his hair should be the gold of ripening corn. He should be like the god of the harvest, solid as apples on a tree. Green in September is alien. When I woke up this morning, I thought he was John Barleycorn. I had forgotten it was another planet.

"Sarah."

She found herself stammering, as if she didn't know him. "I came to make the picture." It could have been an apology.

"It's very wet out there. Come in."

No! Quick as her own reaction, she knew that he had heard her. "I'm sorry." She was stammering again. "It's not that I don't trust you. But it's so different from yesterday. The weather."

"Of course."

"If I come in . . ." She hesitated, afraid of offending him but even more afraid of what she did not know. "If I come in, will the tent still be in the same place?"

He smiled at her as if he'd caught her meaning, and was relieved that she meant nothing more complicated. "It's not a spaceship."

"No, it doesn't look like one. Not that I'd know if it did. I just wondered if reality might be something else inside."

"But of course." That did puzzle him.

"It won't hurt me?"

"Sarah." He was holding his hands out to her again. "I have

23

no power to hurt you, none at all."

Oh yes you do. You're a man, aren't you? With a flicker of anger she saw that again he had picked up her meaning at once. "Aren't I allowed to have any secrets?" she said crossly.

"If you wish, it shall all be a secret."

"Listen," said Sarah sharply, "this gets us nowhere. We found that out yesterday. No talking. All right, I'm coming in. I've got my fingers crossed."

She stepped past him into the tent.

He certainly didn't carry all this here on his own, was her first thought. Then how? It was very comfortable, like a nest. If she had wished for all the colours of autumn, she had been given them in abundance. It was all reds and golds and ripe browns, high piled cushions, hangings in rich profusion, patterns like leaves in a forest, domed walls with circles and spirals and mazes, colours fading into one another, paths like branches disappearing over her head into a canopy of leaves or ripples upon water, so that she might be looking up to the surface of a golden pool. She stretched out her hand as if to feel for a boundary, for the circle of the tent itself. To her eyes everything was infinite and complicated, lines softened into nothing, endless patterns with no solid shape as if it were all shifting, changing in the uncertain light.

There was a light. She looked down and saw a small wick floating in a pool of green oil, in another of those full-bellied pots embellished with whorls and rings. Hardly space-age technology, she thought with a flash of irritation. It's all too confusing. And there's no point even in asking.

She heard his chuckle and snapped at him. "Stop reading my thoughts, if you're capable of stopping. I can't stand it!"

"Sit down, please," he said soothingly.

"Don't patronise me!"

"I don't think I can be doing that."

"Why not?" she said crossly.

"Because I don't know what it means."

"I thought you were pretty fluent, even though you can't account for it."

"As fluent as you, naturally. But if you present me with a concept which is totally new to me it's very difficult to give it a meaning."

Sarah sat down on a cushion and buried her face in her hands. "I can't bear it. It's like grasping at the very edges of what I think is going on, but how can I be sure? What do you expect me to do if I can't ask? How can I have taught you to speak? What don't you know about me? Last night I thought I must have dreamed you. Lin! I can't even ask you. I don't know if you're real."

"Sarah, I warned you. I told you you would need to take care." He was kneeling beside her, and his hand was on her shoulder. "I was afraid for you – for me. But you came back. The important thing is that you came back."

"Important for what?" To her fury she realised that she was again on the verge of tears. "You can't care that much about me. Why should you?" She spoke roughly, and she wouldn't look at him. I don't want to look at him, she thought. I'll only see how green he is, and that won't make me feel any better.

"You make it very complicated," he remarked presently, "or something does. There is something very difficult about the world in which you live. I am beginning to feel it, you know. To do with the fact that I am a man, and you are a woman."

"Well done," she said nastily.

"No doubt it seems very clear to you," he said. "I hope you'll be patient with me. I never encountered such resistance before."

"Resistance to what? To your manifold charms I suppose," said Sarah, realising that if she was not horrible to him she would cry. And she had already cried in front of him yesterday.

"I don't quite understand 'charms'," said Lin. "I meant to myself. I am Lin. I don't think we ever met before."

"Of course we didn't. I would have noticed."

"This language is extraordinarily difficult. I am trying to convey to you that you treat me as if I were somebody else.

25

Or any number of people. As if you expected that I should behave in a certain way, and you were not very pleased about it. As if there were some reason why I might hurt you. You have no reason to think that, unless from the moment you saw me you had me confused with something that had happened before."

"I'm beginning to see what you're getting at. Go on."

"Oh no," said Lin. "I have never put so much into words. I find it very tiring, and the meaning comes through so very clumsily. Couldn't we do something else?"

"Such as?" asked Sarah suspiciously.

"Be silent," he suggested.

"Then do you mind if I paint?"

"Of course not."

Sarah unpacked her rucksack. She felt a familiar sinking feeling of anticipation, a mixture of delight in indulging in the one activity that made her feel entirely herself, when she forgot who she was, and anxiety that today might be one of those days when the spell didn't work, when the whole thing became meaningless, infuriating and frustrating as nothing else on earth could be. The strangeness of her surroundings resolved itself into an observable situation. It might not be livable with, but it had to be paintable. Sarah sat on her cushion, her knees hugged to her chest, and observed.

The low light threw huge shadows that curved in response to arched hangings, domed walls. No definable outlines, no edges, but colour rampant. Colours in varying shades and shadows, a curious greenish dimness, like a cave, like phosphorescence, she whispered, and the word seemed to echo back to her as if the shadows could catch a sound and hold it, as if the word and the vision were one, which is never possible, thought Sarah, and the thought made her unhappy. Her eyes rested on the man who sat crosslegged beside her, a green statue under a canopy of red and gold. He was watching her. His green eyes were gentle, almost luminous, for they held in their pupils a flicker of the lamplight, a reflection like two candles with green flames, like a cat's eyes caught in sudden torchlight. A man green as jade, as obsidian, as emerald, a man carved out of rock, a statue with eyes like jewels and dark green draperies, fir-tree-coloured, his hair as bright as holly. Her eyes narrowed, seeing him now as an image, a form without life, a stone semblance of a man. Yet a pulse beat in his throat, and his eyes were watching her, or perhaps only seemed to be watching her. A half-formed fear rose in her mind and before she thought she reached out and laid her hand against his cheek. His skin was smooth and warm, and when she touched him he smiled at her. Reassured, she went on watching and a picture began to shape itself inside her mind. Presently she opened up the box that held her paints.

It was the sound of rain that brought her back. Heavy rain, drumming on the tight-stretched tent like the patter of a million footsteps, the endless sound of rain on water, splashing on to the loch outside, rain muffled by grass, rain splashing and soaking down into the sodden ground. Sarah registered what it was, and the world outside flooded back into her mind. She looked round with a slight sense of shock, of fear for all the unguarded hours that had slipped away from her while she forgot.

"Sarah."

His voice was soft as falling rain, but it startled her, as though the hill itself had spoken. He moved, and the picture fragmented. The thing she had painted was nothing any more; only the pale copy of it was caught on paper, of something once seen already ceasing to exist.

"Are you hungry?"

"Yes," she said, and realised that she was ravenous. "What's the time?"

"Yours," he said, laying food in front of her, like a tribute, she thought, still dazed.

He broke a green loaf in half and gave one piece to her. She watched him eat the other piece, and found that she was shivering. A shudder ran through her, and her teeth chattered so it was hard to swallow. She held up her hand in front of her and saw that it was shaking. "I'm cold," she said. "It must have got cold in here. I didn't notice."

"It's not cold."

"For all I know," she said to him, "you have been here all the time."

Silently he poured drink into a cup, and offered it to her.

"For all anybody knows," said Sarah, "you have been here for ever. You might have been here before the railway was ever built."

He offered her the cup and, as she drank, the thick rim clattered against her teeth. She shuddered and swallowed, and handed the cup back to him. "Alternatively, you may never have been anywhere before I thought of you."

Lin took the cup from her and raised it to his lips.

"But why me?" she reflected, and this time she was not asking him for the answer. "Why did you come here – or be here – because of me?"

"I would like to see the picture."

"Oh," she said, as if she had forgotten it. "Yes. Why not?"

Lin looked at her picture for a long time. Very deliberately, Sarah phrased her next statement so it was not a question. "I would like to know what you think of it."

"Oh, I understand," said Lin. "It's a thought. I have never seen a thought done this way before."

"Better than speaking?"

It was the first time she had meant to make him laugh, and she found it very satisfying when he did. "A lot of things are better than speaking," he said.

"It's only a beginning," she explained. "When I get home I shall have a lot of work to do on it." She was packing up her paints carefully. "But now I shall remember everything."

"I can see that." He had stepped across to the entrance, and now he lifted back the flap. A cold grey daylight drifted in like a mist.

"Is it raining hard?"

"Yes. It'll rain until night. But the morning will be fine."

"I have to go home soon. It's school tomorrow."

"Yes."

"I suppose school means nothing to you but I have to be there by nine o'clock. I have first years until break, then third years. I have trouble with third years."

"Third-year boys."

"Did I tell you that?"

"Yes," said Lin. "I found it incomprehensible. If third-year boys are about fourteen, as I understood, I would have expected something very different."

"What?" she asked, fascinated.

"But not on this planet, perhaps. If you prefer not to get wet, you can stay here until it stops raining."

"How long will that be?"

He shrugged. "After midnight. Before dawn."

"I don't think I'd better stay that long. I'll need to get some sleep."

"This is a good place to sleep."

"But then I won't wake up."

"There is no danger of that."

"Early enough, I mean. I'd have to leave about six."

"I shall wake you if you like."

"Lin, do you sleep here at night?"

"Certainly I sleep sometimes. I am a man, you know, and men must sleep."

"And you'll sleep here tonight?"

"Some of the time."

"And the rest?"

"You're very curious," he remarked. "Is it never dangerous?"

"Is what never dangerous?"

"That was another question," he said. "I'm learning it from you, very quickly. It seems delightful, quite adventurous, but there is a hint of danger in it. If one asks questions, one doesn't see where they're going to lead. I'm surprised no one suffers for it."

"They do suffer for it."

"And yet they think the question is the greater good."

"I think it's more that they can't help asking. If I stay, what else is going to happen? What would you be doing if I were not here?"

"Sarah, you are as human as I am. You must have dreams."

"Of course I have dreams."

"Then I don't see what the question is. I'm going out now. I won't be long. If you fall asleep, I'll wake you in time for you to get home before school."

"Thank you," she said, wondering if she had really committed herself to staying. The thought of leaving at six horrified her. She hated to get up early, especially on a Monday morning. It made the transition from this to school much too quick. If her mind failed to adjust, God knew what would happen. It was useless to get into school in a meditative or vulnerable state. She needed to be shut off, quick and efficient, with her wits about her, which was why art could not flourish, however good a teacher she might be. And nothing was done at home, nothing left tidy, no shopping list made. The insistent demand to think clearly and be ready for another world tugged at her mind and the peace of the tent was disturbed by it. She got up and looked outside.

It was not inviting. Rain swept over the loch in great grey gusts, and the water turned black and dappled beneath it, the swish of water falling on water mingling with the soughing of the rain-sodden wind. Lin had vanished. If the tent ceased to exist, she thought with a shudder, she would be standing bareheaded in the midst of a rainstorm and there would be no shelter in the hills. She let the flap drop, and the tent enclosed her once more.

There was nothing to do here. No books or pictures, no words, images or thoughts. Nothing to do but sleep, or dream. Or go on with her picture. She glanced at it, spread out by her box of paints, but her eyes were heavy, and she had done all that could be done that day. It must be very early still, there was no hint of dusk in the raw air outside. Too early to sleep. She lay down and pulled a cover over her. Nothing stirred, only the rain beat down on the roof not so very far above her. Dim green shadows drifted in the flickering light. Sarah closed her eyes, and slept.

He was back again, or she dreamed that he was back. This time it was night, and when he drew back the whole side of the tent there were only the stars. The moon had not yet risen and the air was pitch black, but she knew where the hills were by memory, or instinct. When she stood up she saw the place etched in faint outlines below her, an empty world, contours of hills, silent forests, and a black lifeless sea, all stretched out before her eyes, slowly circling, converging, making slow cycles round the still point where her senses touched this world. She recognised the place, the thin line of the railway, the tilted shed above the loch, the bent reeds in the water. She put out her hand to feel for the hangings of the tent, to draw close the veil between her planet and the other, but the tent was gone from under her hand and the wind eddied at her back. There was no shelter.

"Lin!" she tried to call out to him, but her voice had lost its power, and there was no sound in that whole world. "Lin!"

As she watched, the moon rose slowly over the hills, a full September moon, red for the harvest, circled with a halo of mist. A red moon that tinged the silent earth with a curious shadowy light, illumined the dark shapes of dying trees with the colour of blood. A land laid waste, bound by words, spells, questions, concepts in the minds of men. "Lin!" she called out with all the strength she had. "Lin! I didn't do this! I am not responsible for this!"

No answer, only slow clouds gathering, shifting, diffusing, so that the face of the moon grew pale, slowly dissolved and remained but an aura of misted light, spirit-pale. She saw that all the stars had vanished.

It was very dark and she realised she was half blinded by tears. So many ghosts laid at her feet, so much cast away and dismissed into a world of shadows. Beings grown insubstantial for want of food and offerings, small deities denied their due, guests bringing gifts from beyond the stars drifting upon the hills because there was no one left to receive them. "Lin!"

31

she called out, and her voice was thin as the north wind on the water. "Lin, come back."

She began to run, tripping on hummocks of grass, slipping and sliding, splashing through bogland and water, stumbling against stones and rocky outcrops. A slope rose in front of her, firm and symmetrical, and she recognised the neat outline of the railway embankment. "No!" she shouted aloud, and turned away from it. It would get her out of this, but that would be to lose too much.

"Lin!"

She ran straight into him, and he caught her. She clutched at his cloak, her head against his chest. He was substantial under her hands, the warm body of a man against her. "Lin," she said on a sob, and clung to him.

"No," he said. "You can't. You can't do that. I can't make anything real for you." She felt him grow cold, slipping away from her grasp, as if he would slide into the mists like a ghost and disappear.

Sarah stood up straight and caught at the edge of his cloak. "I won't then," she said. "I don't need to be rescued. You don't have to do that. But you have to stay."

He paused, poised for flight, ready to drop the cloak she held.

"Come back!" said Sarah, and her voice was strong and human. "I command you to come back."

He dropped on his knees at her feet. "I have come."

3

When she woke again the light had burned low, so that the tent seemed enormous, a cavern of green shadows. She lay on her back with her eyes open, staring upwards. If this were a dream she would wake again in her own bed, and if it were not then perhaps all illusion would vanish and she would find herself lying half naked on the wet hillside. There was no sound of rain. She propped herself up on one elbow and looked sleepily round the tent.

Lin was sleeping with his back to her, curled up like a cat, the red-patterned cloak covering him, outlining the curve of his shoulder. When she looked closely she could see the rise and fall of his breathing. If it were a dream, she thought, I'm sure he had the same one. I don't even need to ask. I wonder what the time is.

Lin stirred as if he could feel her eyes upon him. Then he rolled over and opened his eyes. When he saw her he smiled, and her heart jumped with sudden desire. Oh God, thought Sarah, not that as well. I can't go through much more of this. But whether it were a dream or not, it happened, and he knows it happened.

"I'm hungry," said Lin.

"But it must be the middle of the night!"

"Not quite," he said, and sat up. "Sarah."

"Yes."

"There is a word you use which confuses me."

She checked the question just before he caught her. He chuckled. "I'll tell you what it is. Let's eat."

He's quite keen on eating, she thought, but at least he

produces the food himself. This time it was a sort of porridge, but green, inevitably. He gave her a wooden bowl and spoon, and waited for her to begin before he tasted his own.

Presently he said, "You're thinking it again. The word is 'love'."

"Oh Lord," said Sarah. "It would be."

"It displeases you, that word."

"Do you have a meaning for it?" she asked.

"There are too many," he said. "You're trying to describe a rainbow, when the only colours you can see are indigo and violet. The word will not work for you because of that."

"Do you know what I was thinking about it?"

"You think many things I don't understand."

There was a long silence. Sarah watched him eat. He ate delicately but very thoroughly, scraping the very last of the porridge from his bowl and licking the spoon with careful attention, like a toddler given a mixing bowl to clean up. These images of childhood are irrelevant, she thought, or else I only think them to make things easier for me. There is nothing child-like about him at all, except possibly innocence, and I don't want to start defining that. She felt pleasantly tired, as if she had been for a long walk, or a swim. What had happened was exhausting, but also purging. She seemed to see him with exceptional clarity. It was simple enough. She was a woman, and he was a green man.

She had thought him attractive even while she was still overwhelmed by the fact that he was green. Now that green had become normal to her she found herself seeing him just as a man. His physical presence was growing easier. It seemed natural for him to be demonstrative, or rather it was not that he demonstrated anything she could account for, merely that from the beginning he had communicated by touch, apparently unaware of the connotations. Like a child, she thought again, and then no, not like a child at all. I find myself very conscious that he is a man. She wondered how he saw her. Very pale, was her first thought. Pale and skinny, like a tight bud, not yet ripened by the sun. An image flashed into her mind of the little terracotta statues that are dug up all over the world, images of women, squat fertile women with breasts and genitals preponderant. Likenesses fashioned out of earth, red-brown women, women as they are, or for what they represent, or as seen by people who were thinking about something more important than desire. Woman come to fruition, woman the colour of harvest, ripe as berries that burst under the sun and scatter their seeds, warm as turned soil when the spring sun reaches it. The fact that I desire him is getting in the way, she thought, so what can he be thinking about me?

She watched him, trying to catch his thoughts, the way he seemed to do more easily than speak. He was standing at the tent door, the flap raised in his hand, looking out. A pale moon caught his features in a greyish light, but the lamp behind him cast him into sharp relief, so that his outline loomed over him, a deep, curved shadow that towered up and was lost among the hangings. He was looking out, presumably over the loch, for she could hear the incessant rustling of the wind catching among the reeds. The world outside was still her world and that reassured her. He was very tall. The lamplight at his feet seemed to make him even taller, and he had that trick of stillness which imposed itself upon her painter's eye. He might stand like that for centuries; the lamplight would flicker through the ages in homage at his feet, like the small gods of the hills to whom offerings were made in caves and round hollows in the hills, for whom the oil of the lamps would be replenished and the flame kept lit. Perhaps he had stood thus, watching over this loch and these hills through all the ages before Ninian landed at Whithorn, in the same century that Augustine came to Kent. A long and patient watch, while the wilderness shrank back into the hills, and the creatures of the forest retreated into such land as was left empty for them. No one had laid claim to this place yet; they had merely traversed it, and passed on.

At last he turned round, letting the tent flap fall back into place, and smiled at her, but as if he were still seeing

35

something else. His hair was thick and curly, blown by the wind, and his eyes were huge and dark where the shadow caught them. He came and sat down, but he was still abstracted, his thoughts uncollected, wandering open and vulnerable. Desire shook her. She held out her hands to him and he took them automatically, but still with that strange lack of knowingness, because for him, she thought with a twist of bitterness, implications simply did not exist. But though it made no sense, she wanted him. Though he had suggested nothing, she wanted him more than she had ever desired a man in her life. In fact, she realised now, she had never properly desired a man before in her life. She had merely responded to their need. Lin seemed to feel no need, and she wanted him.

"Lin," she said to him at last.

He looked at her. "Yes."

"I want to know," she said. "In my world, there is this matter of sex."

"There is always that," he agreed politely.

"Are you familiar with it?" she asked, and as she spoke she realised the question was remarkably silly.

Certainly it made him laugh. "Oh yes," he said. "Surely you must know that."

"So when you're with me it must just seem to be irrelevant?" She wanted to sound interested, as if they were pursuing an academic discussion. She hoped she had succeeded, but rather doubted it.

"I've not been thinking about it."

"Not at all?"

"No."

"I find it difficult to stop thinking about it," she said breathlessly. There is something back to front about all this, she thought. I'm a woman, supposed to be dealing with the fact that I'm alone with a man. I'm supposed to be ready to defend myself, and what am I doing instead? Only what I choose to do, she answered herself.

Lin regarded her thoughtfully, apparently interested in this

36

internal debate, of which, she realised with dismay, he had probably picked up every word.

"I hadn't thought about it because I hadn't thought about thinking about it," said Lin.

"What?"

"It wasn't relevant," he explained. "Now you say that it is. Very well."

"You don't have to think about something just because I tell you!"

"I don't understand that."

"I don't want to be humoured!"

"I don't know what that means. You say that there is this matter of sex. I believe you."

"But what about you?" she said furiously. "What do you feel?"

She was answered by a look of complete incomprehension. His bewilderment pierced her frustration, so that she caught his meaning, a sense of a man caught up in a sudden whirlwind, buffeted by emotions and connotations which meant nothing to him, yet still seeking the clear path and eager to follow it.

"I hate this," said Sarah. "Do I have to spell it out to you? I desire you. I desire you sexually. I want you. Are you able to understand that?"

"Oh yes," said Lin. "Completely."

"And now I want to know what you think about that."

"There is nothing to think. You offer me a . . . it's hard to grasp your word for it. I know . . . you offer me a sacrament?"

In her astonishment she snatched her hands away. "You've looked up the wrong page I think," she said. "Certainly not!"

"Then tell me right."

"A sacrament," said Sarah, shifting on her cushion so she was looking away from him, down into the lamplight, "is a sort of ceremony, a changing of state. There are five of them: baptism, confirmation, holy communion, marriage and extreme unction, which is when you die. I don't believe in

37

marriage, I should tell you. I'm not religious any more, but it makes me uncomfortable when you bring sacraments into it. It feels blasphemous."

"This is becoming extraordinarily confusing. You are speaking of the sacred rites."

"That's more like it. That suggests quite a different idea of religion. More anthropological."

"Religion is all one."

"Oh shut up!" Suddenly she found herself yelling at him. "I get all my courage together and tell you I love you and you get me involved in a great theological argument about bugger all! Just piss off will you? Just fuck off and leave me alone! I don't have to know you, it'd be much easier if I didn't. It's all too much. I can't stand it!"

"Sarah."

"Yes?" she answered uncertainly, a little ashamed, for he had shown no emotion to match hers.

"Don't be angry. Tell me what is to happen."

"No," she said. "Not like that. How can I put it into words?"

"I thought that was the way you liked to communicate?"

"Not about sex."

"Very well."

He was watching her again. I don't know what to do, thought Sarah miserably. I don't know what he feels. It's very humiliating. I feel a complete fool. And yet he must know about sex. He said so. Walking round like a bloody fertility symbol and not showing the least sign of making love even when I put it to him. I didn't ask him, to be fair. Why do I feel like this? It doesn't matter, anyway. It would be much easier to forget it. I can't make love with him. It's the last thing I thought about being ready for, and he certainly doesn't look the type to have had a vasectomy. And how would I cope with a green baby? Forget it. I don't have to say another thing. Lin need never understand. Better not.

"There wouldn't be a green baby," remarked Lin.

She jumped round. "You've been watching what I was

thinking!"

"It's very difficult not to," he said apologetically. "You do nothing to hide it. And you said we weren't to use words."

"You're so literal."

"I would like you to explain to me what the problem is."

"In my world," said Sarah, "sex is a big deal. We are led to expect that men are always thinking about it. There are images of sex everywhere. It's extraordinarily important, and yet it's very seldom discussed straightforwardly. Everyone has too many feelings about it."

"Sex is a celebration," said Lin, "and a delight."

"The images," Sarah went on, "are of women. Women presented as objects of desire for men. Sex is a power struggle, the domination of women by men. This is exemplified in marriage, which is basically a contract for the exchange of property, women ceasing to be the property of one man, and becoming that of another."

"The final image of the world," said Lin, "is the figure of a woman."

"Not in the game we play. In our world, everything is created in the image of man, and woman is something other."

"Everything is born of woman," said Lin, "and there is no Other."

"Sex is a game. Men and women don't tell each other what it is for. It's just assumed by everybody that they need it."

"I am here," said Lin, "to be whatever you wish."

"I want to make love with you."

"Then I am here."

She shrank back against the cushion. "But what do *you* want?"

"Nothing."

"You'd rather not?"

"I like the idea very much. I think it's very sensible of you."

"I give up," said Sarah. "We're never going to understand each other."

"As you say," said Lin. "Tell me when you'd like to begin."

39

"Well," said Sarah, embarrassed. "It's not usually like this. I mean . . . well, supposing you take your clothes off."

Lin pulled his shirt over his head. His skin was preposterously green, very smooth, gleaming a little in the lamplight. He untied his trousers, and they fell gently round his feet, and he stepped neatly out of them. Sarah looked hard at the flame flickering in the lamp, and said, "Three hundred years ago, or less, women got burnt at the stake for copulating with devils. If a man did it, it was with a succubus, and if a woman did it, it was an incubus. They were tortured until they confessed to it."

"Since people first came to this place," said Lin, "there have been five thousand harvests. Barley once grew at the foot of Airie Hill where the sheep are grazing."

Sarah looked cautiously at him. Naked, he seemed more like an image than ever, an image carved out of living earth, but proportionate and lovely, like the statues hidden in the hills of Parnassus when the oracle was despoiled.

"There have been gods," said Sarah, "of the sea and of the harvest. Pan has become a devil, and Poseidon was thrown over the cliffs at Sounion and discovered at the bottom of the sea."

"Before any god was thought of," said Lin, "there was the image of a woman, and she was the whole world. I think you wear too many clothes yourself."

Without looking at him again, Sarah pulled off her jumper and began to unbutton her shirt. "They used to plough the earth and sow corn, and into the furrows they spilled the blood of a man to make the corn grow."

"Corn grows," said Lin, "when the seed is scattered."

"Women have strong imaginations," said Sarah. "They have often been accused of self-deception. The word for it is hysteria, which is the Greek for womb."

"In every language," said Lin, "the same words have been spoken, and the same rites have been enacted."

Sarah took her shirt off. It was not cold in the tent, and the lamplight shone palely on her skin, giving it a faint greenish tinge.

"There used to be sacred places," said Sarah, and sat down to take her socks off, "on the tops of hills, or in hollows, or by water."

"I know," said Lin, "for we have never gone away."

She stood up and unzipped her trousers. "There are people who see images in the sky," she said. "Circles and spheres, and strange shapes hovering in the places where people used to watch the stars."

"It is difficult," said Lin, "to forget everything."

She turned and looked at him again, naked as he was and very much aware of herself. "I think I have forgotten everything," she said. "Or perhaps I have only just remembered."

He held out his hands to her, and she put her own hands in his. "I am afraid," she said, "of being afraid."

"I am afraid," he answered, "of ceasing to exist."

"You exist," she told him, and took him in her arms and kissed him.

Under her touch he was man, as human as she was. His skin was smooth like hers, his body substantial. She closed her eyes to forget the greenness and knew him immediately as someone recognised, like and yet unlike every other lover she had had. He seemed more familiar, though strange, as if there were nothing in him that was not attuned to her. A person living entirely and only for this moment, she thought, for him now there is no past and no future, and so of course he knows me. And I? I have too much memory, too many thoughts, but I love him. I love him more than indigo and purple. I love him in all colours, beyond colour. She looked at him again, gazed at him as if trying to encompass him, and he looked back at her with eyes that had turned dark green and passionate. They sank down into the cushions like one being.

"Sarah."

He was heavy on top of her, heavier than any figment of imagination could ever be. He touched her with a respect that frightened her, because it reminded her of worship.

"Lin?"

"Yes."

"What is this? Who do you think I am?"

"Sarah," he said, and his head went down on her breast, so that when she bent over him green curls brushed her face and tickled her nose.

"Yes, but who is Sarah?"

He looked up at her laughing. "I think you could ask questions for a thousand years. It must be very important, this knowing of yourself."

"You know yourself."

"I am content. And you are Sarah."

I give up, thought Sarah, and heard him chuckle. She turned over with her arms around him, so she was looking down into his face.

"I love you," she told him.

"There is no need," said Lin.

"I would like to know myself."

"It is what I am telling you."

To let her mind go free and hear him with her body; she felt vulnerable, but this man had no knowledge of inflicting pain, he was innocent. It was like having a huge burden lifted from her, that she need no longer be on guard. Innocence is a savage thing, she thought, for Lin, having given his attention to sex, was sexual to the roots of his being. There was nothing to hold him back. If she had not known him, she would have been afraid; as it was she delighted in him, and found herself. Sarah, who is Sarah? Sarah is maid and mother and priestess, Sarah is she who has been named in every language that woman ever spoke, Sarah is she who has been worshipped and reviled by men, she is woman made in the image of herself. Sarah now is sex personified, Sarah is desirous, untouchable, giver and withholder, Sarah is paramour and virgin, born of the earth, her body is the image of the earth, given to a man but never possessed by men. Sarah is the desire of men and the image of women. Before the first green god materialised upon this spinning planet, she had given birth to all that knows itself.

His mouth was on hers, his body vibrant within her body, his skin soft under her hands. For a moment she saw the vision of her dream, the slow planet circling, fluctuating around the one fixed point, the bridge and the tilted hut and the loch beside it; this place where she and he became one being, and the earth turning again under their touch. The end of the dream became her own body, life exploding within her, all the colours of the earth illumined, his seed springing in her in response, and his ecstasy echoing to hers. She saw trees growing again through the centuries towards the sky, and the greenness unfolding every spring, the whole earth green again because she would not have it different. I am Sarah, I am the daughter of innumerable harvests, and whatever he gives me, he is given.

The tent gently re-formed itself around her, so that she was looking up again at the hangings, quiet reds and browns in dim shadows. Lin lay across her, heavy and damp, still breathing fast, his face now hidden in her neck. She turned towards him. Her face met holly-coloured hair, and green curls caressed her cheek. "Lin?"

He raised his head and faced her, resting his cheek on his elbow. "Another question."

"No."

He kissed her. "Freckles," he said, as one committing a new word, or concept, to memory.

"They'll fade in winter," she told him.

"Of course."

"You're heavy," she said regretfully.

He rolled over sideways, taking her with him. "Sarah," he remarked, and curled himself around her, and went to sleep. "Sarah. Sarah."

It felt like the same minute, but it was not the same. He was still entwined around her. The covers were drawn tightly over them, but he was looking at her with wakeful eyes. The lamp was burnt out, and the flap of the tent hung down, so that a meagre grey light trickled in with all the chill of a

September dawn. Sarah turned her face away from it and shut her eyes.

"You wanted to wake up in time for school."

"Oh my God. It can't happen."

"I don't understand."

"Don't you ever have any bother switching realities?"

"No," he said, puzzled.

There was a pause, and Sarah opened her eyes again. "Is it cold out there?"

"Almost certainly."

"You're not much comfort, are you?"

"Comfort," he considered the word. "No, I think you would need a nurse for that."

"Don't start that," said Sarah sharply. "All right, I'm going to get up."

It was cold. She found her clothes strewn among the cushions and pulled them on fast. "Do you happen to have a toothbrush?"

Lin frowned. "Oh yes, I understand. I can give you an apple, or a raw turnip."

"That just about sums it all up," said Sarah. "I'll settle for the apple, thanks."

He got up and found her an apple. The cold seemed to make no difference to him; he seemed quite unaware that he was naked.

"I suppose I shall have to go," she said uncertainly.

"To be in time for school," he agreed.

"Goodbye, Lin."

"Sarah," he said, and in an oddly formal gesture he bowed over her hands and kissed them.

"Will I find you here again?" The question sounded pathetic and forlorn, even in her own ears.

"When you are ready. Do what you need to do first."

"Oh yes, the picture." She looked around. "I'd almost forgotten it. May I come back then, Lin, when I've finished the picture?"

"It's not for you to ask me."

With a stab of fear she remembered his kneeling at her feet. "I shall come back," she said firmly, and picked up her things. If it does depend on me, she thought, I only hope I am strong enough. She felt like crying, but desolately she admitted it would be useless. Take care, Sarah, he had said the last time. And now there was so much more to lose. "Lin," she said, and dropping her rucksack she put her arms around him and hugged him as if it were for ever.

"Sarah."

She picked up her rucksack and slung it on her back. Then she walked away without once looking round, until the curve of the hill hid her from Lochskerrow Halt.

4

Paint. A broken world. Sky split, pale distance. A way in. Fury. Black. Red. Hills, transmuted. Like Mars, red planet. No trees. No life. Green distance remaining. In perspective. Distance. Very frail, through the black. Then a red moon over it.

Her hands were engrained with paint, black paint under her nails, and green streaks across her forearms. Her overall was wet where she had wiped the brush on it and stiff with paint all down her front. It was beginning to get very cold. Sarah stopped at last and stood looking out of the window. She felt bemused with work.

It was dusk already. She could see the trees down by the burn, bare and still, almost purple in the fading light. It would freeze hard again tonight. The sky was a hard cold blue, with an edge of cloud high up, threatening hail. There was no one on the road. The tarmac was still wet from earlier rain, gleaming in the last of the light. Black ice. It would be a treacherous night out, even if she wanted to go anywhere.

She untied her overall. There was paint on her jersey, where it had soaked right through. It was a bad habit, wiping her brushes on herself like that, but she never noticed herself doing it. She switched on the light. The colours of the picture leaped up at her, wet and raw. A landscape of despair. No, not completely. The green part at the back offered hope, and remained unobliterated. She studied the shapes that almost covered it. The line of a hill had come from somewhere, a part of her being. She had known it had to be like that, and now she saw it. Airie Hill, the shape it was from Lochskerrow Halt.

She stared, and the picture turned flat as the passion she had poured into it suddenly drained away. It didn't look like anything any more. Maybe it was good. Maybe there was nothing there at all. While it was still wet, she couldn't really tell. It had been a long day's work. Had she had lunch? She couldn't remember. It was very cold in here. She could just see the cloud of her breath when she breathed out. That was not much good for drying paint. Had she let the fire go out? She couldn't remember that either. Sarah brushed her hand across her tired eyes, and left a streak of black paint across her brow. Time to see to the fire, and get something to eat.

The kitchen seemed flat and unreal, the colours harsh under the electric light. The stove was still in, but only just. Sarah piled on more logs and opened up the draught. There was some bean stew left in a plastic box in the fridge. She tipped it into a pan, added a dash of cold water, and stuck it on the hob. Then she cut a slice of bread. She was almost out of bread. She pushed the kettle into the middle of the stove, and looked around for the milk. There was a drop at the bottom of the bottle. Tomorrow she would have to shop. It seemed a waste of time. The picture kept on shifting inside her head. The hill would not be all black, not really. Now the red moon had come, there would be a reflection, like another possibility. One planet turning into another. No, it wasn't a Mars landscape after all. That was just an image, an analogy. It had merely been a step on the way. Sarah took a wooden spoon and stirred her stew, which was beginning to sizzle at the edges. These worlds were merely images of one another.

She had never gone back to her painting of him. At the time she had thought she knew what to do with it but, in the event, it had merely been a starting point for something else. This was the third picture which had grown out of it. There were more, she had no doubt about that. But his figure had not recurred. It was not that she had not remembered, only that the images had presented themselves in a different way.

Nor could she go back until they were done. She hadn't expected that, either. The day she had set out for the Halt

47

again, just after she had started on the first picture, it had suddenly become quite clear to her. It had been an overcast October morning, with a leaden sky, and sodden yellow grass along the railway track. She had wanted to go, but she was frightened. Suppose he were not there? What then? It was imperative now that things should not be different, because of the picture. If she had arrived and found the place quite bare of him, empty of his presence, then she would not have been able to go on.

She walked a mile, turning over the probabilities in her mind. It seemed a huge risk to take, now that the picture had begun to exist. When she met the people, it had actually been a relief. They were only fishermen, trudging along to the loch with rucksacks and rods slung across their backs, but their presence would make the whole thing impossible. The excuse to turn back had come as a reprieve. Perhaps it was a message. He had understood the importance of the picture. That was three months ago, and now there were more pictures to come. She didn't know how long it would take, but she knew that this was the most important work she had ever done.

Sometimes she thought it would be preferable just to be loved. Sarah took her pan off the stove and poured her stew into a bowl. She ate standing up, leaning against the stove to get the heat. Perhaps she should leave the oil stove on in her studio tonight. Paint would never dry in this cold. Her feet were numb with standing so long. She might go for a walk before bed or she would never get warm, not even with a hot water bottle.

If he had been human, she would have been tempted. Even if it meant not finishing the pictures, or risking all that they might become, a night of love and warmth would have been very comforting. But he was not human, and that made the temptation less. For all she knew, the whole experience had simply been the reason for the pictures. No, she corrected herself, that could not be right. The pictures had to be about her life, not her life about the pictures. First things first. The stew was not quite heated all through. It didn't matter. She bit off a piece of bread. She wasn't even sure now about the pictures. Just now the one on the wall looked like nothing, just a mass of paint. But that was not true. She knew what she had put into it. He was in there, too. In a way, they were all portraits. She had to find a point of contact between something which could not have happened, except that it had, and everything which she had always known to be real. If she went back, without succeeding in doing that, she would either end up mad, or, perhaps worse, disappointed.

There was a knock at the back door.

Sarah wiped her mouth on the back of her hand, and went to open it. It was Linda, her nearest friend, who lived up a track a couple of miles away.

Linda stood in the kitchen, taking off layers of winter clothes and boots. "No one's seen you for weeks," she said. "I thought I'd just come along and check you were all right."

"Of course I'm all right. I've been working."

"Can I see?"

"I suppose so."

It was hard to be gracious about it, although Sarah knew Linda was her best critic.

"It's not finished," she said, while Linda stood before the painting and looked.

"It's quite different from anything you've done before," said Linda, and relapsed into an uncharacteristic silence. Then she said, "More surreal. Or more emotional, or something like that. I don't know."

"Something changed," said Sarah.

"Well, obviously. What happened?"

There was a long silence.

"What happened?" repeated Linda. "What made everything different?"

"I can't say," said Sarah at last.

"Why ever not?"

"I just can't. It would be like a betrayal."

"Betrayal of what?"

Sarah felt desperately uncomfortable. "I can't say."

"Well the paintings will say it for you, won't they?"

"No," cried Sarah, as if willing her words to be true. "No, I've not given away anything in them. Only how it seemed to me."

"I don't understand. But they're good, anyway, you don't need to worry about that. Better than anything you've ever done. Why should you be ashamed of what you've done?"

"I'm not, it isn't that. It's just . . ." Sarah struggled for words. "If everyone knew, they'd go there, and the other kind of world . . . it's too fragile. It would be destroyed. I won't be responsible for that."

"I suppose I know what you mean. It always makes you feel vulnerable, coming out and stating what's inside your head."

"It isn't what's inside my head. It's a place as well."

"Oh," said Linda doubtfully, looking at the painting. "I suppose it does look like somewhere I might recognise. Is it here?"

"It isn't anywhere," said Sarah and almost pulled her friend out of the room.

5

The windows of the gallery looked out on to green slopes and, standing there, Sarah could see the whole outline of Arthur's Seat, rising like a living being out of a sea of grey rooftops which gleamed in the sun with recent rain. It was very comforting – and suitable – to have visions of green slopes between the pictures. She pushed her hair from her hot forehead and turned back into the room.

Linda was balanced at the top of a ladder, adjusting a picture hook on the high rail. Jessica stood back, her eyes measuring, looking right through the picture, seeing only the angle to the floor. "A bit up on the right," she was saying. "A bit more. No . . . down a bit. Stop! I think that's it. Come down so we can see properly."

Linda descended carefully and moved the ladder. It was the second landscape, *Landscape with Red Moon* Sarah had called it for want of anything better. I never had much of a gift for titles, she thought. So what, it's only words, isn't it?

"That's amazing," said Jessica in an awed voice. "When you see it up it's absolutely amazing."

Well, thought Sarah, exhausted, other critics have said as useless things with much less love. "It looks right there," she said. "Now there's the other one. The one with the trees. Yes, that. We'll bring it over if you go back up the ladder, Linda."

Afterwards they sank down on the floor among the scraps of packing. "God, I'm tired," said Jessica. "Where's the kettle?"

"What about those?" asked Linda, pointing.

"The three small ones? They can go between the windows."

"Any particular order?"

"It's written on the back. One, two and three. I'd given up on language by that time," said Sarah.

"You look worn out. Have some tea."

Sarah took a steaming mug from Jessica.

"Sorry there isn't any milk."

"It's like labour," said Linda. "I feel as though I was assisting a delivery."

"Forceps please," said Jessica, and Sarah, who knew her very well, passed her the sugar spoon.

"Thanks."

"So it's just those three, then we can sweep the floor."

"They're amazing," said Jessica again. "I suppose you realise, Sarah, it's quite amazing."

"You did tell me." She was too tired to go on being polite.

"No wonder you've shut yourself up all winter. I was getting quite worried about you. But it'll work, you know. You'll get what you want with this."

"What do I want?" asked Sarah, genuinely curious, for she seemed to have forgotten.

"Recognition. You said so sometime last summer. After your little exhibition. There's no way you won't get it now."

"We are never recognised," said Sarah unhappily, staring down into her murky tea.

Linda looked at her with concern. "I tell you what," she said. "It's a good thing you're going on holiday. You need the sunshine. Away from all these twilit Celtic dreams. You'll have to look after her, Jessica."

"I'm not an invalid," snapped Sarah ungraciously.

"Drink a lot," advised Linda as if she hadn't heard. "Retsina. Ouzo. Get drunk. Have your dinner very late in small restaurants overlooking the sea. Watch out for dolphins. You'll come back feeling quite different."

Sarah stood up. "Shall we finish?"

It didn't take long. At the end Jessica stood in the middle of the room, broom and dustpan in her hand, and turned herself around in a slow circle. Nine pictures, nine paintings in various sizes, nine canvases bedaubed with paint, nine symbols that she recognised as hovering on the edge of consciousness, as if her friend had wandered into dim regions beyond the compass of the waking mind, armed with nothing less prosaic than her brushes and a box of paints.

"Sarah," she said. "It's like another world. How did you find it?"

"It's only thoughts," said Sarah. "But I never did a thought quite like this before."

"No," Jessica. "Where did you learn it?"

"You see that one there" – Sarah pointed – "in the middle it has the railway line, and a tilted hut and the loch behind it."

"Oh? I thought it was an abstract."

"It is abstract. Anyway, that was where."

"I've got to go now," said Linda, tying up a black plastic sack of packing. "Are you two going for lunch? I'll see you at the opening."

"Fuck the opening," whispered Sarah.

The other two exchanged glances. Linda's said, as clear as words, look after her, and Jessica nodded. "Come on, Sarah," she said, taking her friend by the arm. "Lunch!"

"Oh," said Sarah, and looked at them as if it were hard to focus. "Thank you. I do appreciate it really. Thank you very much."

They had lunch in Crawford's. Sarah wasn't hungry, but she ordered a cheese salad. Jessica watched her pick at it.

"I got our tickets," she remarked presently.

"Well done," said Sarah uninterestedly.

"We arrive in Athens about six. I thought we might stay there a day or two. Or do you want to go straight into the country?"

Sarah looked up and said clearly, "I want to see the place where Athena struck down Poseidon and banished him from the city."

"Oh?" said Jessica. "You mean the Parthenon and all that? It is pretty amazing. You wouldn't want to miss it."

"No."

"Then we can choose. I'd like to visit some of the islands. Or there's the Peloponnese. If we did that we could go north and visit Delphi. I've always wanted to go to Delphi. Would you like that, Sarah?"

"In Delphi," said Sarah, "the courts of the temple lie in ruins, the god no longer has any sacred grove to shelter him. The voice of the oracle is silent in the laurel, and in the fountain even the voice of the water is silent." She put her head down on the table among the Crawford's coffee cups, and burst into a passion of weeping.

When the first people arrived at the opening, Jessica thought Sarah was better. The gallery was clear and bare, and Arthur's Seat was radiant outside in the golden dusk of a cloudless May evening. Sarah was thinner than she had been before the winter: her skin was taut and pale, the freckles faded after long days indoors, quiescent months spent at work, long dark nights giving way to pale spring days, and the slow return of the sun. She seemed drained, as if there were no energy left in her, but the pictures that surrounded her were alive, a celebration of colour and pattern in eternal renewal, images through which she had made her earth definable, images of life, very specific, each perceived by the eye of the painter but recognisable as something already met and known. They were strange pictures, as from another world, or the same world seen through other eyes. Jessica remembered Sarah's first exhibition, small landscapes drawn from the surrounding woods and hills, portraits of people she knew. In contrast this was terrifying, but no less real.

There were quite a lot of people at the opening. The easiest ones to deal with were Sarah's friends. Some spent a lot of time looking at the pictures, others spent more time talking to one another. There were people from the press there too. Jessica kept a wary eye on them in case they upset Sarah.

54

There were people who had to do with the local art scene, or thought they had to do with it. They looked at the pictures together, and discussed them in low voices.

To Sarah they were all just people, an endless meaningless procession, fools chattering while the pictures loomed silently in the background. The pictures looked very flat to her now, one-dimensional, vessels uselessly containing the hollow tale of something that had already been said. They did not feel like hers any more. In Mossdale they had been hers, in the little room with bare floorboards, and windows looking out on the trees and the river, where she lived through the long days and nights in a passionate solitary struggle to communicate, to follow the thought, to bring experience to birth and name it an idea. Her part in this was over and all she wanted now was to sleep, and to forget.

Someone said her name, as if it were a question.

"Yes?"

A small red man, talking, gesticulating, demanding her attention, forcing her into some kind of response. Apparently he liked her pictures. He seemed to think she would find it important that he liked them.

"The Celtic Renaissance," he was saying, and she blinked at him. Ancient motifs. The maze, the spiral, the dragon and the dance. Carved stones and stone circles. Yes? No? Images drawn from pre-Christian mythology. A pagan Celtic dream. Where did she come from? Was she Irish? What did she think about the Picts?

"I thought the Picts were dead," she said vaguely, and moved on.

It was a woman this time, a tall fair woman with beautifully arranged straight hair and a string of amber beads. She thought that Sarah's art was so delightfully primitive, and yet reflected all the complexity of the dilemma of modern man.

"But I don't know any modern men," said Sarah.

Another woman would like to be her agent. This was the time to have an agent, apparently, when one hovered upon the brink of fame. This would not stop in Edinburgh.

London, Paris, New York, the art world. Life from now on would involve money, competitions, interviews, exhibitions. Did Sarah know anything about commissions?

"No," said Sarah. "Nothing was promised. It seemed unnecessary."

A man again. A tall stooping man, with black hair receding and turning grey. He was talking about imagery, abstract landscape, mythological figures, the vision of the artist. He mentioned Blake and, later on, Dali.

"But Dali only draws his own signature now," said Sarah drearily.

The dusk was gathering. The hill had become a vague twilit shape outside; the sky thickened, clear eggshell blue turning to dark, night creeping in. "You know," said Sarah to the man standing next to her, "in Shakespeare's time they thought that dark had substance, that it was not an absence of light, but a being that crept across the earth when the sun went down, and robbed the world of colour."

"No," he said. "But I see the idea. You're talking about the painting?" He pointed to one of them, she didn't see which.

"No," said Sarah. "I don't really have anything to add about the paintings."

"I'm from your local paper," he said. "I came to see you at home after the first pictures were shown in Dumfries. You remember?"

"Yes," she said, looking at him. "I remember now."

"It was this one that interested me." He took her by the elbow and steered her across the room, which was emptying now, a knot of people gathering near the door. "I thought it seemed familiar," he was saying, "even though it might as well be on another planet. It was something about the line of hills in the background, with the forest. And this could be a hill here on the right" – he pointed – "and the line, like a railway, with the loch behind it. I know it's all completely transposed, but just now I was looking at it, and I recognised it."

"You recognised it?"

"I used to go fishing there when I was a boy. The hill is Airie Hill, and it's Loch Skerrow, isn't it? Lochskerrow Halt."

"Please," said Sarah, and there was sudden urgency in her voice, "don't say so. Don't tell anybody. It was simply an image. There's no need to make it any more specific. It would be much better not."

But the words were repeated behind her in another voice. Their conversation had been overheard and was passed on. The room was suddenly thick with it, a piece of information, vital, irrelevant, one specific fact which could be grasped by all of them. The words seemed to resound in her ears, a chant, a threat, a spell that would find her out, find him out and destroy him. "Lochskerrow Halt," the voices said, and repeated it again to one another. "Lochskerrow Halt. The place is Lochskerrow Halt."

Jessica and Sarah drove back from Edinburgh together.

"You ought to be pleased," said Jessica. "It's what so many people dream about. No more school."

The Border hills surrounded them, the road lapped around them, twining upwards to green passes, and down again beside waterfalls and rivulets into sheep-studded valleys, where stone bothies crouched in the shelter of the folded hills, and bracken unfurled in pale green fronds against the greener grass.

"They were very nice to me at school," said Sarah presently, "letting me take time off for all this. And no fuss about my resignation. The headmaster said they'd buy one of the pictures to hang in the hall." The prospect appeared to afford her no pleasure.

"Sarah," said Jessica, after another long pause. "What really happened?"

Sarah jumped and looked at Jessica. Her friend's profile told her nothing. Jessica's eyes were fixed on the road, and she followed the bends and dips easily, undistracted.

"I don't mind your asking," said Sarah. "It's just that it's pointless. The answer isn't the response to a question, if you follow me."

"No," said Jessica. "I don't."

"Green," said Sarah, "is a very interesting colour. Look at the hills. Everything is green, or could just as easily be green. Green upon green upon green. Do you realise that if there were no green we would all be dead?"

"Yes," said Jessica. "It's called photosynthesis."

"If nothing died there would be no space for anything to be born," said Sarah. "Do you think anything really dies, Jessica?"

"I think you need a holiday," said Jessica. "I don't believe in reincarnation, no. But I suppose recycling in general is a fairly obvious fact. I suppose I believe in a sort of metaphysical compost heap."

"There is a picture by Blake," said Sarah, "in which you see all the souls waiting by the river, waiting to go down through the water and be born. They clamour to be born, Jessica. Can you understand that?"

"It doesn't say much for the alternative," said Jessica.

"I'm quite all right," said Sarah. "It's just that I've been letting it simmer all winter. If I follow the thought into a picture, people say it should hang in the Tate. If I tell it in words, they think I'd be better locked up."

"Oh come on," said Jessica. "Don't dramatise. Did you ever hear from John Macgregor?"

"Who? Oh him. No."

"Perhaps you need a lover."

"No," said Sarah. "I don't think so."

"That article in the paper," went on Jessica, "that one that upset you, because it went on about that place. You know, the place with the railway . . ."

"I know."

"It was good, I thought. Certainly appreciative. I don't understand why you minded."

"It doesn't matter where it was."

"So why bother?"

"It frightens me."

"But why?"

"No good will come of it," said Sarah. "It used to be forbidden to name names."

"Sorry, I don't follow."

"I never meant to tell, though I never promised I wouldn't either. I don't know if he understood the danger."

"Eh?"

"I slept with a man last September," said Sarah. "I thought I might be pregnant afterwards, but I wasn't."

"Did you mind?"

"Oh yes."

They drove on in silence. Presently grey shower clouds loomed over the hills, and raindrops splashed down on to the windscreen.

"Shall we have tea in Moffat?"

"All right. Then I'll drive."

After Dumfries the rain grew heavier and they churned along the main road in the wake of a trail of container lorries bound for Stranraer. The lorries behind them at last, Sarah accelerated and the shower passed, a fitful sun turning the green of the fields from grey to gold.

"What's all this then?"

"Army lorries."

Sarah slowed down again, and they drove along obediently in the wake of a long procession. Soldiers grinned down at them from the open-backed truck in front.

"There's an awful lot," said Jessica. "You don't think something's happened we don't know about?"

"Like what?"

"It could," said Jessica, momentarily stripped of self-possession, "at any moment. Even if we do prefer to believe it's all a fantasy."

"Rubbish, it'll be another NATO exercise. I think someone said there was going to be one. Glentrool again I suppose," said Sarah without enthusiasm.

"We need petrol."

59

"I'll stop in Crocketford."

"What's going on?" asked Jessica of the woman at the garage, pointing at the green lorries thundering by.

"It'll be another exercise. It was in the paper. Mossdale way."

"Mossdale?" Sarah swung round, her eyes round with alarm.

"Somewhere there. Up above Mossdale. Bennan, I suppose."

"Jessica," said Sarah, "come on. You drive. I have to get home."

"What now?" asked Jessica. "She said it was only an exercise."

"Not there."

"Well, it's hardly war."

"Go faster please. Faster."

There were lorries at Mossdale, Land Rovers and trucks. There were soldiers on the bridge, men in khaki carrying rifles. Soldiers on the bridge over the river and more soldiers where the road spanned the old railway. Trucks were parked on either side of it. "Jessica, I have to get out. Let me out!"

"Steady on. Come home first. What is it?"

Sarah was almost crying. Jessica pulled up in front of the house and Sarah ran indoors. Jessica followed, frightened now. "Sarah, what is it? What are you doing?"

"Don't you see? Don't you see what it is? I painted the picture. I did this." Sarah was scrabbling about in a cupboard; she backed out, her hiking boots in her hand. "Where are my socks?"

"Where the hell are you going?"

"You must see," said Sarah, and as she pulled off her shoes her tears splashed over her hands, "I am responsible for this."

"I see nothing." Jessica stood in front of her shouting at her. "It's rubbish. It's total paranoia! You can't believe the bloody army came out here because you painted a picture! You're mad! There can't possibly be any connection."

"Everything is connected," wept Sarah, lacing her boots.

"Stop it! You can't go out! You're ill. Sarah. Sarah! Wait!"

"No!" Sarah pushed her off, and Jessica went reeling back against the wall. When she recovered her balance Sarah was gone, the gate swinging behind her.

6

They wouldn't let her go along the railway. There were soldiers picketed where the track from the village joined the railway.

"Sorry, miss," one said. "It's an exercise. They're using the old railway. You'll have to take your walk somewhere else today."

"But I live here. I have to go that way."

"Sorry, miss. Not today."

"But I have to. I have to see somebody."

"Not this way, miss. Sorry."

Sarah retreated back to the bridge and thought. The quickest way then? North, into the forest behind Stroan Loch. Under the cover of the trees. The bridge in the forest and the track through the trees that reached Loch Skerrow from the north. That would be fastest, and was hidden. She crossed the field to where the wood began, a small hillock grazed by bullocks hiding her from the men by the railway. There was a fence to climb at the edge of the forest. She came up to it, her hand was on the fence post, but there were shouts behind her. Men in khaki circling the fence. Sarah backed down, stepping into thick bogland where she could not run. Water squelched over her boots. Above her was the railway.

"Stop! Stop there!"

There were men across the bog, between her and the railway – no way back that way. Heart thumping, Sarah ran a few yards and peered into the gloom of the spruce trees. Her hands were on the fence again, and the dark safety of the forest beckoned. There was a crack from within, a trodden branch or a shot. Sarah jumped. The forest was alive, no harbour but a nest of eyes that watched, waited for her, blockaded the hillsides, a hidden army within the blue shadows of the trees. And now the men running by the fence were within yards of her. She turned, cornered, and made a break for it, in the small fast-closing space between the ranks that converged on her.

They let her through, back to the village; obscene shouts and curses followed her. She didn't go in to the village, but followed the wet field round the back and scrambled through the fence on to the road.

Failed. It couldn't be done, not that way. What now? North, the forest stretched for several miles. There were many tracks made by the foresters, but not right through. It would mean scrambling under the cover of the trees. Track-less, very slow. She had no compass. There were men in the forest. How far? No knowing. Maybe guarding the north slopes right across. No way through. South. A mile down the road. A road off. Private land. Safe. She'd have to go right down to the road to cross the river. The only bridge was guarded. She'd have to walk past them. Legitimate business, down the road. Then the track over the hills leading to the last house. They couldn't guard that, not with a house. Private land. But in sight of the railway and the soldiers. So, turn off up the hill before Airie, up through the new trees. Back in soldiers' land, but the top of the hill was only a mile from the Halt. She would be sheltered by the trees, and she could see the loch from the summit. That way then.

She crossed the railway bridge with all the nonchalance she could muster. Men leaned on the stone parapet, smoking.

"Evening," they said.

"Evening," said Sarah, and walked past. Muttered comments followed her, but she didn't catch the words: only about her body, she could tell. They didn't see her as a fugitive.

The bridge over the burn was humped, overshadowed by great beech trees. There were men there too. Sarah crossed quietly. They were on both sides of the bridge, so she had to walk down the middle of the road to avoid them. They stared as she passed. There was a low whistle.

"Evening," said Sarah.

There was a muttered reply from the men who leaned over the parapet, not watching the water but watching her. They were in the place where she used to come in the evenings when the light grew too dim for her to see the colours clearly. She used to come and lean over, her tired eyes watching the quiet water bubbling under the bridge, running between banks of naked birch and alder, the river swollen by winter rain so that the bare branches trailed in the water like brown gnarled fingers.

She could feel men's eyes on her back, staring her out of sight. Their gaze was cold between her shoulder blades. She shuddered and forced herself to saunter slowly on.

The big bend in the road had never seemed so slow, curving out of sight of the bridge as if reluctant to plunge back into the shelter of the woods. She waited until the trees were thick on her right, then looked back. The bridge was out of sight. No soldiers. Sarah began to run.

The road had never seemed so long. It would have been quicker to go back and fetch the car. She could have taken it right up to the Airie track. Too late. She cursed herself and slowed down. She could run so much, but there were miles to go. Even straight down the line it was five miles. She remembered from her childhood: twenty paces walking, twenty paces running. She tried that for a bit, the counting soothed her, brought back her spinning brain from the edge of terror and wild speculation to the simple problem of using her body in the most efficient possible way. She had been tired out when she and Jessica got home. She wasn't tired now, but there was a shaking in her chest, and her legs threatened to tremble under her. She couldn't allow that. Not efficient. She went on counting.

The burn drifted away, back from the road, only the sound of it came faintly through the trees. At the turn a small signpost – Private land – she could walk here unmolested. She settled to a walk. It was a mile or so before she'd reach the Airie track, she guessed, and she couldn't run all the way.

The evening was resplendent above her. Trees towered over her, a dim memory of the true forest that once covered all this land, so that the first clearings made by people were up in the hills, in the open ground around the lochs. Places that had been harvested for five thousand years while these valleys lay unawakened, while boar and badger rooted in the forest and eagles flew over the vast canopy of trees. The sun was low to the north-west, long fingers of June twilight reached down in golden shafts through the silent trees. The day had been hot. The smell of damp earth rose slowly into the cooling air, and little curls of mist drifted over the puddles by the road. In spite of the violence and the shock, the forest soothed her. She walked on steadily. Dormant thoughts uncoiled themselves inside her mind, a longing which had been suffused with pain all winter, drowned in a grief that could not be endured, only painted.

She had not gone back to Lochskerrow Halt for nine whole months. She knew there was no point, and it would have been too hard to bear to stand on the edges of the railway track, to look down on the loch fringed by ice, its cold shores brown and empty, frost-riven, offering nothing. Sarah shivered, though the sun shone down on her back between the dappled beech leaves so that as she walked she was flecked now with light, now with gentle green shadow. Why be afraid for him now, if he were gone? Two wood pigeons cooed and nodded to one another in the road, and Sarah stepped round them.

So why now?

Lin?

The danger now is that I have given you away, thought Sarah. I never meant to, but I have betrayed the one thing that should never have been told. Whose hills are these, Lin? Who is responsible for the harvest?

I have brought you back into the minds of ignorant people,

Lin, I have shown them the vision which was yours and inadvertently I have drawn their minds down to that one spot where your world touches mine. I have dragged you on to another planet, forced you through the veil, and now there is no safety for you. I have stripped you of shadows, I have made plain pictures out of thoughts that had been hidden in safe places where consciousness could not reach them. I have handed the key to those who are not to be trusted with it. The place is in their thoughts, Lin, and you with it. If they command you, you will kneel at their feet and they will have no mercy, for they know not what they do.

The track led upwards past a herd of grazing cattle who stared at her with liquid eyes, then lowered their heads again to graze. The sun's last rays caught her, but when she looked up she saw it was setting, sinking in a crimson ball behind the contour of the hill. The hillside was slowly draining of colour, green dimming to grey and, when she looked, the twilight drifted over the northern slopes like pale smoke. I have no torch, thought Sarah, but it shouldn't get too dark. It's June already. I wonder what the time is.

Yours.

Lin, Lin. How can I ever communicate with anyone in this bleak world again? Gifts beyond price you gave me, full measure, pressed down and running over. You even gave me time, presented it to me like a plaything on a golden plate. Shut up, Sarah, she told herself. This is getting you nowhere, and if you cry again you'll see even less.

Soon it would be better to leave the track. How soon? It was the easiest way to go, she could move the faster, but when the slope dipped down again it would bring her dangerously close to the railway. Maybe there were soldiers on this side of the hill. Very likely. Where would they go? To the top of the hill, where they might see down? Then she couldn't. Up to her left was young forest. Not much cover, but some at least. The open was easier, but might not remain so safe.

There were sounds on the slope below her and she stiffened. Cattle maybe, the shifting purposeless movement of grazing cattle. Or men. Sarah left the track, and retreated like a shadow into the hills.

The hill had recently been planted with spruce in regimented lines. Sarah took a line up a firebreak and struggled upwards through torn marshy ground, ploughed over by forestry tractors, and then grown over with bright bogland grass and bracken and dark green alder. The wood was full of sounds. She stopped, poised and listening. Shufflings and scramblings in the undergrowth. Badgers? Deer? Men? Who is the hunted and who is the hunter? Lin? The light was fading very fast. I am more afraid of the hunt than of anything in the world, thought Sarah. A hare leaped out from cover just under her feet and she started back, a small cry escaping her. The animal bounded away, leaped from hummock to hummock, eyes staring, ears flattened, and vanished into the heart of the forest.

She could see the river flowing below her now, the same river that she had crossed by the road bridge, and in the fading distance the straight line of the viaduct where the railway crossed it. There would be soldiers down there. Even as she thought, she saw beams of light passing below her and heard the drone of engines. Not trains any more. Trucks. Terror struck her in the chest like a blow, and once again she began to run.

What if a man were hunted, a green man? She imagined him standing in the twilight, the hills at his back, hidden below a safe horizon, sniffing the air, head cocked, alert and listening. And the dogs after him, hounding him down through uncounted ages, the terror of the harvest, the blood spilt in the furrows and the land laid waste.

There was movement ahead of her. She stopped, crouched down among the alder, breathless, blood pounding through her body so that it drummed in her ears, and she felt that they must surely hear it.

There were men moving about at the top of the firebreak, a little way ahead of her. They were quite close. They were spreading out, moving downwards. She heard loud scrapings and scratchings, heavily dressed men moving through trees that entangled them and tripped them, pressing them back, protecting the hill like a hedge of thorns. Shelter for the hunted, and yet no shelter. The men were moving through the wood, and there was no cover under the young trees, and not enough room to run. Safer to stay in the firebreak. Easier to keep silent. Sarah squeezed herself flat under branching alder scrub. It was very wet. Her kness sank into mud and water trickled down into her boots. They were coming down the firebreak, a line of soldiers. Very close. She heard their voices.

"I'm fucking knackered."

"What d'you expect, up and down these fucking hills all day? Can't see a bloody thing."

Only soldiers after all. Only men. She had an absurd desire to jump up and show herself, to prove how ridiculous this was. Only men, and only one planet. The soldiers knew that there were no gods in the mountains. The soldiers knew that women . . . the thought trailed away, and she sank further into the grass. Her reality was not the same as theirs. She wanted to beg them to agree with her, or she with them. That was not sanity. That was defeat.

The deer gather on the hillsides, the stag is alert. The hinds rustle behind him, nervous. He stands silhouetted in the high places on the mountaintops and sniffs the air. His life is in danger and the stars are circling over his head, unheeding.

Life consumes life.

The kestrel hovers over the forest, which extends below her to dim horizons, a sea of spruce that covers the slopes of the hills, right down to the little loch where the water has gathered in a hollow in the hills. The wren flitters across the clearing, for there are fledgelings in the nest. The hawk dives like a stone, down into the forest, where no eye can follow. Blood flows down into the furrows of the fields, forgotten fields where people once ploughed the hills, and scattered the seed of the barley.

The people change. People come from the shore, make their way into hidden valleys, to sheltered slopes lost in the folds of the hills. Other people make way for them, then fade away, hidden in the safe places in the forest, until they are lost to the world.

Life demands life. The seed has been sown and the green man must die. And I, Sarah, have named the place. I have dragged him back into this world, and forfeited his life for a ruined harvest. This is the wasteland, Lin, the trees are already dying. The loch is dying, poisoned with acid. The water that flows down from the hills is death. There is nothing for you to do, Lin. There will be no more harvest.

Flee away, Lin. She formed the thought with all the power she possessed. I command you, Lin, flee away. Go back to your own world. Ignore the call, forget the commands that have been laid upon you. Have nothing more to do with this. Lin, I command you to leave me.

No answer, just the stirring of a faint breeze among the darkening trees, and the scrambling of men passing her far away down the hill.

Cautiously Sarah stood up. The hillside appeared to be deserted. She was wet and cramped with squatting. There were no more voices, no scufflings in the undergrowth. An owl called from the woods behind her and she jumped. The answering hoot came echoing back across the valley. She climbed on up. The spruce trees were mere outlines now, but a pale moon was rising.

At the top of the firebreak the trees thinned out, and the bare outline of the hill was in front of her. She climbed on slowly. The hill seemed to be empty, and the line of the railway was hidden from here. She must only be a mile away now, but there was still the hill between.

I wish I could go with you, thought Sarah, out of this world, Lin, wherever it is you are, or will be, or have been. I have nothing left of you now, only stale images hanging in a gallery that I shall never see again. People may marvel at them, exclaim and award me fame or money, but my pictures have not changed the world. I suppose that's what I hoped for. I would rather have had your child, Lin, and I wished for it, knowing that it was impossible. Take me out of my world, Lin. My world is dying, and I want to live. Lin!

No!

If I call him back now, he will come. If he comes again to kneel at my feet, they will kill him.

She came out on the hilltop and found it empty.

The valley was spread below her, but it was fading fast, disappearing into the dusk. She could only make out the faint curves of the land beyond the shoulder of Airie Hill, and the thin line which was the railway. There were lights. Her heart jumped. There were still lights all along the railway. If they found her here now, then she was lost. The hope had surfaced that they might have gone away, camped for the night, have ceased to keep their patrol. At least that need not have been real.

The loch was a pale patch of water under the moon. It was possible she could still make out the tilted shed, or perhaps she only imagined it. Sarah stopped to get her breath back, then plunged down the hill. She reached an old wall at the forest's edge. The railway was hidden again, but that meant that so was she. She traversed Airie Hill almost at a run, tripping over the heather stalks in the gathering dusk. She realised as she drew close that she was on the wrong side of the burn. Too deep to cross, unless she waded, and the only bridge the railway bridge. She would have to wade. A thought formed in her mind, and she took the last part of the slope cautiously.

The burn flowed at her feet, separated from the railway by only a few yards. She could hear the scrape of boots on shingle, and voices. Dark shapes of stationary vehicles loomed along the track, their lights dim. There was nothing to hide her now but the dark. Very slowly she edged her way along the side of the burn.

She froze. There was the sound of a match being struck and a thin flicker of light on the other side of the burn.

So they were patrolling the burn, on that side anyway. Sarah dropped down on her hands and knees so her outline wouldn't show and crept on slowly.

The banks were steep just here and the burn flowed swiftly. It twisted through the marshlands in wide meanders, and curved round under the bridge. There was fencing across the opening under the bridge to keep the sheep out. She could hardly see it, but her fingers made out barbed wire. Very carefully she eased it apart, and picked her way through. The bank gave way on the other side, and she slithered softly down into freezing water. It came over her knees, and she felt her boots drag on the stones as the current tugged her. She drew her breath in silently, and edged her way under the bridge. It was pitch dark, but unguarded. Not very wide, the railway track above was straight and narrow. She slipped out at the other side like a shadow, and the loch was in front of her.

The railway behind her was bright with headlamps, but all shining one way, so she was safe off the line, protected by the enclosing dark. There were more voices and footsteps, all further up the line. She ignored them. Quiet as a ghost she made her way along the shore.

In the moonlight the water was pale and still, unrippled. The owls called again across the water, echoing from forest to forest. She reached the place she had been looking for.

There was nothing there.

Nothing. Only a slight paleness among the grass, a dim circle of pale grey. She knelt down and put her hands out to feel. The greyness was flaky under her fingers, feather–light. It took her a moment to recognise it. Ash. Just ashes. A circle of cold ash, formed by a ring of fire that had burnt out. There was not the faintest flicker of a flame now, and the ashes were cold as loch water.

Sarah knelt down in the centre of the circle, her hands over her face.

Nothing.

Perhaps he heard me, she thought. He heard me and fled.

71

Perhaps he did not hear.

She remembered the touch of his hands, the warmth of his skin against hers.

There is always the hunter and the hunted.

There is nothing left worth having, not in this world. The gods have departed.

Unless he was here, and died.

Sarah stood up, and stepped down to the loch side. The reeds were thick now, a mass of dark stalks fringing the water. She stooped down and scooped up a handful of water. She went back to the circle, and poured it on the ground, where it trickled down and was lost among the ashes.

Either this world is doomed, she thought, or it is saved. But my thoughts are my own, and my memories, and the thoughts will be made into pictures, whether they change anything or not, until I reach the end of the journey.

Islands of Sheep

Peter's garden had once been at the bottom of the sea. It intrigued him to remember that. It added a new dimension to his activities, a piquancy to his relationship with this dark soil, from which he slowly enticed a new luxuriance, wresting from it the embodiment of his particular dream. This patch of land was his own, and he could do what he liked with it. It was his personal legacy from a long-forgotten sea.

Just now the garden was struggling with drought. It was May; the sky was blue and cloudless, stretching from horizon to horizon over land flat as water, white-frothed with may blossom around the garden, empty fields beyond covered with a film of green.

His interest in land was something new. There had always been a garden when he was a boy; of course that was different, merely a fact of life. Who had made it, or how it came to be like that, was nothing to do with him. When he left home he had forgotten all about it until he bought this house. That in itself had been an unlikely thing to do. Previously he had lived in a flat in Cambridge, on the top floor of a seventeenth-century building three minutes' walk from his college. His friends had thought it extraordinary that he should leave to go to a boring bungalow stuck on the edge of a village hideous even by Cambridgeshire standards, surrounded by huge featureless fields in the middle of the fen. He had not left because he wanted to have his own bathroom, which was what his mother assumed, nor because he had finally realised that it was time he got some capital into his own property, a motive in which his father erroneously delighted. Nor was it to get away from Judith, which was what Jill had been pleased to decide, nor to have more peace to work on his thesis, though his friends had accused him of becoming an academic recluse. He had actually decided to buy the house last September because of the mulberry tree. It grew in the middle of the back lawn: a strange twisted tree with large lumps bulging off its trunk like arthritic growths. Its big pale leaves had shimmered in the autumn heat, and among them clusters of vermilion berries swelled, turning purplish as they ripened, unpicked. Under the tree, the grass had been sticky with unharvested berries and the wasps buzzed over them as they blackened. Peter had stared up into the gnarled branches. The canopy of leaves was shaken by a small breeze and dappled shadows moved across his face. The house had stood empty for some weeks, and no one had come to pick the mulberries. He wondered if they had cared about leaving the tree. He doubted it. The bungalow was ugly and convenient, with cork-tiled floors throughout. It had belonged to a couple who commuted to Cambridge daily. Very little wear and tear, three years old. The mulberry tree might be three hundred.

There had been other signs. A pear tree, surrounded by nettles five feet high, its fruits still hard and bitter. A mass of raspberries gone wild, inextricably tangled with briars and hawthorn in a hedge guaranteed to defy any passing prince. A bed of neglected rhubarb among the nettles, with exotic spikes of white flowers which showered him with feathery dust as he brushed past. He forced his way among the nettles, until he stood on a low bank, too regular for nature, and looked down into a straight-cut dyke where brown water drifted sluggishly. On the other side a beet field extended almost to the horizon, and the marks of a turning tractor had made wide circles into the exposed soil at the edge. Nowhere to walk here; it was like being adrift in an ocean. There was no reason why the garden should be just here, or the mulberry tree. It seemed arbitrary, unnatural. Yet looking closer he could see the faint outline of the slope on the edges of the blank field. A foot, maybe two feet. Perhaps enough to have made an island, or at least a patch of dryer land among the saltmarsh. Enough to have built a village, with a fine fourteenth-century church arising apparently out of nothing like a lighthouse on a rock. Enough for a terrace of ugly yellow brick houses, and a vicarage and a small shop which was also a post office, and a scattering of unattractive modern bungalows like this one, whose keys he still held in his hand.

Someone must have built a house here, and made this the garden. Someone planted the mulberry tree centuries ago. There was no sign of any house now. Only the tree, a piece of flotsam washed up out of the past in the middle of a sea of flatness which told nothing.

He had gone back and stood under the tree in the welcome shade. The sun beat down on the mocktiled roof of the grey bungalow, and reflected back from the plate-glass French windows. If he sat at that window he would not see the house. He would sit at his desk, just inside, and look out across the crazy paving that the estate agent called the patio, over a lawn which would have been mowed smooth, to the great twisted tree which would dominate his vision. He would watch it change from green to yellow, watch the naked branches silhouetted against the winter skies, and see the slow greening of it in the spring. Oddly, he thought of Judith, who had wanted to live with him and grow famous with him, and of Jill who, he guessed, wanted to marry him and have his babies. It would be restful to live with a tree like that. He put his hand out tentatively, as if seeking some sort of permission, and touched the trunk. The brown wood was rough under his fingers, seamed and knotted. It seemed to receive him with indifference, and complete acceptance. It could not be for the first time. A mulberry tree was a garden tree, a useful, enduring, dependable tree, accustomed to living with people. Next year the fruit need not drop to the ground and rot. Next year would be different.

The first winter had been testing enough. He tended to

work at night, because that was when he could use the university computer, and the last months had been a mixture of long hours in the silent department, followed by bitter journeys on flat icy roads as dark and lonely as the bottom of the sea. The garden had been frozen into death-like immobility, and the house stood square and empty in the frozen fen, uncompromisingly free of thoughts or shadows. Sometimes he thought he had been mad, and Judith had confirmed his suspicions by telling him so in no uncertain terms and by going off to have an affair with a woman instead. Peter affected to consider this development ridiculous, but it had shaken him. He found himself thinking of her more often than he had intended. She talked at him in a manner which made him feel uneasy about himself. He was quite open to discussing sexual politics: it wasn't as if he were totally unaware of the issues involved, or at all unwilling to discuss them. Only sometimes it felt as if Judith hated men, including him. She said that was nonsense, and he told himself that if she did, that was her hang-up, not his. But he had ceased to feel at ease with her, and, worse still, with himself.

Jill did not hate men. Certainly she was very far from hating Peter. In fact if he admitted the truth he was frightened of her intensity. She liked the bungalow. She had come to stay a few weekends during the winter. The first time, she had looked round with interest and a hint of a proprietorial air, while he made coffee in the kitchen and listened to her opening doors and walking with quick efficient steps over the cork tiles. It would make a good family house. Two bedrooms, kitchen/dining-room, sitting-room. Three bedrooms if one shifted the computer. A nice garden for children, if one put a fence around. Peter switched on the percolator and looked out at the mulberry tree. The gaunt branches were reassuringly bare and blank.

When Jill returned he was pouring out the coffee. "It's very nice," she had said. "What does the central heating run on?"

"Natural gas."

"I suppose that's quite economical then. I like the cork tiles.

Were you thinking of decorating the bathroom?"

"No," he replied, mildly surprised. "Should I be?"

"I don't like the wallpaper."

"Why? What is it?"

"Oh, come on, you must have noticed. Mermaids. So some fetishist can lie in the bath and have fantasies about breasts. You could have something more suitable."

"Suitable for what?"

She took her coffee in withering silence. Then: "I'll paint it over for you, if you like."

"Sometime, maybe," he had said vaguely.

The mermaids were still there. Peter leaned on his hoe in the middle of the vegetable patch, and wiped the sweat from his face with a grubby hand. Maybe he should do something about them now, because of Anna. She might think they were his idea. But it was far too hot for decorating, and if she couldn't accept things the way she found them, then she'd hardly be an ideal companion. He realised that the skin on his back was hot and suddenly prickly. He had been out here too long. He trod carefully between the rows of peas and picked up his shirt. There were grubby streaks on his chest where the dust off the dry soil had mixed with sweat. He wiped his face on his teeshirt. A familiar, half-forgotten feeling, to get dirty like this. As a small boy he had liked to be grubby, and had attracted grubbiness to him by the force of sheer delight. Sunburned and dirty, bare feet caked in dust, he used to go swimming in the pond, chugging across the brown water doing doggy-paddle, while the chestnut trees towered over him, dropping sticky buds and petals on to the still water. It was half scary, because he wasn't allowed to swim on his own, and because there were brown trout in the pond which might nibble at him, which was why he was afraid to take off his trunks. He never did swim naked.

Peter put the hoe neatly away in the garden shed, and went into the house to have a shower. Afterwards he put on a clean shirt and trousers, went to the fridge and poured himself a long drink of pineapple juice. He padded over to the French windows. The tiles were warm and smooth under his bare feet.

The telephone rang.

It was Judith. She was going to be in Cambridge at the weekend. She wanted to talk to him about the relationship. Which relationship? he thought bitterly.

"I can't," he explained. "Someone might be moving in."

"Who?"

Mind your own business. Aloud he said, "A girl from the psychology department. She advertised for a place to rent. She's coming tonight to look at the spare room."

"Well, I'm glad to hear you won't be lonely."

"I'm never lonely."

"Rubbish."

"It's true. I never even think about being lonely."

"But you act it out, all the time. I told you before, what you need to do is learn to live on your own, without getting in any woman to tell you you're all right and approve of you all the time."

"I do live on my own."

"Yes, yes, I know. I know all about your 'need to be on your own'. It's because you're scared of commitment. You just want to have your cake and eat it. And being a man, you manage it."

"I don't want to have this conversation again."

"So who's your friend?"

"I told you. She's not my friend. For God's sake, we've only spoken on the phone. All right, come over on Saturday. Anna may be moving in, but I suppose it won't matter."

"OK, see you Saturday then. I'll drive down. You won't have to meet me. Bye for now."

"Goodbye, Judith. I love you."

"What? Oh yes. Well, I'll see you Saturday. Bye."

After she had rung off, Peter put on his sandals and went for a walk. There was nowhere much to walk to in Shippea. There were no footpaths or hedgerows between the fields. The only way to go was along the road, which extended in a straight line from north to south, ruthlessly bisecting the village so that the beet lorries thundered right past the front windows of the terraces, leaving a trail of rich mud along the road in autumn. Just now the road was empty. The shadows were lengthening and the heat of the day was fading into golden evening. Peter's sandals flapped stickily on melted tar. He walked out on to the fen, between grass verges studded with dandelions and campion. Gnats hovered over the dyke that ran beside the road. There was almost no water, and the mud at the bottom had cracked and hardened into desiccated rivulets where some moisture still oozed in memory of forgotten marshes. The slopes of the dyke were rampant with wild flowers. Peter glanced over vetches and cow parsley and stitchwort, and stopped as something more exotic caught his eye. He scrambled down the machine-smooth slope and jumped the dyke clumsily, so that one sandal emerged caked in creamy mud. He wiped his foot on the grass and a nettle stung him. He swore and climbed up again. Sure enough, it was an orchid. He squatted down and turned the flower up to face him with his finger. Purple, with a brown and orange bulge like a bee. There used to be bee orchids at home on the hill sloping up from the brook.

He stood up and looked at his watch. Six-thirty. The woman would be here in an hour, and here he was getting himself covered in dirt again, just looking at an orchid as if he had never seen one before. He jumped back over the stream and walked towards the village. All he could see of it from here was a clump of elms that hid the houses, like a green island in the fen, and above them the church spire, the only sign now that there had been an island there at all.

The doorbell played the first two bars of the Westminster chimes every time it was rung. He'd never got around to changing it. Peter winced and went to answer it. He could see the outline of the woman outside, distorted by the ribbed glass. She wasn't very tall. Peter opened the door.

The first thing that struck him about her was her hair. It

81

was absolutely blond, and he could hardly take his eyes off it. Indeed, it remained a tantalising mystery for several weeks. It was not until he had shared a bathroom with her for long enough to know that no bottles which were not severely practical appeared on the shelf, that he finally convinced himself that her hair was naturally that colour. Until then he took every opportunity to consider the matter more closely when she wasn't looking.

Her skin was pale, with a sprinkling of freckles across her nose, but her eyes were dark, fringed with long lashes which made them look all the larger. Her features were otherwise small and delicate, the shape of her head accentuated by the shortness of her hair. My God, thought Peter, she'd be a raving beauty if she only made the very least of herself. She was small and slight and, if her clothes did nothing else for her at all, they did reveal the fact that her figure was as attractive as her face. She was dressed in a pair of patched and faded jeans, a black teeshirt with a hole in it, and dusty sandals. She carried a canvas bag slung over her shoulder.

"Come in," said Peter, holding the door open wide. "You must be Anna?"

She held out her hand. "Hello, Peter."

He shook her hand, with a feeling of bemusement to which he was not at all accustomed. She had a trace of an accent. He had noticed that on the phone but he couldn't place it.

He realised as he showed her round that he was inordinately anxious to please her, and that irritated him even while he did his best to find favour. Anna seemed unimpressed either by the house or its occupant, but subjected each room to a cool scrutiny. Peter watched her face while she examined the room that would be hers, if she came. Surely she would like it? It was clean and comfortable, if somewhat bare, but no doubt she had belongings of her own. A bed with a Welsh tapestry cover, rather hot for summer but she could always remove it. A chest of drawers from the auction in Cambridge, and a Victorian watercolour of Gloucester Cathedral on the wall above it. Perhaps there should be a mirror. White fitted wardrobe. She'd have to find a desk of her own, and a bookcase. Maybe she'd get a rug for the floor.

Whe they came to the bathroom, he suggested she look for herself, then offered her a glass of sherry while they talked business.

She refused the sherry, accepted coffee, and told him that if the rent was definitely what he'd said before, she'd take the room. Then she asked if she could see the garden.

"Please do. I've done quite a lot to it. I'll have all my own vegetables to eat this year. I don't know if you're interested in gardening?"

She didn't answer; maybe she hadn't heard. She went straight to the mulberry tree. "What sort of tree is that? I've never seen anything like it."

"It's a mulberry." He turned from her to the tree, and regarded it with affection. "It's a beauty, isn't it? I think they only grow in the south of England, so you wouldn't get any in Stirling."

"I was only in Stirling three years. Where I come from, there are no trees at all. I don't know much about them."

"Where are you from?" he asked idly.

She turned and smiled at him for the first time. She looked very young. He realised that if she had only taken her degree last summer, she was probably no more than twenty-two. She was astonishingly beautiful, and had no doubt assumed by now that he was middle-aged. "Well, that's an interesting thing," she said. "I never meant to look at anywhere so far out of town, but it was the name that caught me. I come from an island too, you see, with the same name. We call it Shapay."

That elusive accent fell into place. Peter felt remarkably foolish and thanked God he hadn't asked her if she was Irish, or Italian. "The Hebrides?" he hazarded.

"No, no. Orkney. Tell me more about this mulberry tree."

"There's nothing much to tell. Queen Elizabeth was always planting them in memory of her visits to various country houses. But not this one."

"No? How do you know?"

"There can't have been anything here except a few sheep on a fever-ridden island in the middle of the marsh. I should think the local farmer planted it. There's no house left now. Just the tree."

"And it has fruit?"

"Oh yes, later in the summer. They planted them partly for the fruit, but mainly for the silkworms."

He was enjoying himself. This was his territory and she was his visitor. He thought fleetingly of Judith coming on Saturday. "Silkworms live on mulberry trees," he said, watching Anna. She was touching the rough bark on the trunk, just as he had done, and was looking up into the canopy of broad-toothed leaves above. "That's why mulberry trees suddenly became so important. Before that, silk was imported from China and no one knew how it was made. For centuries it was about the best kept trade secret there's ever been. Then it was discovered and silkworms were brought back to the West, with, of course, the mulberry trees to accommodate them. So by Tudor times everyone was planting mulberry trees."

"I see." She turned back to him, and asked abruptly, "So what's your subject?"

"Geography. I'm doing a book on locational analysis."

"That's what all that computer work you're doing in there is about?"

"That's it." He turned back to the house. "And you? Psychology, didn't you say?"

"Yes."

"Research?"

"I've come to write a thesis." She wasn't following him. Instead she began to wander further down the garden, down to the dyke. Peter went after her. She was staring at the muddy ooze at the bottom of the dyke, and then at the beet field. The sun was setting, long golden rays stretching across the bared earth. "It's about dreams," added Anna.

"Dreams?"

"My PhD."

"Oh yes."

"You can tell it was once an island when you stand here. I find this fenland very alien, don't you?"

"It's not at all like Gloucestershire," said Peter cautiously.

Anna knocked on the door of the computer room. "Come in," called Peter abstractedly, without taking his eyes from the screen. He keyed in another symbol, and started a printout. The machine whirred away and Peter swivelled his chair round, giving her his full attention.

It was worth it. She was wearing a loose white shirt and a pair of shorts, and that seemed to be all. No doubt it was practical attire for unpacking boxes in a heatwave but, even so, she could have stepped out of a travel brochure for the Riviera. Her legs were long and suntanned. "What did you say?" he asked with a start.

"I said, would you mind if I took down the picture of the cathedral? I'd like to put up something of my own."

"By all means. How are you getting on?"

"Fine, thank you." She glanced over his shoulder. "If you don't mind my asking, what's the square spider's web for?"

"What?" He swivelled round to his screen. "It's a map of population densities in the British Isles."

"I see, a rationalised coastline. What a nice idea. Has anyone suggested it to the Commissioners for Northern Lights?"

"I beg your pardon?"

"Not to worry. Where do you want Gloucester Cathedral?"

"Just leave it in the hall for now."

"Thanks."

She was gone, with a slight breath of cool air as she shut the door. Peter wiped his forehead with a handkerchief, and turned back to the screen. It looked drab and grey, with the white heat of the sun pouring in at the open window behind it. He sighed and looked out over the garden. Tonight he'd water the lettuces. He'd put it off for as long as possible, because he didn't believe in watering. It encouraged shallow roots, and once one started one had to go on. But it was a satisfying thing to do in the cool of the evening. He glanced at his watch. Three hours to go.

He'd hoped she might be in that evening, but after her supper she left without saying where she was going, or when she'd be back. He had no right to know, of course, but it seemed odd that she didn't tell him anything at all. On second thoughts, perhaps it didn't. They weren't even friends, yet.

The house seemed empty without her, which was curious, since she'd only lived in it for six hours. Peter made himself a tuna and tomato sandwich, and poured himself a half pint of lager. He ate sitting on the terrace, looking over the garden. The broad beans were coming up nicely and would soon need staking. The peas were more sporadic. It would be worth filling in the gaps with a second planting. That would be the birds, presumably, or perhaps a mouse. He wondered if she knew how attractive she was. Perhaps it was only he that thought so. She seemed quite unselfconscious, or possibly she simply wasn't thinking about him. No, it was more rational to suppose that she was being deliberately distant, moving in with a single man like this. He understood that: it was clearly important to establish a workable living relationship. If the weather stayed like this, it would be safe to plant out the French beans before Monday. Judith was supposed to be coming tomorrow. He felt a slight flutter of panic under his belt and wondered why. There was nothing more to be said between him and Judith. If he replanted the peas, he might try stringing black cotton across the beds. Perhaps he should have helped her carry in her boxes, but she seemed to want to be left alone. She might be driving back to Cambridge in her battered green mini, thinking how churlish he was. It would be interesting to know what had replaced Gloucester Cathedral. Come to think of it, there was no reason why he shouldn't know.

He hadn't precisely intended to suit the action to the

thought so promptly, and when he found himself at the door of the room which was no longer strictly his, he felt a little guilty. Not so much as to blame himself, but just enough to add piquancy to his curiosity. If he had heard a car draw up outside, he would have retraced his steps at once. But no car came. Peter entered the room.

It was no longer his room at all. The poster on the wall was of the sea, a great wave in the act of breaking, with the water beneath it swelling into troughs like mountains. A yellow threatening sky, turning to ominous grey. Peter was drawn closer, until with a shock he sighted the boats. They were long and narrow, pointed at either end, and the bows of the foremost already pierced the foot of the wave. There was no chance they could ride it out: they were trapped beneath the curve of water, engulfed by the swell. But the little figures at the oars showed no signs of panic. They were in their places, all leaning together, while death towered over.

For a moment he was sucked in, the roar of water in his ears and the taste of salt and terror in his mouth. They had their backs to the wave, so perhaps only the helmsmen knew. Peter drew back, and saw the whole thing clearly, merely a poster on a wall, with neat grey print at the bottom. Peter stooped to read it. *The Great Wave of Kanagawa* by Katsushika Hokusai, 1760–1849. And other details, prosaic and definable. He turned away with an irrational sense of relief.

It seemed strange that this should still be the spare room inside his house. It had altered inexplicably, as if much more had been done in one afternoon than the redisposition of a few possessions. He wondered if she were aware of her own effectiveness, or whether she had merely unpacked her boxes as a routine task and casually created this strangeness without giving it a thought. He would almost prefer to think she had deliberately invoked it: there was something alarming about the careless disposition of power, like a child playing with matches.

Peter shook his head, and told himself not to be foolish. Many women had the knack of creating atmosphere. Come to that, he wasn't such a bad homemaker himself. He pulled himself together, and deliberately began to look round.

She liked photographs. There was one big one, an enlargement of an old photo of a lighthouse on a rock. Uniformed men with splendid moustaches posed before it, arms folded, on a granite outcrop. He recognised a colour postcard of the same lighthouse stuck into the corner of the big one. It was taken from further away and showed the whole station: a square of grey stone cottages and outbuildings clustered on a green plateau below the rock. The other photos were of people: a group of fair-haired children posing in a boat, a young man in the same uniform as the others, but with a gentle mouth and no moustache. The same man, older and portlier, with him arm around the shoulder of a woman in an apron, and a Skye terrier at his feet. A different young man in jeans and a patterned jumper, smoking. A little girl, smiling, with white-blond hair in pigtails, and no front teeth. Peter looked at that one twice, and picked it up. She was wearing a gingham dress and a cardigan tightly buttoned across her skinny chest. He recognised her by her eyes. She was standing in a doorway, surrounded by whitewashed stone, and a hen with chicks pecked the worn grass at her feet.

When he came to look, the room wasn't really that full. She had brought a bookcase, but it was empty, with three boxes piled against it, no doubt containing her books. There was a round rug on the floor, all in greens and blues, and piles of papers and files under the window, in the space where there ought to be a desk. She had filled the windowsill with plants: nothing exceptional, just lemon geranium and jade, and the inevitable spider plant. They all needed repotting. There were one or two oddments on the chest of drawers: a green glass trawler float, a snuffbox with a picture on it of a schooner under full sail, and an indeterminate white object. Peter picked it up. It felt like a shell, though it was flat, with five oblong holes arranged around the centre, and a pattern like a five-pointed star. No, too fluid for a star, more like an amoeba. Peter turned it over. The thing slipped from his hand. He winced and shut his eyes just as it hit the floor.

It lay on the cork tiles in two pieces. Slowly Peter picked it up. He could hardly put it back. If only there were a cat, he could offer some excuse. If it just vanished, would she notice? He didn't even know what it was. A wild thought of rapidly importing a cat crossed his mind, to be as speedily discarded. No, better to lose it and play ignorant. He couldn't say he'd been in here, touching things. Peter carried the broken pieces to the kitchen and stood irresolutely over the dustbin. Suppose she searched in there? No, not the dustbin. The compost? Better get the evidence right away from here. Peter went into his room and stuffed the thing into the inside pocket of his work jacket. He could throw it away in the department. She could never follow it there. He breathed a sigh of relief and went into the garden.

"Would you like some supper?"

"Well, if you're making some . . . Thank you very much," said Anna.

"Good. Do you eat meat?"

"I eat anything," she told him.

Peter took some trouble over the meal. He knew he was a good cook and he usually found that women were impressed by his ability. He was pleased with the results this time and regarded Anna with satisfaction as he poured her a glass of wine.

"It's nice to have company," he remarked. "I tend to live on sandwiches in the summer."

"Do you?"

"Though in fact I had a visitor today. To be honest, I was quite glad to see her go. I've had quite a day."

"Dear me," said Anna, after a short pause.

"Well, you know what it's like. Old relationships rising from their graves to haunt one. You must know the kind of thing."

"I don't think so."

Evidently she didn't want to hear about Judith. He could

hardly blame her, though it would have been a help to unburden himself a little. Peter changed the subject. "So how do you find life in Cambridge?"

She shrugged. "Fine. I'm glad I've moved out of college. Too much prunes and custard, you know, like in Virginia Woolf. And I like the space out here, even if I can't stand the fen."

Peter followed this with difficulty. "You don't like the fen?" he asked, grasping at the part that made sense.

"I don't think so." She frowned out of the window. "Do you think this would still have been an island when they planted your mulberry tree?"

She hadn't looked at him once and her conversation seemed to jump sideways all the time. Feeling slightly out of his depth, Peter struggled after her. "Here, you mean? I suppose it depends what you mean by an island. To all intents and purposes, yes. The fen was drained by Oliver Cromwell. In the seventeenth century," he added, just in case she wasn't sure.

"So what do you mean by an island?" asked Anna.

"Wait a minute." Peter got up and went into his study. When he came back she was spreading more butter over her potatoes and looked slightly shamefaced when he reappeared. "Will this do for an answer?" He was reading from a calf-bound book.

> There is in Britain a fen of immense size, which begins from the river Granta, not far from the city which is named Grantchester. There are immense marshes, now a black pool of water, now foul running streams, and also many islands, and reeds, and hillocks, and thickets, and with manifold windings wide and long it continues up to the North Sea.

"That's Felix's description, from the life of Guthlac."
She didn't ask who Felix was, or Guthlac. "It must have

been very safe for the people who belonged here."

"Defensible, you mean?"

"Yes, and knowing that any strangers would die of the marsh fever. Isn't that right? Were they saltmarshes?"

"I imagine so."

"That's interesting," said Anna. "I suppose it seems like the ghost of the sea now, because of the sky. Not quite an optical illusion, more a psychological one. Don't you think?"

"I'm afraid I don't quite follow."

"The sky," explained Anna patiently, "makes you think you're at sea, because there are no horizons. You don't usually see the whole sky like that inland, which is why this place reminds you of the sea. There's nothing uncanny about it after all. It's merely association. At least it's a more comforting theory, don't you think?"

"More comforting than what?" asked Peter, reaching for the wine bottle. He felt bewildered and he didn't like it.

"Thank you," said Anna, as he filled her glass.

"You grew up on an island?" asked Peter, trying to rescue the conversation, at the same time as remembering what he was supposed to know and what he wasn't.

"Yes." He thought she wasn't going to enlarge, but then she added, "My father was a lighthouse man. He's back on the mainland now."

"So you grew up at a lighthouse? It's the sort of thing I used to dream about when I was a boy!"

"Was it?" asked Anna, and looked straight at him. "Why, weren't you happy where you were?"

"What?" He was completely taken aback. "Happy? What's that got to do with it? I had a very happy childhood. But all children like to imagine things."

"That's true," said Anna. "So what made you so happy?"

"I think that's an impossible question," said Peter slightly huffily. "Weren't you happy?"

"Oh yes. Some of the time."

"Then I suppose it's the same for me. I was happy at home. I hated school at first, but in the end I was happy there as well,

91

I suppose."

"Boarding school?"

"When I was seven." If he had hoped she would express sympathy, he was disappointed. After waiting a moment, he went on, "Though I'd never do that to a son of mine. The extraordinary thing about it is, they know. My father went through the same thing. He knew. And yet he still believed it would be good for me. That's the part I'll never understand."

"Perhaps he liked himself."

"What?"

"Payment by results. He can't have wanted you to turn out different."

Peter shook his head. "Insecurity," he said, "not arrogance."

"And a son of yours wouldn't have an insecure father?"

He glanced at her sharply, but she didn't seem to be laughing. He must have been mistaken about her tone. "He wouldn't have an arrogant one, I hope. Have some more wine."

"No thank you," said Anna.

He had made fruit salad for dessert, and he was glad to see that she took a large helping.

"Have you made plenty of friends in Cambridge?" he asked as he passed her the cream. He had been rephrasing the question in his mind while he changed the plates. It was the nearest he could get to what he really wanted to know.

"Some. In fact a friend will be coming over tomorrow, if that's all right. Bringing a desk."

"Ah, I thought you'd need a desk. I'm glad you've managed to find one."

"It wasn't very difficult."

Not as difficult as this conversation, he felt. She didn't seem to be shy, and she certainly wasn't uncivil, but he uneasily sensed that he was being kept at a distance. He was inclined to feel resentful, and would like to confront her with the fact that he knew her better than that. In a way he did, but not at her invitation. Peter thought of the white shell, and felt vaguely guilty. Perhaps she had noticed after all.

"Do you like coffee?" he asked presently.

"Yes, please." A pause. "That was a very good meal, thank you."

"It's a pleasure." The phrase gave him an obscure sense of advantage, and he was brave enough to ask, "The room's all right, is it? Do you think you're going to feel at home here?"

"It's fine, thank you."

She washed up, without making any fuss about offering. She was very quick and neat in the kitchen. That was a relief. Peter had been accused by several women of being fanatically tidy. Anna showed no signs of accusing him of anything, but he would hate to think there was any incipient discord at this stage. He had approached the idea of a lodger with some trepidation, because other people's habits tended to be so irritating. He had decided almost at once that Anna would not irritate him, and had wondered afterwards if he had been too precipitate. There were many questions he hadn't asked. He asked one of them now.

"When do you like to have a bath?"

"What?" said Anna, reaching on tiptoe to put away the glasses. "Oh, I'm not bothered."

"I usually have a bath in the morning."

"Cold?" she enquired.

"Sorry, I didn't quite catch that."

"That's all right. I didn't mean to say it. You'd like me to bath at night, then? That's fine by me. And I'll clean the bath, so don't worry."

Peter turned slightly pink, and said quite crossly, "Nonsense, of course I wasn't worrying. Listen, I need to water the lettuces. Do you want to bring your coffee outside?"

The house still held the heat of the day trapped between its walls but the garden was now cool and restful, the soft air filled with the scent of may blossom. Anna sat on the edge of the terrace and watched Peter watering. He was distantly aware of her eyes on him. In the house he had found her disturbing and was annoyed with himself for minding so much. She was only the lodger, after all, and they had to establish an equable relationship. That was all she was doing; she could hardly be blamed for being young and attractive. Out here things acquired proportion. The rambler rose he had trained against the fence was adorned with dark red buds, and he could catch the scent of lilac from the tree at the front. There were primulas in flower below the terrace, and aubretia and arabis were covering the ugly concrete wall at the end of the house with festoons of white and purple. The mulberry leaves stirred in the evening breeze, like the sound of waves on a distant beach. Tomorrow was Sunday and he would mow the lawn.

When he went to turn off the hose he had almost forgotten she was there, and for a second he resented her. This was his garden, and she had no place in it. He didn't allow the thought to surface properly. He was too used to appreciating the society of attractive women to allow himself to wish one elsewhere. He realised that the garden was enhanced almost tangibly by her presence. Her shirt was almost the colour of the aubretia on the wall behind her and her white skirt glimmered in the dusk like a lily. An Impressionist painter would be groping for his palette, thought Peter. A brief picture of Jill flashed across his mind. Jill, with her taste for camouflage, would be sitting plumply there like a sparrow waiting for crumbs. In fact she would probably not be sitting outside at all. She would still be in the kitchen, tidying up and poking about in his kitchen cupboards. Or she would be questioning him about the vegetables.

Peter coughed. "I don't know if you're interested in vegetables?"

"I like eating," replied Anna, but she looked obediently at his garden. "It looks most impressive. I had a friend who was a gardener."

"Had you?" said Peter politely.

"Yes. He used to prune his rockery with nail scissors. When it rained he always had to go straight home to cover up his alpines. We didn't see much of him, because it rained quite

94

a lot."

"You don't get any pleasure out of gardens?"

"I like daffodils. My mother used to grow them. But I've lifted too many potatoes in my time to feel romantic about growing vegetables."

"I don't feel romantic about it. On the contrary, I find it restful."

"That's an interesting contrary." Anna stood up. "Anyway, I'll say goodnight. I have to have that bath. Thanks a lot, Peter."

It was the second time she'd said his name. She made it sound rather pleasant.

"Goodnight," said Peter, and watched her go indoors.

It was not long before he followed her, and she was still in the bathroom. Peter went through to his own room to wait. He lay sprawled on his bed with the newspaper. There was no point undressing before he had cleaned his teeth. His bed was just behind the door, which he left open, so that if she emerged she would guess that he was still up and waiting for the bathroom.

Presently the bathroom door opened, and he heard quick light steps crossing the hall. Wet steps. Peter raised his head in surprise. There was a crack along the hinges of the open door so that, with his eyes not six inches from it, he could see a section of the hallway, cork tiles and blank white walls. She was coming back again. Without actually moving, Peter adjusted his eye to the crack between the hinges. She whipped into the bathroom too quickly for him to see very clearly but she was wet, and pink, and naked, and very much as he had imagined her to be, only a little more substantial.

Two minutes later the door opened again. Peter had shifted slightly nearer the crack, and he could see better. She was in her dressing-gown this time. He had seen her in it this morning. It was blue, and made her skin seem browner and her hair fairer. She hadn't bothered to tie the belt, but held it loosely round herself. She disappeared into her room and shut the door.

Peter waited for a moment, almost as if he were afraid of being caught, though there was no place where he had a more legitimate right to be than on his own bed. It had been a complete accident, and he had seen quite enough women not to need to go out of his way to peer at them. He folded up the paper neatly, and went into the bathroom.

It was almost disappointing that she spent so little time at home. It was also a relief, naturally, because he had been used to solitude for so long that it was difficult to accommodate himself to another person. On the rare occasions when she was back before him, he was startled by the pleasure he felt. When she was out all evening he felt almost lonely. It was irrational, because she spent little time with him when she was at home. Twice during the first three weeks she stayed away all night. She never said where she had been and he would have given a good deal for the right to ask. It was a time when he could have done with some support, and even some female companionship. The relationship with Jill had fallen apart much more messily than he would have anticipated. He had not thought of Jill as being given to high drama but it transpired that he had been wrong about that. It was unpleasant having one's assumptions turned upside down. Peter realised with something approaching shock that, for the first time in his adult life, he was without a woman. There was little time to think about it. He was up until the small hours most nights, marking exam papers. It would soon be summer and it seemed likely that he would be spending it alone. He could do with a holiday but there was the garden to be considered. He didn't want to leave it just as the harvest was beginning and the weeds were still growing. He hadn't thought, when he allowed himself to become so involved with this patch of land, that it was going to tie him down all summer. Once or twice he almost wished he were free of it but that was a ridiculous thought. He had nothing else he particularly wanted to do and if he stayed he would get plenty of work done. He wondered what Anna was going to do. She would still pay rent, so presumably she would be here at least some of the time. That cheered him. Without the distractions of the term, it really would be like being on an island together. Anything might happen. Peter allowed his imagination to drift a little.

Her friend had found her an excellent desk. It was Victorian, and had plenty of brass-handled drawers. Someone had stripped it down, lightly varnished it and renewed the leather top. Either she had money to spend, or her friend must be pretty generous. There was nothing of much interest inside it. She kept her things very tidily, with one drawer for clean paper, one for other stationery, two for files full of notes carefully labelled in different sections. He was no psychologist; he couldn't make much of it. Her writing surprised him. It was not neat at all, but sprawled across the page boldly, ignoring the narrow lines of the file paper. She did keep her personal letters but Peter was a gentleman, and looked no further. Besides, most of them were only from her mother. The middle drawer of the desk had a key, and to his surprise she kept it locked. That was strange: it seemed quite unnecessary in a house as private as this.

It was the last week of term and he was exhausted. The weather had broken at last, and it was a delight to see the garden absorb the rain, the thick fen soil turn slowly from dust to good, black earth. Peter stood at the French windows watching the rain for a long time. The mulberry tree shone with wet as water dripped from its leaves on to the lawn, slowly forming a long puddle in the hollow under the tree. Peter found himself yawning, although it was barely ten o'clock. He decided to have an early night.

He must have slept well, for he never heard her come back. In the morning he noticed her car parked outside and ran his bath with a lighter heart. It had stopped raining. The garden looked spent and peaceful, open to the leaden sky. Peter whistled as he dressed, and made himself a leisurely breakfast.

He thought about knocking on her door and asking if she wanted any, then decided that if she'd had a late night she might want to sleep in. He boiled himself an egg, and made toast. He waited while the coffee percolated, then sat down on the side of the table that caught the morning sun, and automatically arranged the paper against the milk bottle.

It was good to know she was back. Somehow it disconcerted him when she stayed away without saying anything. Perhaps when she worked late she didn't always want to face the long drive back. It would be worse in winter. Maybe by that time they would be able to arrange things jointly. It would be nice to give her a lift, so that they'd have each other's company on those freezing nights, when the flat fen roads were treacherous with ice, the dykes full of water gaping blankly to receive any car that skidded off the road. There was something particularly cosy about sharing a warm car on a winter's night. It would be illogical not to, and it would be sensible next term to arrange a cooking routine. He didn't know what she had for lunch but she'd need a hot meal on a cold night. Perhaps they could take it in turns. He hadn't seen her do much cooking yet, but in summer it was different: light in the evening, and much more tempting to stay in town. He thought about long evenings by the fire. It was a pity it was only Magicoal, but the sitting-room was very pleasant. He and Anna had not yet sat in it together. It would be a good room for winter. Jill had made the curtains, in a thick red weave, very suitable for bitter fen nights, and he had bought the hearthrug himself, a traditional Persian pattern, warm and red, that he took care to lay facing east towards Mecca. Not that he used it for praying, of course. He imagined Anna sitting on the hearthrug. Somehow he saw her in dark red, completing the subdued luxuriance of the colours in the room. Perhaps her hair would have grown a little longer by then. He thought of it curling softly over her collar. He saw her dark eyes fixed upon his, strange and unfathomable in the firelight.

Peter poured himself another cup of coffee. He had not

been in love with Jill. Really, if he thought about it, she had forced herself upon him, and it was always hard to refuse an attractive woman. And with Judith – well, honestly, it had been her mind that had attracted him. Her body was thin and angular, and she was too tall for comfort. If he didn't concentrate on standing up straight, she might even be considered a little taller than he was. She was certainly not beautiful and in bed he had sometimes been slightly repelled by her boniness. Anna was not at all bony. Anna would feel slight but soft. Her hands were small and delicate; she had a precise way of touching things, very neat and careful. It would be an extraordinary thing to touch her and have her touch him back. Most particularly it would be good to touch her hair. It was so short, it seemed to have a feathery quality to it. He would like to run his hand over it. But it would be pleasant to have it grow a little longer. Perhaps if anything – it was hard at this stage to specify exactly what – if anything did happen between them, he might persuade her to let it grow. On the whole he liked women to have long hair.

He heard her door open, and turned round at once, so that he could see her as she came into the hall.

It wasn't her. It was a tall young man with black curly hair, scantily draped in a bath towel. He looked disconcerted but only for a moment. "Good morning," he said.

"Good morning," said Peter. By the time he had recovered his wits, the stranger had glided into the bathroom as though he owned the place.

Before the stranger came out again, Peter had left, cramming his books into the car and grabbing his jacket from the bedroom. He didn't want to see either of them. Before he could begin to think he was on the road to Cambridge, driving much too fast. It was outrageous. In his house. That was the worst thing of all. In his house. Without a word to him. Not so much as a by your leave, not a word. As if they owned the place. How dare she? In his own house!

The road ran straight along the edge of an embankment, where the canal flowed above it. There was a blind corner at the end, and a low arch under the canal. Peter swerved at the corner, and accelerated under the arch without a pause.

There was a car, still coming on, just under the arch. Couldn't stop. Peter swung the wheel round and missed it. There was an ugly scraping sound and his car skidded away from the arch, jerking to a stop on the opposite verge.

Peter took his hands from the wheel and saw that they were shaking. He turned off the ignition very deliberately and got slowly out of the car, moving like a stiff old man.

The other car had gone. If it had seen him hit the arch, it hadn't bothered to stop. Why should it? It was Peter's fault and he knew it. He had been driving too fast, just assuming the road was clear. As it usually was, he thought bitterly, surveying the damage.

There was a scar right the way along the passenger side and a dent where the arch had caught the edge of the passenger door. He wished rather grimly that he had a battered green mini and more money in the bank. No point thinking about that. No point thinking about that bloody girl at all. She wasn't his. He was being quite irrational; he realised that now. He had never told her about his private life and it would be a ridiculous condition of tenancy for him to censor her lovers. She had never pretended to be virginal, but if she weren't then she had no right to look so – he groped for a word – untouched. But she should have thought more of herself. She was worth more. That boy was too complacent and too bloody young.

Peter walked round his damaged car, flung himself into the driver's seat, and slammed the door. He drove into Cambridge at forty miles an hour, while images of Anna seethed mockingly in his brain.

He came home late and found the house empty. The kitchen and bathroom were both immaculate, except that two mugs had been left to drain in the rack. There was nothing to complain about, yet something indefinable had changed. It didn't feel like his home any more. The peace had evaporated.

He felt violated. Peter put the kettle on and found his hands were shaking again. It was too much. Without warning, tears pricked his eyelids so that he had to blink them back. He sat down suddenly on the kitchen stool, horrified at his own weakness. No woman had reduced him to tears since he was sixteen. He had vowed then it was for the last time and, up until now, so it had proved. So what was all this nonsense about the bloody lodger? Peter didn't wait for the kettle but went into the sitting-room and poured himself a large whisky.

It was impossible to settle down. The garden didn't need watering. Indeed, a soft rain was falling again, along with the dusk, so he was trapped in the house. He couldn't work. The computer presented him with rows of figures which seemed to make no sense. He tried a new calculation but it made nonsense of itself, so finally he pressed the escape button and thankfully watched it vanish. The evening stretched ahead, unrelieved.

He was standing in front of her desk, with no curiosity as to how he got there. Her bed was made; whatever had happened in here last night had been expunged and smoothed away. There were no clothes lying about, except a pair of fleecelined slippers on the rug beside the bed. He had never known a woman who left fewer traces of her dressing and undressing. He had only ever seen her clothes when she was in them, or when they appeared on the washing line. Even that revealed very little: she mostly hung out teeshirts and pants, usually black or white. He had deduced that she wore no other underwear and nothing at all in bed. Occasionally a skirt would appear, a pair of shorts, or jeans. He knew she always went barelegged, and barefoot as well around the house.

And here was her room, telling him no more than usual. It seemed to be cheating him. It knew so much more than he did, had witnessed so much more of her. The air seemed charged with the secrets of the past twenty hours, so that he felt quite stifled by it. He stared down at the desk. There was

101

nothing on it except a blank notepad and her portable typewriter. On an impulse he tried the locked middle drawer.

It opened and he almost jumped. There wasn't much inside it. A small cardboard box. He opened it with trembling fingers. It contained two red pebbles and a lump of quartz. An address book. That might reveal much but he only glanced at it. There was a fat black notebook underneath it and, slowly, Peter drew it out.

He was right. It was her diary. Her current diary. The first date was April of this year. He fumbled through the pages until he found the date of her arrival. He read slowly, with puzzlement, and then faster, almost frightened. It made no sense. It was crazy. She was crazy. It was not what he thought at all. It was a diary but it was mad. A mad diary. The woman must be mad. He skipped through it, reading here and there, desperate to make it rational, but there was nothing rational about it at all.

> I was on the coast of Carolina, and the mist was creeping in so thick I could barely see the place where the waves broke upon the shore, yet, from the noise they made, that could hardly be two yards away. The sand was dry and cold, slow to walk in, at each step I sank so deep. And the foghorn never stopped, before or behind me, sounding mournfully right along the shore like the ghost of all the drowned ships that must have met their end on this lee shore.
>
> The lighthouse was not so far away, though no light pierced that gloomy fog. I don't know why I had to reach that light but the urgency was there. The fog lay thicker still and the sand grew soft and heavy so I couldn't run. I could hear waves breaking, slow and muffled on the hidden shore. Why Carolina I don't know, but the word rang through my head like an echo. There was something ominous about it, some terror that lay inland, where I couldn't see.

Barney was in Culpeper's herb shop, the one just by the bus station. It was dark blue in there and all moving. The mermaids were behind the counter and we had to buy what we needed from them but the shelves were drowning too fast. The tide was coming in over rocks on the shore, the seaweed rising and falling, a brown jungle of life belonging to some other dimension. But the mulberry tree stood clear and firm at the cliff top, the light between its branches a star for seamen shining across from horizon to horizon.

I was afraid because I had trodden across his garden. The stakes he had put in for his peas and beans were all knocked apart and I could see my own bare footprints on the raked soil. The black cotton had snapped, and something had pulled out all his onion sets. At first I was trying to smooth over my own footprints, and then I was trying to put back the onions but the earth didn't seem to hold them. It was floating away too fast and the boats on the dyke were being washed up into the garden.

Long, white corridors all lined with cork tiles, so long that the two walls seemed to join together in a point at the far end. The corridor seemed empty at first, but soon I was overcome by the cathedrals. Someone had been taking photographs of cathedrals. I could feel the danger. I was calling for Barney, over and over again, but there was no sound in that place. My voice seemed to have no sound at all.

Islands of sheep. Islands of sheep. The sea so calm and still, flat as a field on a summer's day. The islands were bright green like toys, like the scenery on our model railway at home, and the sheep were white as plastic snow. Islands of sheep like lily pads, floating towards the sun. A very gentle languorous kind of a place. It was easier to stop counting, to let the boat dissolve beneath me and drift into another kind of sleep.

At first it seemed to be Barney but when I came closer it wasn't, it was Peter. He had grown old and crabbit, wrinkled, with a beard but, even so, I could not run. He was drawing me towards him. Perhaps he was laughing at me. The horrible thing was that it was sexual. I felt as sexual as if it had been Barney, as though I could not stop. I could hear the foghorn groan its warning from above but I was still drawn forwards, while I hated him. There were mulberries everywhere. The ground was slippery with red juice like blood, and the old man standing in the middle, leering at me.

That time I woke up shaking. This house seems full of nightmares and yet it has no character at all. I am comfortable and uneasy; I like this place and I hate it. Something is happening that eludes me. Why are these dreams so full of danger?

She never came home that night. Peter slept late the next morning. He woke feeling hot and sticky. The garden was no relief, it was too close and humid. Clouds of insects hovered over the muddy dyke and spread themselves across the garden. Peter was driven indoors, where he daubed himself with insect repellent before returning to his weeding. It was really too hot to work. The soil was so dry it came away in hard lumps with every weed he pulled, or broke the roots. Presently he gave up and went to spray the pear tree. There were hundreds of tiny pears forming already, some already adorned with ominous little scabs.

Peter pushed through the long grass to the dyke and looked out over the fen. It shimmered in the heat, its horizon fluid, almost lost in the heavy haze. The dyke gave off a pungent smell of drying mud. Peter found himself sneezing, although pollen never usually affected him. The air was too heavy, and the hedgerow seemed almost dangerously lush, as though unknown tropical poisons lurked in its depths.

He tried sitting outside in the shade of the mulberry tree, but his skin felt moist and itchy and small crawling things seemed to be finding their way around the insect spray. He sneezed again. The air hardly seemed to retain enough energy to carry the sound, so that it fell dully round his ears. It was all too much, in England. Peter got up again and went indoors, carrying his garden chair under one arm.

In the afternoon he slept a little, which was most unusual for him. Lying on his bed with the curtains drawn, he closed his eyes and realised that several little hammers were beating rhythmically inside his head against his temples. Even indoors there was no darkness and white light seemed to beat against his eyelids, turning them fiery red. He should have been in the department, but exams were finished and there would not be a soul there anyway.

When he awoke the sun had shifted, so that the shadow of the window frame had moved a few inches across the curtains. Nothing else had changed. Peter sat up rather shakily, then padded across to the kitchen. His bare feet made small squelching noises on the tiles. The floor felt unpleasantly warm, like drinking lukewarm white wine. He fetched a carton of orange juice from the fridge, and drank it from the packet, gulping the whole lot down without stopping. It left him feeling slightly sick. The headache was back, if it had ever left him. He supposed he ought to eat something, but the idea of something specific nauseated him. He wondered if he were feverish, and wandered into the bathroom to take his temperature.

It was quite normal. He felt frustrated at being baulked of a rational explanation. It would have been quite simple to go to bed with an aspirin, but that was no solution if he were not ill. He drifted into the sitting-room, and switched on the television. That was most unlike him: normally he only watched the news while he had his supper.

He was still there when her key turned in the lock. He heard her go into her own room and shut the door. He wondered if she would stay there. His stomach churned, and his hands, pressed tightly together, were cold and clammy.

Two minutes later she appeared at the sitting-room door.

"Hello," she said.

"Hello." His voice came out too harshly, and he coughed.

"Isn't it hot?" said Anna. "Are you feeling all right?"

"Why shouldn't I be?" It sounded surly but normal enough.

"You look a bit pale, that's all. And you're usually in college on Tuesdays."

"Just a bit of a headache," he said, trying to smile. "I thought it would be even hotter in town."

"It was. Well, I'll leave you in peace. Would you like a cup of tea? I'm making one for me."

"Yes, please," he said, and at once wished he hadn't. He didn't need favours from a girl who would no doubt be just as sympathetic to her great-grandfather. But that was ridiculous. She wasn't to know what he was thinking. It would never cross her mind that he knew what he knew, and it mustn't.

He received a mug of tea with a good grace. He heard her go back into her room and switch on the radio. She was always careful not to turn it up too loud, and he could only just hear it. Radio Three. Vaughan Williams. Some people would say he was very lucky in his tenant. In fact two men he knew had said precisely that after only one look at her. Peter sighed deeply and picked up the newspaper, which he had already read.

She was at the door again, breathless and troubled. He sat up quickly. Too quickly, he thought, his heart pounding. What had she found?

"Peter," said Anna. "Have you seen my sand dollar?"

"Your what?" His bewilderment was quite genuine.

"My sand dollar. It was on my chest of drawers, leaning

106

against the snuffbox. I know it was there. You haven't seen it?"

"Well, no, not if that's where it was. How should I? Anyway," said Peter more easily, "what's a sand dollar?"

"A kind of shell. Sort of round, with five holes and a pattern. I don't think I've seen it for a while." She really seemed quite upset.

"It was important to you?"

"Barney gave it to me. He picked it up on the beach in South Carolina. He brought it home for me because he said the place reminded him of me. I suppose it doesn't matter. Only it was . . . well, it was important. Sentimental value, I suppose you'd say," she added with an irony that he recognised as her usual manner towards him. Strange that he hadn't noticed it before. She must be flustered to be telling him so much about herself. He should have felt guilty, but the fact was he felt light with relief. It could have been so much more serious.

"Who's Barney?" asked Peter, looking sympathetic.

She stared at him. "You met him yesterday morning! At least, he said he'd met you."

"Oh, so that was Barney?"

"I thought you knew," said Anna vaguely, frowning. "Oh well, never mind. I can't understand it, that's all. No, you couldn't know. Don't worry about it."

She left him quickly, cutting short his helpfulness, and went back to her room.

The evening brought no coolness. On the contrary, the night fell thick and cloying, without so much as stirring the saturated air of the garden. Peter refused her offer of supper and went to bed early. He thought he would lie awake for hours. He lay sprawled under the topsheet, trying to keep cool by lying spread out and still.

Temperature or no temperature, he must be ill. He hadn't felt like this since he had the 'flu, five years ago. His memory of it was vague, but apparently his temperature had been 104° and he had become so feverish he had started to hallucinate. It had been a sort of waking dream, falling in and out of consciousness, like drowning. He'd been told some of the things he'd said, afterwards, and he couldn't recollect them at all. What was her name now? Sue, that was it – his girlfriend of the time had nursed him through it. Come to think of it, she'd been a nurse, which was useful. He could remember the cool touch of her hands on his hot skin, and wished someone would do the same for him now. His mother had never been any good at things like that. She used to tramp up to his bed, usually with some revolting medicine, and ask him how he was feeling with abrupt suspicion, then question him about why he was always ill on the same day as maths coaching, or his dancing class. He didn't want his mother. He wanted Anna. If only Anna would come now. She had cared about him. She'd offered him tea, and supper, and asked him how he felt. Suppose he knocked on her door and told her he was ill? He imagined the quick sympathy she would show, her coming through in her dressing-gown, feeling his forehead, knowing what should be done.

Peter turned over, his body crawling with prickly sweat. He felt desperate. Perhaps he should go to the bathroom and take his temperature again. It must have been wrong before. Perhaps the thermometer was broken. He remembered having his temperature taken at school and holding the thermometer under the hot tap when Matron wasn't looking. She'd read it, and turned her callous gaze upon his shivering body. "Did you hold this under the hot tap?" she'd asked him. She couldn't have seen him do it and yet she knew. He had denied it, of course, had lied his way out of it as he had had to lie his way out of everything in that place.

It was school which had first given him something to hide. At home they might not have thought much of him, but they accepted him as he was, with resignation on his mother's part, and an absent-minded tolerance on his father's. At school he had very quickly learned that he had to pretend to be different. That was nearly thirty years ago. Thirty years in terror of discovery, of dreadful anticipation of the day when all would be found out and he would be exposed.

Escape was always such a relief. Leaving school, leaving college, leaving relationships. Leaving every time with his reputation still intact. But Matron had known about the thermometer, and he had known that she had known. All women had been like that. They pretended not to know, and he pretended he didn't know they knew. He knew he had been unfair to Judith. More than that, he had hurt her. But she seemed to know so much about him. She implied things that made him smart with indignation. Naturally he had denied reading those letters he had found in her flat, just as he had denied seeing Anne, pretending that he had gone home for Christmas after all. Perhaps Judith even guessed that the caller who always put the phone down was him, making sure she wasn't lying to him and that she really had decided to stay at home. She had told him that she had complained to British Telecom and had informed the police. Perhaps she was lying as much as he was. Perhaps she hadn't done either of those things but, because she knew, had found an obscure way of threatening him.

It would be so much easier if there were no secrets. But it had never been like that. At school, even crying at night could not be done in secret. They used to pull a boy out of bed and shine a torch in his face, if they suspected him of weeping. The only way to be safe was to turn bully himself. He had become adept at creeping up and pulling a small boy out of bed. It meant that the younger boys hated him, and that made things no easier. Maybe Judith hated him now.

What if he called Anna now? Would Anna know that he was guilty? Would she guess how he was really feeling? How could he pretend to her that he were ill, and get away with it, unless he really were ill? Perhaps he really was, otherwise his thoughts would not be in this confusion.

The sheet was damp and hot. He tugged it away from the foot of the bed and tried to get a fresh bit over him. It would be a strange thing to grow up familiar with the inside of a lighthouse. He had only once been in a lighthouse himself. He remembered climbing in a long spiral, the steps painted red and the brass so polished it seemed to shine like lamplight. The steps winding on up, growing gradually smaller, and the walls coming in closer, so that it was hard to remember what size anything was supposed to be any more.

He saw a girl with bleached blond plaits tied with two red ribbons, climbing slowly, one step at a time, pulling herself up by the brass banister rail that was the height of her shoulders. She looked so small in that huge tower, with the light far above hanging over her, pulling herself doggedly up, her grey cardigan buttoned tight across her chest.

The tower grew in his imagination, stretching out hugely, its curves distorted so that the spiral in which she climbed seemed to stretch itself into another dimension, bending out over a raging sea. Water pounded upon the rocks, and malignant spray leapt up, flinging itself against the tower. But the light shone out steadily. The child stood silhouetted against the great lantern, magnified by mirror upon mirror of glass.

He was very close against the rocks now and his boat was of no use. It was a punt and there was nothing he could do with a punt in a sea like this, except to try to stave off the hungry rocks with the pole, as the sea dragged him nearer. The light was mocking him, shining like a beacon of safety over the very scene of his own destruction. He struck out with his pole and the girl flinched back under the blow. He struck her again and woke in a sweat of shame, realising the enormity of what he was about to do.

He could hear the wind outside now, howling like a ghost against the concrete corners of the house. It was worse to sleep than wake. He had to stop thinking about her. Perhaps he should go to the bathroom and take a couple of aspirin. Did aspirin cure a man of dreams? Peter shuddered and buried his head under the pillow, as if the world could be shut out. He had lain like that at school, huddled and terrified, surrounded by movements and muttering that made no sense to him. He didn't want it to make sense. He didn't want to know anything about it at all. But when they had dragged him out of his hiding-place, which was not a hiding-place, and forced him to see, and know, he had not resisted. There was nothing left to do but lie, and never to admit to anything. He must not know what he felt. Peter sat up, eyes still closed, and hurled the pillow from him. A dry sob shook him. He didn't recognise it for what it was; it was so long since he had felt anything of the kind. He ignored it and lay down again, pulling the sheet up to his chin. He was exhausted. A flurry of rain beat against the window. Somehow that was a relief. Finally, he slept.

He awoke feeling sick and heavy, as if no time had passed at all. The curtains billowed out into the room. He could see their vague shapes welling in the gloom. There was a sighing outside like distant waves. He was burning hot. He rolled over on to his stomach and pulled the sheet over his head.

Whether he slept again or not, he was aware of himself, an inert body huddled on the bed like a twisted corpse under the stretched white sheet. He was frightened, seeing his body there, but he didn't dare to leave himself. The bed heaved under him, slid into a trough, and started rising. At the top it hovered precariously. He held his breath, waiting for the crash, but none came, only the slow descent, gaining momentum, so his stomach seemed to leap into his throat. He tried to clutch on with his hands, but it was all too fluid, liquid yielding even as he touched.

There was wetness everywhere. He was on the terrace, the rain splintering across his hot flesh, soaking him in a moment. There was a roaring in his ears, crashing of the sea against rock, sea sucked down into the caves under the island and dying away to a trickle. The light flashed, and the whole garden was silhouetted, purple under a black sky, branches tossing in the wind, and the bean rows bent before the storm. Rain splattered on the terrace, drumming footsteps coming nearer. He backed off, wet grass brushing his feet, while the sea crashed down again and drew back with a thunderous sucking sound, dragging malevolently at the foundations of the island.

The flash revealed a garden in torment, shrubs beaten down, frail stems broken by the rain, and the bean rows falling, twining shoots torn away, the poles cracked and bent apart.

He was there. He was there among the ruins of his plants, speaking to them soothingly, only he had to shriek to be heard above the water. The next crash was right overhead, the rock beaten down, the light flashing, and the tower falling, falling towards him endlessly. He heard the voices of the drowned screaming over the waves behind him, the high-pitched scream of a woman who was hardly more than a child. The light from the falling tower blew apart, fiery bolts tore into the sea. Then the tower broke, and crashed, washing him down with it into the hungry sea.

A white Metro drew up outside the bungalow, and stopped. The driver appeared to be consulting directions written on the back of an envelope. Evidently satisfied, she got out and, after a moment's hesitation, locked the car door behind her. She pushed her hair back behind her ears, and readjusted her glasses. Then she stepped into the porch and rang the bell. The first two bars of the Westminster chimes rang out cheerfully. The visitor winced, then peered through the ribbed glass as a figure approached on the inside. It was difficult to see into the darkness of the house but it seemed to be a woman, not particularly tall.

The door opened. The woman inside was much younger than she had expected. Her hair was startlingly fair, curling down so that it just touched her collar. She was dressed in jeans and a dark red jersey, and fleecelined slippers. The newcomer held out her hand.

"Mary Barnes," she said. "I think I spoke to you on the phone."

"That's right. I'm Anna. Come in."

Mary Barnes looked round the bare hall approvingly. The place could hardly be cleaner. She was equally pleased with

112

the well-appointed kitchen, and the bathroom.

"Though I'm not sure I fancy those mermaids," she remarked. "Don't you ever feel like they're looking at you when you've got nothing on?"

"I don't suppose they get a big surprise if they do," said Anna. "This is the room. Go on in."

Mary stood in the middle of the room which might be hers, and looked round. It was bare but pleasant. There was a plain grey carpet, and double windows facing on to the terrace. A good-sized double bed filled all the space behind the door, neatly covered by a white candlewick bedspread. There were white fitted cupboards right along one wall. Mary opened the doors and examined them inside.

"They're all empty," remarked Anna, "except the ones at the top. All the owner's things are stored there."

"I wouldn't be needing them anyway."

There was a chintz-covered armchair, and a large mirror on the wall. The reprint over the chest of drawers was a Monet: *The Jetty at Le Havre*, borrowed from the public library. It was a satisfactorily blank room, one that could soon be adapted to an individual taste.

"Well, I'm interested," said Mary. "Did you say there was a garden?"

"Come and see."

Mary stood on the terrace for a minute or two, surveying the scene. "Well," she said at last. "Well, that is a pity."

"The mulberry tree, you mean? Yes, it blew down in June, the night of that big storm. It's a shame. It must have been hundreds of years old."

"And the garden too," said Mary sorrowfully.

It was a pathetic sight for any gardener. The tree had crashed right on to the vegetable garden. Its leaves still clung to it, though they had turned a livid yellow. The trunk had cracked across the middle, exposing raw wood in great splinters. Among the wreckage of the tree was a tangle of broken bamboo poles. Only the beans had not suffered; they had twined up over the treetrunk like some exotic tropical

113

creeper, their leaves still green and lush, as yet untouched by frost. Someone had sawn the branches back where they had lain across the lawn, and there were trails of sawdust across the wet grass. The lawn itself needed mowing but that would be difficult with the tree in the way. Weeds were rampant, going to seed in all the surrounding flower beds.

"Well, at least it's September," said Mary. "That puts time on our side. You can tell it was once looked after."

"It was," said Anna. "Do you like gardening?"

Mary shrugged. "In moderation. I'd like to do a bit here, it could be so pretty. Would that be in order, do you think? The owner wouldn't mind?"

"I'm sure he wouldn't."

"Well, I must say I'm very taken with the place. Thanks for showing me round. I'll go back to the agent and say yes, I think. You've not had anyone else round yet?" There was a note of anxiety in her voice.

"Not yet. You were very quick. You must have phoned as soon as the paper came out."

"I did, just about. It's pretty desperate, looking for a place just before the beginning of term." Mary followed Anna in through the French windows. "And the owner – he's on sabbatical, I heard?"

"He was ill. A nervous breakdown due to overwork. That's what the doctor said. He's gone abroad now with a friend."

"Oh, so he wasn't quite alone?"

"No. Jill – that's his friend – fixed up to take him to a friend's house in Spain. He'll be all right," said Anna dispassionately.

"Well, I'm pleased to hear that. I'll nip back to the agent's now, and confirm all this. Very pleased to meet you, Anna, and I'll look forward to sharing with you." She looked at Anna hopefully. "I'm sure we'll get along."

"I'm sure we shall," said Anna politely.

Conditions of Employment

The young woman in the duffle coat lay face down on the slope above the waterfall, sobbing her heart out. The ground was soaking wet and last year's sodden leaves clung to her clothes and hair. Her cheek was smeared with mud but she ignored it. There was no comfort in a wet wood in January, but she didn't want comfort. All she needed was the noise of the falls, to give her permission to cry as loud as she liked. The burn roared on, imposing no time limits. She wept passionately, until her throat hurt so much she could sob no more and her whole body was shaken so she had to gasp for breath. The waterfall was as loud as ever, mocking her weakness. Suddenly she stood up, glaring at it, wiping her wet cheeks with grubby hands. A smear of mud trailed across her nose.

"Shut up!" she screamed. The waterfall ignored her.

She was scrabbling at the bank now, squatting at the edge of the moss that marked the reach of the spray. There were boulders there, and small rocks. She prised a rock free and levered it up. It was slimy, and as heavy as she could hold in two hands. Somehow she picked it right up, shoulder-high, then hurled it with all her strength into the white water.

"Shut up! Shut up! Shut up!"

The water absorbed it without a sound, without seeming to yield an inch.

She was pulling out another rock, round and moss-covered. She stood up, right at the edge of the slippery bit. She was scarlet in the face now, regarding the burn with pure hatred. She was about to raise the stone, and then she paused.

She was speaking now, slowly and deliberately, loud enough for the burn to hear, over its own noise.

"Either . . . " she said, the stone clammy between her hands, "either I have something . . . just one thing. Either I get a job, or, if not a job, a lover . . . Either that, or something will happen. Something that hurts. Like this!" She raised the stone and flung it.

This time it wasn't taken in at once. It hit a rock halfway down the fall, and bounced up again. It descended into the burn in a couple of heavy thuds and landed in the pool below, with a great splash that was just audible.

She stared after it. "Preferably both," she said. "You hear that? It has to be one or the other, but I want both. Otherwise . . ." She grappled with the third rock. It was bigger than the other two and it left a larger scar, bare mud with a trickle of wet sand at the bottom. She could hardly lift it but, panting, she got it clear of the edge and threw as hard as she was able. It landed heavily in the pool, leaving a momentary ripple, even over the turbulence from the falls.

"If I don't," she threatened, looking down at the pool, "someone will get hurt." She wiped her eyes again, her flush subsiding. It seemed a silly, pointless thing to have done.

"Presumably me."

The Job Centre was just the same as it was every Friday. She saw at a glance that almost every card on the rack was familiar. They still wanted a school leaver to stack shelves in the supermarket for £1.20 an hour. They were still looking for a qualified night care assistant in the home for the elderly at £1.50 an hour, pay for your own uniform. The fashion company was still wanting machinists to work at home, supply your own sewing machine, £3 for every finished garment. They still wanted a forestry manager with at least five years' experience. The job in the solicitors' office had gone. She wondered vaguely from where an experienced legal secretary had landed who wanted £3 an hour that badly. It couldn't be anyone who was up on the local gossip.

She stuck her hands in the pockets of her ancient duffle coat, and looked along the racks in the same order as every week, aware of the indifferent eyes of the two assistants following her. They never seemed to have much to do. They were probably looking at the mudstains on her coat, and the new patch on her jeans. She had ripped them the other day, throwing stones.

There was a new card at the end of the rack.

Experienced steeplejacks, no doubt. She glanced at it cautiously, with a feeling she was being watched from the desk behind her.

"Well guardian," it said. "No experience necessary. Excellent pay. Interviews by arrangement. Residential . . ." and so on.

She stared at the card for a minute or two. The wording did not change. Then she braced herself, and turned to face the secretary, who quickly shoved her magazine into a drawer and looked up enquiringly.

"What is a well guardian?" she asked diffidently.

"Name please," said the secretary, turning to the files.

"Miranda Duthie. What is a well guardian?"

There was a pause while the secretary looked through a file. "Yes," she said. "That only came in a day or two ago. Do you want me to fix you an interview?"

"What is a well guardian?"

"It doesn't seem to say. I can arrange an interview if you like."

It seemed a very odd arrangement for a job interview. Miranda stood at the crossroads at the place where the spruce plantation ended and the land opened out into a moor. It was a clear blue day, like a mirage of spring, only the wind off the hills had the bite of frost in it, and the peaks themselves were sprinkled white, glinting cruelly in the sun.

Three roads met at the top of a little plateau, so that the whole moor was spread out in view, open and frozen. The night wind had burned the roadside frost into beautiful intricate patterns. Miranda walked on them absent-mindedly, her feet inside her boots numb with cold, despite three pairs of socks. Below the plateau there was an old packhorse bridge, just wide enough for a car to pass on the thinly tarmacked road which led south. The burn chattered over the stones beneath it, shrunken with cold, and a row of icicles adorned the arch of the bridge. Miranda wandered down to the bridge and stared at the water. She glanced at her watch. Nearly ten. It was the strangest place for an interview. If it turned out to be a joke, she'd be furious. If she complained to the Job Centre they'd probably take no notice. She could write to her MP. The last time she'd done that he'd replied very gently, as if she were a shorn lamb led astray by Bolsheviks.

Ten o'clock. She began to retrace her steps to the cross-roads.

"Miranda Duthie?"

She swung round. She knew the road was deserted. She'd seen that it was.

It wasn't. A woman stood on the bridge, smiling politely.

"Oddny," she said.

"I beg your pardon?"

"My name is Oddny. You must be Miranda?"

"Yes." Miranda tried hard to pull herself together. "I've come to be interviewed."

"Of course."

There was a short pause while the two women looked each other over. Miranda was not impressed. She knew she was shabbily dressed herself but there was some excuse for that, as she'd never had a job in her life, and not for want of trying. However, she didn't go for the ethnic homespun look at all, and this woman seemed to carry it to extremes. She was dressed in a heavy undyed woollen skirt, with a plaid draped around her like the old prints of Highland dress that adorned the lounge bar in the local pub. Her boots were all too obviously homemade, being clumsily cut and sewn together with big stitches of leather thongs. Her hair was dark, very long and thick, with two strands woven into plaits and fastened at the back of her head.

I bet she smells of garlic and woodsmoke, thought Miranda resentfully. I don't think I fancy this.

"Will you come and see the well?" suggested Oddny gently.

"The well? Oh yes, of course. The well."

"It's just along here."

It gradually became clear that Oddny had country notions of distance. They walked for half an hour in silence. After a mile or so they left the road and skirted the moor. Presently the country became wilder; the hillocks that edged the mountains became rougher, scarred by small precipices and sweeps of scree. The two women picked their way carefully across. The high peaks themselves were drawing nearer and, as they did so, the wind grew keener, bringing with it the smell of snow. It was a desolate place, caught between mountains and the silent ranks of spruce below. At this time of year the grass was yellow and sodden, interspersed with withered clumps of heather which scratched at their boots as they passed.

They scrambled round the foot of a precipice, and found themselves on the flank of a corrie. The ground fell away steeply from the hills that surrounded it on three sides, so steeply that in places the slope turned to outcrops of rock. It might have been a dismal place, only the corrie faced south, looking out over the tops of older trees, birch and rowan and hawthorn, over a wide expanse of lowland broken by hillocks, mostly blanketed in trees. There was a loch down there, gleaming grey in the winter sun, and the smoke of a village beyond, lying like a pall under the weight of the still air.

As they climbed cautiously down they heard water. A burn flowed southwards, to the trees and the blue distance where the sea lay. The spring must be in the corrie itself, for no water streaked the steep sides. Miranda couldn't see until they came close, because the source of the water was hidden by a smooth grass-covered mound and a scatter of boulders. She could hear the burn sounding quite loud. The spring must be in the shelter of the rocks. She could see a little grove of trees, mostly rowan, shielding what must be a pool. Then she glanced up, and her heart gave a painful thump.

There was smoke rising from beyond the boulders, apparently from the grassy mound itself.

"Is that a fire?"

"Oh yes, I kept the fire in. Come down to the well first. It's actually the spring; you can see that."

It was a deep pool, overhung by rowan, surrounded by moss-covered rock. The brightness of the moss struck a chord in Miranda's mind, and with a slight shock she realised that this must be the same burn as the waterfall by which she had lain . . . was it only last week? She stared down at the pool, vaguely aware of some connection, but it made no sense. The water was brown and deep, bubbling under the rocks where the spring must surface. Her thoughts were all confusion.

"I don't quite see what the job is," she said.

"No? But this is all," answered Oddny, with a sweeping gesture that somehow included the pool and the rowans. "Just to look after the well. I can't tell you more. It's unpredictable, really."

It made no sense, but Miranda made herself recollect some of the questions she had prepared on the bus, before the long walk from the crossroads had begun to disorientate her. "You said it was residential?"

"Of course. Come and see."

Oddny led her along a narrow treacherous path above the pool, round to the back of the green mound. There was a doorway. Oddny ducked and entered. Miranda hesitated. She was not particularly superstitious but there was something about that configuration of rock, one horizontal slab balanced upon two vertical, with the dark rectangle of the threshold between, that stirred some atavistic memory and made her shudder.

"Please come in." From inside, Oddny's voice sounded

thin and hollow. Some instinct made Miranda cross her fingers. She stepped inside.

There was very little light but it was quite comfortable. The fire had sunk into a mass of glowing embers. Oddny was busy raking them together and laying on fresh peat. The place smelt of garlic and smoke. Bunches of unidentifiable dried plants hung upside down from the ceiling. There was a spinning wheel in one corner, with a stool beside it. A carved chest stood on one side of the fire and a sleeping platform on the other, piled high with woven blankets. There were pots of varying sizes ranged by the door. That was all.

"You could bring anything of your own that you wanted. It goes with the job, so it's all yours."

"Thank you." Miranda knew that she was soon going to have to explain that this was hardly what she was thinking of, but curiosity prevented her for the moment. That, and desperation. She had been unemployed for too long to have retained any rigid expectations. She decided to test the situation by asking another of her questions.

"What about pay?"

The young man in the antique shop turned back from the window and put down his magnifying glass. He regarded Miranda across the clutter on his desk, in some bewilderment.

"There's no doubt about it," he was saying, almost reluctantly, "they are genuine, first-century Roman coins. In fact they must be some of the earliest Romano-British coins minted." He looked down again at the coin in his hand, as if it might be spirited away at any moment. "Quite genuine," he repeated. "I only hesitated because of their condition. They must have lain in a hoard for God knows how long. You'd think they'd never seen the light of day."

He laid the money out on a sheet of writing paper. "Quite remarkable."

Miranda waited for a moment for him to take his eyes off her pay packet, then she coughed politely.

"A thousand?" he said suddenly.

Miranda gaped. Pence? she nearly said, but stopped herself just in time, and changed it to, "What?"

"A thousand pounds," he said, and grinned, a little crookedly. "It's a good thing you came to a reputable dealer, you know."

"Why?" she asked suspiciously.

"You're supposed to cultivate a mask-like expression. A thousand. I daresay you can use it."

Miranda decided not to resent that and looked him over. He seemed quite pleasant, though rather faded-looking, presumably as a result of spending his days in this place. Brown hair, brown jacket, brown corduroy trousers, much too baggy, and scuffed brown shoes. He even had brown frames to his glasses.

"A thousand it is," said Miranda.

He left her and disappeared into the back of the shop. Presumably he had a safe there. This shop didn't seem too hot on security but perhaps he thought she had an honest face. The doorbell was loud enough to warn of an intruder. He came back with a cheque book and stopped to wipe his glasses. "Can I ask who sent you here?"

His eyes were not brown, but quite startlingly blue. She realised for the first time that he was worth a second glance. "The shop on the High Street. They said you specialised in coins."

"Ah." He sounded gratified. "It just shows. Water on a stone: how powerful it can be. If you persist long enough, you get there in the end."

"Where? Fame?"

"Anything you want. Here, you'd better check this."

Miranda read through the cheque carefully. Then she pocketed the advance on her first month's salary. She saw his hand held out and, slightly taken aback, shook it.

"You'll come here if you get any more like that?"

"I expect I shall," said Miranda.

It was a week or two before there was any work to do at all, and then for quite a time it was only routine matters. Her first visitor was a girl of about ten, who had a large wart on her thumb.

"Goodness, I don't know," said Miranda, startled by the simple request. "Why did you come here, anyway?"

The girl was a plain freckled child in a polyester anorak and tight jeans. She gave Miranda a look as brown and unfathomable as the depths of the pool at twilight and explained patiently, "We've always come here."

"Oh," said Miranda, and thought fast. "Well, go down to the pool and dip the thumb in three times. Then turn in a circle moonwise and go straight home without saying a word to anybody. Show the thumb to the full moon when it rises next Thursday and that should do the trick."

The child left, apparently satisfied, and Miranda returned to her green mound to eat prawns and avocado, and read *The White Goddess*. It was the first new hardback she had ever bought.

The following day brought a boy with acne. She advised him to bathe his face in burnwater every moonlit night and to give up fried foods and chocolate. Then came a girl of twelve who was worried because she didn't have a boyfriend. Miranda taught her how to read tea leaves, and gave her a reading list of romantic novels. After the girl had gone, she worried that perhaps that wasn't right but it was too late and she was presently interrupted by an old man whose cow was sick. Miranda told him a charm to St Bride, made up on the spur of the moment, and suggested that he ring the vet.

That night she sat down to chicken in aspic and a half bottle of vin rosé, thinking she had earned it.

The next day brought a girl of sixteen, pale and agitated, who bore a marked resemblance to her first visitor. She gave Miranda a box of After Eights. "From Jenny. The wart went. The morning after the full moon it was gone, just like that."

"Of course," said Miranda. "And can I help you?"

The girl explained.

125

Oh dear, thought Miranda, this is getting controversial. Well, I can only do what I'm paid to do. "How many weeks late?" she said aloud.

"Two."

Miranda breathed a sigh of relief, and reached up to cut a little bunch of pennyroyal which she handed to the girl. She explained how to make a tea. "Drink it tonight," she said. "Bow three times to the waning moon, and call upon every goddess you can remember the name of. Look them up in an encyclopaedia if you don't know any. If nothing happens, go and see the doctor the very next day. If nothing happens with that, try this phone number." She scribbled a name and number. "But don't put it off. It must all be done before the moon has waned."

The girl thanked her profusely and left. Miranda went back to her brand new copy of *Folklore of the British Isles* and sat by the fire, munching After Eights. It was a long time before she turned a page. She was not used to responsibility and she found it weighed an uncomfortable amount.

"Norse," said the brown young man. "Danish coins. Tenth century, I should judge." He closed the book he had been consulting, and peered at Miranda through his glasses. "Of course, this area was Norse at that time but, even so, we can safely say that this is a unique find in south-west Scotland." He cleared his throat. "May I offer you a cup of coffee?"

"Thank you," said Miranda, and hesitated. "Can you give me a price?"

He looked uncomfortable. "I can, of course. Wait while I put the kettle on . . ." Miranda followed him to the back of the shop and watched him rinse two mugs, then measure out coffee. "It's a difficult question, value. There is a monetary value – of course there is – and I'm sure it's all fair and square. But . . ."

Miranda didn't help him. They sat down, one on each side of the large desk.

"I'm quite interested in archaeology myself," he said. She

noticed that his normally pale skin was somewhat flushed. "The historical value of these things is in its context, I'm sure you know that. Can I ask you . . .?" He paused, then the words came out with a rush, "Where are you finding these coins?"

"I'm being paid. Monthly. Every new moon. I was told to find them in a hollow rock above a well, when the new moon has risen. And I do."

There was a long silence.

"Could you tell me a little more, perhaps? If you don't object, that is?"

She thought it over, and realised somewhat to her surprise that she didn't object. In a way it would be a relief to check her own sanity against some external standard. He could have cheated her before. Maybe he had, of course, but she doubted it.

"It's all fair and square," said Miranda. "If I tell you what I'm doing, will you promise not to interfere in any way, whatever your view of the matter may be?"

He shook his head slowly. "No, I don't think I can."

"Why not?"

"Not if I thought it was doing harm. I couldn't promise."

She frowned. "And if it isn't?"

"If it isn't, then I promise."

Miranda stirred her coffee, and looked down into the swirling liquid. "Very well, then. Listen."

Three days later, she had another case to deal with.

She had been out shopping again. Dusk was falling by the time she had walked the five miles from the village where the bus stopped. It had taken her a long time to climb the hill, because she had so much to carry. She was no longer wearing her old duffle coat, but a smart new jacket with a new red jumper underneath. On her feet she had new boots that didn't leak. Her bag was full of books and groceries: in the still evening air she could pick up the faint scent of freshly ground coffee from the parcel jammed in her left pocket.

127

The sight of a horse quietly cropping the brown turf above the pool stopped her in her tracks. It was a very large horse, and its white coat glimmered in the twilight. It was saddled and bridled, and it struck Miranda there was something ornate, even outlandish, about its tack. She thought back to her days of hanging about the local riding school. None of the horses had been dressed up like that. She approached cautiously, for horses made her slightly nervous at the best of times.

The man was sitting in her favourite spot on the dry rock above the pool, out of reach of the encroaching moss. He was gazing south into the darkening valley, apparently deep in thought. She had half expected that he would be wearing armour, but he wasn't. He was dressed in a plain woven tunic and leggings but he wore a large sword strapped to his belt. His hair was dark and fell to his shoulders. For one brought up on Malory he seemed disappointingly scruffy.

"Hello," said Miranda, trying not to sound irritated, although she had been looking forward to a quiet evening, and he was sitting in the seat she regarded as her own.

"Good evening, mistress." He stood up and bowed deeply, just as she had expected him to do.

"Can I help you?" asked Miranda cautiously, putting down her shopping bag.

"I hope so."

"Well, wait a minute then. I must just put all this away."

She wondered if she should invite him in, but it was a mild evening with no breeze and she wasn't sure if he'd want to come. When she had made up the fire and put her things away, she went outside again.

It seemed to have got much darker in a few minutes, but she could make him out quite clearly, still sitting on the rock above the pool.

"I'm here now."

"Yes." It was a relief that he didn't speak in Pictish, or ancient Gaelic. "I came for a prophecy," he said.

Well, tough luck, she thought. "Oh yes?" encouraged

Miranda politely.

"I'm sorry to keep disturbing you," he said, apparently misreading her tone. "We have no other way of knowing what has changed."

"Not at all. You haven't disturbed me before, anyway."

"It is most civil of you to say so. I know that last time you told me to have patience for at least five generations, but I think that time has now passed, and I hope you won't be angry if I trouble you again."

Miranda could think of nothing intelligent to say, so she didn't speak.

"We hear nothing," he went on, "and we see nothing. But there are undercurrents which reach even under the earth. The air grows foul, even where we breathe it. There are sounds in the hills where there were no sounds before. Many have departed, bird and beast and spirit. The hills are bruised and empty, and there is rumour of ugly things further off. I find myself beginning to wonder if it is time."

"Time for what?"

"When the Sleepers shall be awakened, and this long vigil of mine shall be fulfilled."

"Oh my God," said Miranda, beginning to understand. "You don't mean it? Where are the Sleepers?"

She could sense his surprised gaze upon her. "The Guardian of the Well knows the Sleepers," he said. "They are under Cairnsmore, as they have always been."

"Oh yes, of course. It must have slipped my memory."

"But what say you, mistress? Is it time?"

"God knows."

She saw him bow his head. "Indeed that is true. The gods know, and therefore I have come to ask you for a prophecy."

"Well, it's very hard to say. You want to know if the final peril is upon us, so that the hour comes when you must awake to rise again and save this land?" Not a bad speech, thought Miranda to herself. Maybe I could squeeze out a prophecy if I put my mind to it.

"Even so. How do you judge matters? How is this world? I

perceive that there is peril, and my senses tell me that it may be mortal. Is this my country's hour of need, think you, when I should waken the king?"

Miranda replied, "Well, it's an hour of need all right. I'm not sure how much help the king would be, though. I mean, it's very reassuring to know he's there – at least, I've always found it so, but it's going to take an awful lot of explaining."

"How so?"

"Well, just to put you all in the picture. And what can he do about it all? He can't stop radioactive pollution, or the war, or change the economy, and would he even want to save the National Health Service, or put money back into education? What would he do about the unemployed? You know, I'm not at all sure that it's a practical proposition."

"Is this the prophecy?"

"No. I'll have to think that over. This is merely a preliminary discussion."

"You are very wise." His tone was humble, she realised.

"I wish I were. I don't even read the papers. And not having any radio up here – well, anything could have happened. It probably has. I'll tell you one thing, though. You're quite right about the mortal peril. Let me think . . . Why don't you come back in three days – that'll be Friday, and I'll let you know whether it's time?"

He bowed. "I will do your will, mistress. On the day of the goddess I will come, as you say."

"I said Friday. Oh I see."

"Farewell, Guardian of the Well."

"Farewell, Watcher of the Sleepers."

There was some information about the Sleepers in the library but nothing local. They seemed to be reposing under a good many hills of varying sizes across the country. They were rare north of the Border, in spite of the relative importance of Lothian and Orkney in *The Matter of Britain*. There was no mention of Galloway at all. Miranda sighed, and piled up the volumes from the Royal Commission on Ancient Monuments. Not that the cave was likely to be a monument. She'd tried everywhere she could think of.

She hadn't thought of asking the man in the Post Office but, later that day, when she called for her post on the way home, they got into conversation. When she mentioned the cave on Cairnsmore, he didn't seem particularly surprised. He knew at once which Cairnsmore she meant.

"Do you know exactly where it is?" she asked him.

He looked at her sideways. "If you've a map, I could show you. There's only the mound, and a pile of rocks. Nothing much to take photos of, or anything like that."

"I haven't got a camera. Here, it's an old map, but nothing will have changed up there, will it?"

"Only the hydroelectric, and that's far enough from where you want. Now look here . . ."

There was nothing to see at all. Certainly there was a mound, roughly where he'd put a cross on her map, and also a pile of stones, if one could call half a mile of scree and boulder a pile of stones. Miranda sat down on the edge of the mound and considered.

It was difficult to think because of the wind. It had been a wild day down in her corrie, the bare rowans bending to the gale, then tossing up to their full height again between every gust, with a sound like a distant sea. Up here it was a full gale. There was nothing to move before it; only the grass lay even flatter in patches, as if a herd of mammoths had been lying across the slopes like cows in a meadow. Higher up there were grubby patches of snow, glistening in the sun as they melted reluctantly into the hill. Miranda moved round to the leeward side of the mound, into the shelter of a large rock. The little pocket of stillness caught the weak sun and held it, extracting a faint warmth in spite of the draughts that eddied round the rock.

In the prosaic light of a March morning it was difficult to justify her search. She had to believe all that had happened, because there was her job, her home, and her pay, all there to

131

prove it. She had wanted something to happen for years; indeed, recently she had become quite desperate about it. She was beginning to wish now that events would locate themselves more solidly in a world she recognised. It would be easier, thought Miranda, if I were doing something I could write home about. It was impossible even to try to explain. Her mother had asked if she had a nice boss and her father had asked if there was a Union and, if so, whether she was paid up.

What could she say? "I wish I had something I could explain," said Miranda aloud. "I wish this cave would produce some evidence. Just so I know where I am."

There was a slithering sound above her and a couple of stones skimmed past her, bouncing down the slope. She looked up.

"Godammit!"

Miranda jumped to her feet. It didn't sound like a Sleeper, but there'd been no one else in sight all day over the entire mountain.

"Hello?" she called nervously across the wind. No answer. She began to scramble upward. "Hello?" she called again.

A shout came back from above. She couldn't hear the words. She tackled the rocks on hands and knees, and clambered back on to the mound.

It wasn't a Sleeper. It was a plump middle-aged woman in a scarlet anorak, arrayed in what looked like the very latest hiking equipment. She seemed to be clutching part of a camera. The camera appeared to be in trouble. A fallen tripod lay pathetically across the rocks, and the rest of the camera had rolled further down. The woman had presumably been scrambling after it but now she seemed to be stuck.

"Can I help you?"

She could indeed. She could help the woman to her feet, and retrieve the camera. Miranda did all this and more. She got the camera fixed back on the tripod, made sure everything was steady in spite of the wind, then together they tested the camera with a couple of shots.

"Well, it sounds all right. I won't know the worst till I get back to town." The woman looked up. "Say, I'm grateful to you, I truly am. My name's Helen Louise Caldecott, and I'm truly pleased to meet you."

Miranda muttered her name, so that the wind whipped it away instantly, and shook hands.

"Sorry, I didn't catch that. Miranda, did you say? Well, that's wonderful. It's a wild place for a hike, isn't it? Do you hike in these mountains a lot? There don't seem to be many trails."

"That's because not many people do any trailing. If they do, they go straight to the summits. This is a bit out of the way."

"So what brought you here, Miranda?"

Miranda hesitated. But what harm was there? Americans were supposed to like antiquities. "I was looking for a legend. I mean a cave. There's supposed to be a cave round here, with a king sleeping in it. And a load of knights. Just under here, somewhere." It was easier to sound flippant, a bit stupid, even, in case she was about to be mocked.

"You don't say!" But the woman wasn't looking at the mound. She was looking at Miranda. "Now where did you hear about that?"

"In the Post Office."

"You're not telling me it's a matter of international security?"

Miranda looked sulky, in case the joke was at her expense.

"No, wait a minute. I'd like to hear about this. I'm quite serious," the woman replied.

Miranda looked up. "I have an interest in this matter myself. Can we sit down out of the wind somewhere?"

Miranda led her back to her sheltered spot. She felt a little overpowered, but the woman was quite friendly and even seemed to know what she was talking about. Miranda hurriedly revised her impressions of Americans on tour, and began to listen. She was offered a share in a flask of coffee and some smoked salmon sandwiches, after which she even began

133

to talk a little herself. The woman seemed impressed.

"So you've been studying Iron Age burial sites yourself?"

"Not exactly. I mean, I don't know anything about it. It was just what I read in the library."

"You seem to have done a lot of reading."

Miranda finished her sandwich. "Well, it's because of my job. I mean, I don't have to but it seems to be relevant."

"So you've been reading it up on your own initiative?" This with a nod of satisfaction. "Well, this is interesting. Like I say, I'm doing a book about Arthurian sites, with a chapter on the legends of the sleeping knights, or whatever you choose to call them . . ."

"It won't be Arthur here. This is Galloway."

"I'm not bothered what they call him in one place or another. He's still the king."

"But there's quite a few of him."

"It's going to be a big book. And I didn't know anyone had got on to this site except me. There was a manuscript in the Museum of Antiquities but nothing ever published. And your source was local anecdote? That is very very interesting. Are you a historian?" The question came suddenly, making Miranda jump.

"What, me? No, no. But I did History at school."

"Liked it?"

"I liked History and English. And Art. I wanted to do Art but they said I lacked imagination, so I sort of gave up."

"So what did you do?"

The sulky look was back, making Miranda look very much younger. "Secretarial," she muttered, almost inaudibly.

"How was that?"

"Well . . . if I hadn't hated it, and loads of other things hadn't been happening at the same time, I suppose I'd have done all right."

"So this job is different?"

"Oh, it's not that sort of job. I applied for thirty-seven jobs, and then I sort of gave up for a bit. And now I've got this."

134

"Like it?"

Miranda's face changed, as if the wind had forced the clouds back off the sun. "Oh yes, I like it."

"Permanent, is it?"

Miranda shrugged.

"I only ask, because I was thinking about hiring an assistant. A keen young person who'd be willing to lug that goddam camera about, and help me with my research. Lots of travelling, and a fair salary. Expenses paid, of course. I'd do the driving. You wouldn't be interested?"

Miranda stared at her for a minute. "I don't know," she said slowly.

"I have thought," announced Miranda dramatically.

She was quite pleased with the whole scene. A crescent moon pierced the cold sky behind her, and Venus shone like a beacon over the silent rowan trees. The land was silent, gripped by frost, but the burn was loud, filling the corrie with sound, as the last light faded nightwards. The Watcher of the Sleepers stood before her, head bowed, like a suppliant at the feet of the oracle. She felt a little drunk. She was wearing new clothes too, black from head to foot. In the shop she had felt sophisticated in them; here, she felt invincible.

"I await your doom, Mistress of the Sacred Well."

Entirely as it should be. "I have thought," repeated Miranda, "and inspiration has come to me. Do you have a front door key?"

He only hesitated for one moment. "But assuredly, Mistress, the great oak door lies ten feet inside the tunnel: a double door six inches thick, bound with fearsome spells and hoops of iron, so that no evil thing may enter and none untimely. And I, the Guardian of the Sleeping King, and the sleeping flower of knighthood, I hold the key."

"Excellent. I want a copy."

"What?" That shocked him.

"You hear me. The day of peril is at hand. Evil stalks this land, and cannot be appeased by human power. Death threatens the earth on every side, and though the people are afraid they do not act. The day of awakening may be close. You need one who is vigilant, who is aware and who walks the hills, who buys a daily paper and who listens to the *News at Ten*. I am that one, and I will come to your cave and bring you word, when the hour strikes for you to rise."

"I hear your word, Mistress, but I am troubled."

"Prophecies are always troubling."

"I was charged to hold the key, and deliver it to none until the world is ending."

"Fair enough. You can do that. Did anyone say you weren't to get a copy?"

"No."

"Then you know what you must do."

"I suppose so."

"Repeat it."

"I must go to the smith of the gods who forged the key, and wove the spells surrounding it, and ask him to make a copy, which I will deliver to you at this well."

"Very good. Next Friday."

"As you say, Mistress." He straightened up, and seemed to relax a little. "Then our business is concluded?"

"It seems so."

"Well, that's good," he said, coming towards her. "And here are my gifts. You forgot to ask for them before."

"I didn't forget," lied Miranda. "It was a test."

"I hope I pass? There is wine here, and apricots, spices from the East, and honey from the Western Isles. There is cloth woven from the finest wool, and amulets of ivory."

"Goodness me, the horse must be worn out."

"No doubt," he said, obviously without considering the matter. He appeared to be thinking about something else, for presently he said, "And if you have the key, how will you know the door?"

"Well, I think it must be in that place where there's a peculiar pinnacle of rock on the slope up from the mound. Those arched slabs below it could be a doorway, if one could

136

squeeze pass the rock at the entrance."

"You found that?" His voice was suddenly sharp. "When?"

"The other day. And soon I'll have photos, if the camera was working. Is there a spell to move that rock? We couldn't budge it."

"Mistress, you see further than I reckoned. When I give you the key, I will give you the word of opening, for I know that I must trust the Guardian of the Well."

"That's very good of you. And thank you for all these gifts. I'm much obliged."

Suddenly he was very near her. "It is my greatest pleasure, lady, to do anything for you."

Miranda looked round at him, startled. She recognised his manner but in this context it took her completely by surprise. She couldn't think how to react, until she felt his arm slide round her waist. Well, she knew how to deal with that; whatever kind of a resurrected knight he might be, this was not on.

"Hey, stop that," she said, wriggling away from him. She confronted him over her pile of presents. "Now look here, Mister Watcher Knight. This is harassment. I'm at work and I don't like it."

"No, no, you don't understand. I love you."

"Really?"

"From the moment I first laid eyes on you. You, I mean. Not you, as you were all the other times."

"Oh." Her head was spinning, it seemed so inappropriate. She managed to say coldly, "Are you sure you're not married?"

"Not for fifteen hundred years."

"Oh?"

"We brought no women into the cave," he said simply. "My past is quite a long way behind. I'm sure we can disregard it."

"And what did the women reckon to that?"

"To what? Well, we didn't really consider it. That is, we didn't ask them. Perhaps we made a mistake."

"I shouldn't worry about it. No doubt we organised our own methods of survival."

"I'm very sorry." It was the humble tone back again, and it annoyed her.

"Now you must go, before the moon rises high enough to touch the water. Stay longer at your peril!"

He retreated at once, and mounted the white horse in one swift graceful movement. At a few yards distant, under the moonlight, he looked quite courtly after all.

"Lady, I go. Until seven nights from now, I go."

"So she wants me to visit the sites with her, helping with the photos and taking notes. There's a lot of routine work I can do in local libraries. If I get on well, she might need me to go back to the States with her. She could get me a visa as a research assistant, because I'm a local expert. She can do that because of what she is at her university. I'd be working at the university too, you see. I think I'd fancy that."

The brown man surveyed the line of coins laid out on a white sheet of paper. He didn't seem to be finding much pleasure in them today. It took him a while to answer. "I'll miss you," he said at last. "I thought you'd be around for a while."

"I didn't say I was going. I can't," explained Miranda. "I'd have to give notice, and that would mean leaving a note at the hollow in the rock. It won't be new moon for three weeks, and then she'd have to find a replacement, I suppose."

"But that's not your problem." He seemed to speak reluctantly. "This sounds like a real opportunity. I think you should take it."

"It is my problem, though. I can't just leave the well."

"Why not?"

"I'm the well guardian."

He raised his eyebrows, as if there were a question about it.

"Now look," said Miranda. "I've done a responsible job for God knows how many centuries. I've got an important project, which I've been working on for fifteen hundred years, and it's just reaching a crucial stage. It's my job. Do you think I'm going to walk out and leave it?"

"Have you really?" He was looking at her rather anxiously, and again she read his thoughts.

"Not I, Miranda, silly. I, the well guardian. Don't you know the difference?"

"It's a little beyond my ken," he said apologetically. He was about to say something else, but apparently changed his mind, for he began studying the coins again. "Though the pay would be incentive enough for some. The two Welsh ones now . . ." He turned back to the reference book. "Absolutely unique in this area, I should say. And the others . . . if they really are Pictish, then you've created an archaeological earthquake and they'll feel the ripples right through to California, so you'll be feeling them in this new appointment of yours for years to come. You do trust me to take them to Edinburgh for you?"

"Of course I do."

He looked at her gravely. "You honour me."

"Oh?"

"I'll do my best for you, Miranda. I don't know . . . I was hoping . . ."

"Hoping what?" she prompted him, puzzled.

"I thought there'd be plenty of time, with your coming in every month like this. I look forward to it, you see. The thing is . . ." He took off his glasses, and began to polish them thoroughly. "I was planning to go on holiday soon. I know somewhere I can get a cheap flight. I thought of Greece. Delphi, you know. Olympia, Epidauros, Mykonos and Delos. That sort of thing. I was going to ask you if you'd like to come."

Miranda's jaw dropped. She sat and goggled at him.

"I speak Greek," he said. "I know my way around a bit. I don't know if you've been to Greece at all?"

"I've never been abroad in my life," said Miranda slowly.

"Well . . ." His blue eyes were large and beautiful. "I don't know if you'd feel like coming with me, but it would make

139

me very happy if you did."

Dear Oddny,
I know it's not a new moon, so I'm not sure if this
will reach you. The job is going well. I just have
to finalise a major project this evening, which I
hope will meet with your approval. Routine matters are going well. The spring has been a bit low
lately because of the snow on the hills. I am sure it
will pick up again, and I expect the burn to be in
spate as soon as the thaw begins. There are buds
on the rowans, and the nettles are growing nicely
by the front door.

If convenient, I would like to give in my notice
as soon as possible. Not having a written contract,
I'm not sure what the terms are. The fact is that I
have been offered a good job and I would like to
start next month. I would also like to take a couple
of weeks' holiday before that. If a fortnight's
notice (or less) is convenient to you, perhaps you
would let me know.

Yours by moonshine,
Miranda Duthie.

Saturday morning ushered in the spring. The southerly
breeze was soft and balmy, and there was a new smell of
growing grass. The first leaves were unfurling on the rowans,
and the pool sparkled in the sun. The thaw had come and the
snow had retreated to the highest peaks. Only the burn was
white now, the pool overflowing with meltwater from the
hills. Miranda stood at the entrance to the mound, her hair
tousled and her eyes still full of sleep. She stepped down to
the well to wash her face, and found Oddny waiting like a
statue under the rowans. Dewdrops shone like beads in the
folds of her plaid and her skirt was dark with spray. Her
cheeks were pink with morning cold. Miranda wondered if
she had been standing there all night, waiting for her to wake.

"Hello."

"Hello, Miranda." Oddny smiled at her. She seemed pleased about something. "Thank you for your letter."

"Oh. That's all right."

"Did you get what you wanted last night?"

Miranda pulled at a silver chain which hung around her neck and extricated something from the folds of her dressing-gown. It was a large iron key. She held it out to Oddny, who took it gingerly, frowning a little.

"It's the key of the door to the cave," explained Miranda. "I also have the words to open the rock. The agreement now is that the guardian of the well will warn them when the time has come, and they will arise at her bidding, and be ready to receive her advice."

Oddny looked at her in wonder. "He gave you such a promise? The Watcher? He said that?"

"Yes."

"That surly youth!" exclaimed Oddny. "I've never got so much as a smile out of him in a thousand years, let alone a concession. You have done a greater thing than I ever imagined, Miranda. Do you want me to write you a reference?"

"I thought he said too much, if anything. Yes please, I think that would be very useful."

Oddny pulled a roll of parchment from one drooping sleeve. She sighed. "I suppose you'll want it in modern English? You may have to help me with the spelling."

"That's all right." Miranda watched her take a quill and an inkpot from the depths of the plaid. She cleared her throat, and asked tentatively, "What about my notice? Is that all right?"

"To tell the truth, I was delighted," said Oddny, a little absently, scratching away with the quill across the parchment. "It was good to have a holiday – I haven't had one for centuries, but I was beginning to miss the place. I'll be glad to be home again."

"Home? Oh I see. I didn't realise . . ."

"But it was the right thing to do. You have achieved something which I now see was most urgent and necessary. I thought you rather demanding at the time and, really, I can do my job quite well without having rocks hurled at me. But we are here to help, and no supplicants can ever be ignored once they take the trouble to ask. I should have remembered then that there are two sides to everything. If you hadn't been needed, you wouldn't have come. And you are satisfied?"

"I have everything I want now, thank you."

"For the moment."

"Yes." Miranda watched Oddny writing. She did it slowly and beautifully, but Miranda had a feeling that her script would prove quite illegible to any normal employer. Luckily her next employer wasn't too conventional. "So you feel all right about the key? I mean it felt like a responsibility. I've started reading the paper, you know. I never bothered before. And I got a little radio. I can leave it with you, if you like."

Oddny raised her head. "Whatever for?"

"Well, you know . . . I thought if I was holding the fate of the country in my hands I ought to take it seriously. I mean, I'm quite willing to save the world if necessary, but there's loads of other things I don't want to miss. There's a lot of things I want to do, but . . . you don't mind being left with the key?"

"The key belongs with the well guardian. The well guardian takes it into her hands, and the well guardian will use it when the time comes. Here's your reference. Do you want to read it? And check the spelling, if you would. The alphabet changes so fast it's hard to keep track of it. You do right to go, Miranda. See the world, and respect water. Water is much more powerful than you think."

The Cold Well

She sat under the waterfall, letting the burn wash over her. The falls were white and full, churning the pool into a froth of air bubbles and brown water. Little waves lapped against the rocks, which were scoured into a smooth curve at the pool's edge, following the circling water. The water itself was soft with peat, bitter with acid, flowing over her with a touch like a northern breeze on a spring day, even while her shoulders ached under the weight of it.

It was snowing. The flakes were huge and wet, falling silently into the pool and melting instantly. The air was damp; she could smell it even over the spray from the falls. There was a gap between the black trees where she could look right over the valley. The landscape beyond the pool seemed curiously inverted. The sky was dark grey, heavy with the weight of unshed snow. The earth beneath was white in the daylight that seeped in under the clouds. Each tree was highlighted by blown snow which clung to its northern side like a shadow. Black trees, white shadows. Dark sky, bright earth. She chuckled, swallowed icy water, and choked.

The snow thickened. She could hear the wind rising behind it. The trees swayed and bent. The valley was blotted out: nothing to see but whirling whiteness. It was bright and dark all at once, like the pool and the waterfall, and herself. She laughed out loud, and stood up.

As soon as she came out of the water, the snow settled on her, and melted as fast as it came. She stuck her tongue out and tasted snow. She could feel the tang of it on her body, and stood still by the pool. When she moved she left two bare footprints on the rock. The snow pounced at once, obliterating them within seconds.

She climbed up the rock, careless of the fact that there was no trace of any foothold under the blanketing snow. She knew them all by heart anyway, and when she reached the top she followed the path between the rowans without hesitation, although there was no trace of it. Once she left the shelter of the pool the wind caught her, so that she was swept into an invisible world of wind and snow. She blinked snow out of her eyes, though even then she couldn't see more than a yard ahead. It didn't bother her. She twirled herself around on the path, naked under the north wind, letting the snow catch her all over, and melt in a stream of water drops that trickled over her skin. Her feet stung a little as they sank into the snow. She couldn't even feel the ground. She laughed again, and twirled faster, winding her way among the trees in an invisible dance. She couldn't see the trees but she could hear them groaning under the wind loaded with snow. She caught the last one by the trunk and spun round.

The path brought her into deeper snow. She could make out the outline of a mound of earth, a small hillock overlooking the burn, its contours as familiar to her as her own body. It looked alien now, a thin line of white beyond the flying snow. She circled it until she reached the entrance: a black rectangle of dark leading into the heart of the hill.

She was about to enter the tunnel when a different sound was blown down to her, neither wind nor water. It might have been a human voice crying across the mountains, but she knew better. She stopped at once, frowning a little, then raised her cupped hands to her mouth, and called back.

She was answered at once by a cry as high and wild as her own, wordless and inhuman. If other creatures were out on the hill in this blizzard they might think that it was the crying of birds, or some animal driven out of shelter, or, if over-imaginative, might think of ghosts. She didn't spare them a thought. If anyone were out on an evening like this they would be the more likely to die.

A shadow rose out of the storm just in front of her and became substantial, a dark shape that loomed over her, bowed by the blizzard at its back. Snow swept between them, blinding her, but she could see as well as she needed to. She nodded as though satisfied, and turned back into the tunnel.

It was pitch dark inside. It didn't matter, because she knew exactly where everything was. It was calm, every small sound suddenly loud and precise after the undifferentiated roaring of the weather and water. There were faint sounds of movement, the scraping of wood on wood, and the clink of metal on stone. There were other sounds too, that of another body entering: the heavy tentative steps of one less familiar with the way; and quick breathing, as if the newcomer had been running hard.

A small flash, white and sudden, then a glow of orange, the crackle of flame on tinder, and a fitful light which grew and settled, until a soft glow filled the whole place.

The chamber under the mound was round and low, the walls built of corbelled stone, rising to a narrow roof of slabs with a black space between where the smoke escaped into the snow, and stray flakes drifted downwards to melt and vanish as they approached the fire. The room was already filled with peat reek, so that only near the floor was there any clarity. Kneeling by the fire she could see quite well but if she looked upward there was nothing substantial, only vague shapes through the smoke which appeared to move, though perhaps it was only the smoke and the falling snowflakes which changed and the rest was illusory. It didn't bother her: it was her own place and she knew what it contained. Down by the floor the room was bare, furnished only with a bedplace and a chest, with a spinning-wheel between close by the fire. There was a rough stone shelf holding rows of pots against the wall, and a few tools propped nearby. The floor was of trodden earth strewn with dried bracken away from the fire. As a dwelling it seemed poor at first sight, but curiously it never seemed to become plain by adjustment to the dimness and the smoke. On the contrary there was a hint of richness in the shadows, a glint of brighter colour, the suggestion of brilliance which could never quite be brought into focus. Gradually, as the fire grew in strength, the illusion of comfort became stronger, if illusion it were. But the woman by the fire was not attending to such everyday matters. She appeared to be concentrating entirely upon nursing the small flames into a blaze. If she were aware of her visitor she gave no sign of it, and the figure by the door waited with apparent patience.

At last she was satisfied with her fire, and looked up.

"I thought you might come down with the weather," she said. "I saw the deer had gone into the forest."

"None too soon," was all the answer she got, but the stranger came forward with the words, and crouched down on the opposite side of the fire.

If there had been any spy concealed in the shadows under the mound they might easily have given themselves away at this point. The stranger seemed to be a man, certainly, but not entirely so. He was man enough to be terrifying, in human terms, more so by his human-ness than by the lack of it. If he had been a ghostly, alien thing, it would be no more than anyone should expect if they dared to make their way into a hidden mound under the earth. But this was no ghost: on the contrary, he made every human thing seem a shadow by contrast, for he seemed all substance, a stronger presence than most human things expect to bear. He was big and dark, his face half hidden by the tangled hair that fell over it. There was snow caught in his hair, turning to bright drops which gleamed like diamonds in the firelight. There was driven snow across his shoulders, like the snow shadows beaten by the wind against the trees, which was also melting in small rivulets that streamed down his chest and back so that his skin shone fitfully in the firelight. He did not seem to be clothed; it was hard to take in details precisely. He was more animal than a man should be, and the eye does not readily absorb what the mind has learned to be impossible. But the antlers were clear enough, accentuated as they were by the shadow they cast on the curved wall behind him. As the fire flared they seemed to grow and vanish into the smoke like bare branches into twilight. The man leaned forward and laid another log upon the fire. Flames spurted up, green with the new wood, turning to red and orange. He looked up at the woman sitting opposite, and the gleam of light was reflected in his eyes, yellow and black, like a cat's.

"So you'll stay down till the storm passes?" The question was almost a statement, as if she didn't expect an answer.

He shrugged.

"Well, if you do that, remember what I said before. People come to the well even in winter. I don't want my folk frightened out of their wits. You'll have to lie low."

"Have I ever frightened them?" He sounded indignant. "Not once in a hundred years!"

"And that's not so long ago either. You can do what you like on the mountaintops, but this is my country."

"You don't need to remind me. Anyway," he sighed, "it makes no difference. They see what they expect to see, which means no one will see me. I don't know why you worry about it. There are some who'd give their left hand to be believed in. Does it make the people safe not to be frightened?"

"I'm not going to talk about that now. Do you want supper? I worry because I have to do with people, which is more than you do. Perhaps I see them too much. Sometimes I think the true part of myself is falling away, and I'm becoming only what the people make me. It's very dispiriting."

He laughed aloud. "Not you! Look at you now. You think I know nothing about it, but I see them in the mountains sometimes, even here. They don't look at all like you. They wear clothes for a start, usually a vast amount of clothing in ugly colours. Their hair is very dry, and so are their feet, and their minds are driest of all. You have nothing to worry about."

149

She shook her head, smiling. "No, no, that's just what you see. It's true they lack the influence of water, and so of course are impoverished. But underneath they're just like you or me, I assure you. Only they don't undress on mountaintops, that's all. If they did, you'd see the similarities."

"I knew all that several thousand years ago. They wore much less then, if you remember. I'm speaking of essence, not substance."

"Well, if you could apply your mind to substance for one moment: I asked if you wanted any supper?"

"Essentially, yes."

She stood up. "Very well, but it was you that mentioned clothes, not I. I know what I look like, but I don't necessarily know what I'm becoming. I have my people and I can't afford to despise them. They are all the mirror we have, you know that."

He scowled. "Speak for yourself. Isn't the well mirror enough, and don't the deer know more of me than any man?"

"Water doesn't speak, and neither do the deer. We are what they say we are, and nothing in this world can change that. If you're not satisfied you can always seek another."

"I'm not even so sure of that now."

She had turned to the stone shelf to lift down a pot but she looked back at him, startled. "Not sure of what? There are more worlds open to us than anyone has dreamed of yet. If you cease to believe that, how can you live at all?"

He shook his head, his face hidden.

She put the pot down, then came and stood over him so that water dripped from her hair on to the top of his head. "There's something more, isn't there?" There was no trace of compassion in her voice but he had all her attention. "You didn't come down just because of the snow. You brought despair with you. I can feel it. You have no right to bring such a thing into my house."

He was silent at her feet, not looking up.

"There is no room for despair in this place. If you cannot twine yourself from it, you must go."

"Aren't you the guardian of the well?" he cried out. "Will you no longer give help to your own kind? Or do you keep all you have for those who destroy us?" He glared up at her and involuntarily she stepped back. "I never thought you would turn traitor, not in all the years upon this mountain. I would never have believed such a thing as that!"

She left him and went to open the chest. "Believe what you like. I'm not here to defend myself." She picked out a rough plaid of loosely woven wool, and wrapped it round herself. "If you came for help you should have gone to the well."

"I came to see you." He sounded sulky.

"To bring your trouble into my house?"

"To bring myself. You didn't always object to my company."

"I am always glad of your company, when you offer it. But your trouble is another thing, and I want none of it."

He stared at her with wide eyes. "So you refuse to help your own? If that is so, there really is no future in this world."

She sighed impatiently. "Understand me! I help any who come to the well, as far as I can, because I am the guardian. Any human, beast or spirit. But you did not come to the well."

He seemed puzzled. "No, I came to you. Because I know you."

"And I will have none of you, so you had better go."

He stood up slowly. "Very well. If that is all, and I'm no more to you than any passing stranger of any kind, I will go and take my trouble with me. Clearly it means nothing to you now."

"You talk like a man," she said with withering scorn. "But the water still rises from the earth, however low you fall. The burn still flows to the sea, whether I care for you, or you for me. What have you learned yet, if you don't seek the help you need where you know you can find it? I'm not here to listen to your troubles. So go."

She took a stick and began to trace patterns in the ash beside the fireplace. When he left she never raised her head but

151

seemed absorbed in her task. She drew slowly and carefully, lines and curves and circles. By the time she had finished the sound of his footsteps in the tunnel had died away and there was no noise at all, except the muffled echo of the wind on the hill and the crackling of the fire. There was also the sound of falling water, but she never heard that; there was no more noise in that than in the blood flowing in her body. It was as much part of her and therefore imperceptible.

"The army?" she repeated. "In our hills? But the Covenanters have all gone. Religion is no longer important, I believe."

"No, no, Oddny, you have it wrong." The man standing outside the Post Office sighed. "It's not a religious army."

She frowned. "The English, you mean? But don't they have what they want already?"

"It would help if you tried to keep up with things between times," he answered with a touch of impatience. "Up there in the hills you just assume nothing changes, until the place is overrun with khaki. Then you expect a potted history of the last three hundred years as if it were a week. You'd better come in. It's freezing out here. The wife's not in. I'll put the kettle on for you."

"Freezing?" Oddny cast a puzzled look at the sun, which bravely flung its light across the snow-patched hills, although all its warmth was whisked away by the wind before it could touch them. It would have been pleasant to feel the light on her skin, instead of having to dress herself like a decent body in a long skirt and plaid. "No. It stopped freezing shortly after dawn."

"In a manner of speaking." The man shuddered and pulled his jacket round him. "I know you're not keen to come in, but I'm not speaking for long out here. I tell you, there's a wind you could cut with a knife, and that's a fact."

"All winds can be cut with a knife," remarked Oddny, but she followed him into the Post Office without further protest, just as she answered to the name by which he addressed her. These people had applied it to her for the last twelve hundred years. She had used many names: this one served its purpose as well as any.

The Post Office was also a small general store, crammed from floor to ceiling with shelves full of groceries, iron-mongery, stationery and fishing tackle. The actual Post Office was a small desk behind a glass panel in a little booth. The door into the sitting-room was beside it. It felt cramped and strange indoors, with too many angles everywhere. She'd been here before in this man's grandfather's time, but the place had changed. The high wooden counter had gone, and the sacks on the floor, and the glass jars on the shelves. Everything was brightly coloured and covered with writing, like a jumble of unwholesome spells. Oddny tried to re-establish her bearings. "Don't you sell bootlaces any more?"

"Bootlaces? Of course. In those orange packets there."

"What's a packet?"

"Come in," he said firmly, holding the door open. "NATO is one thing, and that'll probably take all morning. Forget about packets."

She felt more at home in the sitting-room. The open range had gone, and so had the fat Empress cast-iron stove that had followed it. Now there was a sleek white Rayburn that took up the entire fireplace. The smell of peat was the same, only fainter. There was still a picture of deer on a hill over the mantelpiece, still china carthorses on the windowsill. The stone flags were covered now, as was the green linoleum. Instead, there was a brightly patterned carpet on the floor. Oddny regarded it with awe. The almanack by the kitchen door had changed, but that was only to be expected. No useful information this year, just a photograph of two kittens in a stocking, which seemed curious. The table had acquired a cloth, but the two upright chairs that flanked it were as they had always been. The resting chair by the fire had dis-appeared, and so had the rag rug. Oddny sat down cautiously on the edge of one of the matching armchairs, watching the man make tea. He did it as it had always been done. She sighed with relief.

"So," she said, "the army. I admit I was glad to find you safe, my friend. Aren't you afraid? And you with a wife and family? Grandchildren, it must be by now."

"Oddny, you'll have to take this in. It's not that kind of army."

"No?"

"They're doing an exercise."

She looked blank. "Tell me this, then. Are people no longer occupied with killing one another? They're now thinking of the good of their health? Is that it?"

"No, it's not," he said shortly. "Listen."

Oddny listened attentively, and consumed two cups of the revolting tea that people had never failed to produce for her for the last hundred and fifty years.

"They asked the Commander-in-Chief why he chose Galloway," her friend was telling her, "and he said because this was the only place they could think of in NATO where conditions approximated those of a Third World country. They're pretending to evacuate us, you see, after an invasion."

"Wait. You'll have to explain some of that more clearly."

"Oh God," he said. "Let's have a dram." He reached into the airing-cupboard next to the stove, and produced a bottle of whisky. "Let's get this clear. Did you know we had had a war in Europe?"

"Of course I know that. It began around the time the well was given a guardian, and has never ceased since. War came with the people, and when the people have gone, the well will no longer need me. How could I not know that?"

"It's no good," he said. "I have to tell you straight, my dear. I reckon your time is over. It's a different world now, and you can't expect to have any influence, not any more."

"The hills are still the same."

"Are you so sure of that?"

She hesitated. "No, I'm not," she said at last. "That's why I came. It's my own place that worries me, for what can I do about anywhere else? They say the gods have departed, gone

154

away into the shadows, and that such as I survive only here and there, in small pockets of land that are too poor and barren for the people to bother themselves over. It's true enough, there are fewer folk that come, and the troubles they bring are smaller, as though they don't expect that water can heal anything great. But they are troubled, I know that. I tell you something, my friend, I feel like one besieged, and I think the assault will come soon. It's not the army. I thought there might be a connection but the soldiers have come before, and gone again, and the folk of the hills remain. But something else has happened which is beyond my understanding."

He looked at her with more attention, as though he had changed his mind, and now expected her to say something relevant. "What kind of things have happened?"

"The deer are sick," said Oddny.

"Sick?" There was a new sharpness in his tone.

"But there is nothing new. It's not the acid. We know about acid. We feel it in our skin and in our lungs. It's not the plantations. There is space enough still in the mountains and we understand the new trees better now, even the spruce, which I cannot learn to love. There is nothing new we can feel or hear or see, but there is a new danger in the mountains. There is one who knows the deer, who feels their sickness, but cannot sense the cause."

"One?"

"Not to do with you," said Oddny. "But so many have left already. If the deer are no longer in the mountains, then I will be alone here as I have never been before. I wouldn't be the last of my kind if I could help it. You tell me we are no longer necessary, so perhaps it doesn't matter to you if we are driven out at last?"

"I didn't say that," he said slowly. "I can't understand what effect it may have. I'm a practical man. Only I'm afraid it would mean the end of something more. That's all."

"Then if you care, you will explain to me what it is that you must know."

The snow was still thick on the ridge. It was a calm cold day, and standing on the summit it was possible to see for miles. To the west and north there were more mountains. There was a valley just below the ridge, high and bare, divided by the grey line of a burn. Further down there were trees, huddled in a dark mass against the white ground. To the east, the mountains fell away to rolling lowlands, a wild broken country touched with frost against the brown and grey of winter bracken on granite. Beyond the lowlands lay the sea, not so very far away, out of sight beyond the long line of hill that people called the Skreel. Between the Skreel and Criffel, lying half hidden by rainclouds, there was a long gap and through it could be seen the mountains beyond the sea, white-capped, delicately etched against the sky, only a little more solid than a cloud.

Oddny stood on the ridge with her back to her own land, and stared at those other mountains as if there were something vital to be learned from them. She had known their names once but those names were maybe changed and, as far as she knew, the land was now deserted. There had been no message from any of her kind for so long that she had gradually begun to assume that they had gone. Now that she allowed herself to think about it, it was possible that there was no one out in the world at all, that there were none of her folk left upon the planet, except in these hills that had lain out of the way for long enough to be forgotten. Though she knew the world was large, she remembered what her friend at the Post Office had told her about the other countries so unlike her own. It was a curious thing, there were worlds upon worlds which had once been open one to another but the people now believed that there was only one, and that was dying fast enough. That frightened her. People had one power that other kinds did not, which was the power to dream things and make them happen, or the power to destroy, merely by the act of forgetting. Her mountains were only safe because they had been forgotten. She realised now that that was no security at all.

156

At last Oddny turned her back to the south-east and faced north-west into the heart of the hills. She was met by silence and the sun gleaming upon snow. She looked down into the valley, a long hard look that was presently rewarded.

The deer were below, grazing the thin winter grass through its frozen covering. There were only two or three of them, dull-coloured like the rocks around them, so that even the snow did not destroy their camouflage. The rest wouldn't be far away. Oddny cupped her hands to her mouth and called.

It was a long time before she was answered. She waited patiently, sitting cross-legged in the snow, gazing downwards. The sun rose to its highest, just topping the peak to the south of her, and lying in long gold rays across the hill, so that the snow was suddenly dazzling, the sky blue as the sea in summer. Then the sun dipped again, and the shadow of the mountain fell across her. A thin wind sprang out of the west, ruffling the plaid that wrapped her round and playing with the ends of her hair where it fell over her shoulders. Oddny never moved, except now and again to call across the silent hills. Two hawks wheeled in the still air below, then hovered motionless over the patch of woodland. She watched them for a little, then scanned the further peaks, while they drifted into a grey shadow. Presently she called again.

Twilight was in the air, an opaqueness settling over the horizon, bringing the frost down with it, when at last she had her reply. An answering call echoed faintly across the valley out of the white emptiness of the slopes beyond. Oddny stood up, alert as a dog after a sudden scent. She surveyed the hills one last time and was off, plunging down into the valley by a direct, precipitous route, leaping barefoot down the rocks and slithering through patches of snow. The floor of the valley was rough and rock-strewn; its smooth whiteness seen from the summit was entirely deceptive. Oddny bounded from rock to rock, forded the burn without hesitation, giving only a quick gesture of respect in acknowledgment of whatever might dwell amidst its waters, and was up again,

157

climbing fast on to the mountain, scattering water drops as she ran. Burnwater froze on her hair and plaid, leaving her bedewed with brightness.

By the time she reached the next ridge it was almost dark and the wind was rising. She could feel it burn on her skin when she turned her face westward, a warning to any mortal folk that the hill this night would be deadly. Snow was winnowed thinly from the ridge top, fanned out into new drifts, and the ground where she trod was delicately patterned like sand after the retreating tide.

Oddny faced north and called again, half against the wind. The sound was blown away from her, driven upwards into the darkening air, where it was torn apart and vanished. Even so, she was still heard. The answer came clearly down the wind, closer than it had seemed before, just to the west of her. She faced the wind again and ran across the ridge, flitting like a small shadow across the face of the hill into the very teeth of the night.

The ridge ended in a cairn, the stones black against the snow on the eastern side, with a sharp drop below into a valley where the dark lay so thick already she couldn't see the foot of it. Oddny skidded down, bringing a slide of snow with her, and landed on her feet at the bottom. There was a big drift banked against the hill; if she had been any less lightfooted it would have swallowed her up. She ran lightly across the top of it, leaving a faint trail of bare footprints, and reached solid ground again in a mass of frozen heather which crackled like kindling under her feet.

She heard him call again very close by. Before she had finished answering him he was visible, a darker shape emerging from the gathering night. Then he stood in front of her, breathing hard. The night was falling so fast that everything visible had an unreal quality to it, as though she had only to blink and the whole world would vanish. For a moment she was disconcerted, as if she doubted herself so much that when she looked at her own folk with her own eyes, they gave her the lie. But if she was there, so was he. Oddny shook her head a little, and smiled with relief.

He had been watching her, a touch of anxiety in his face; clearly he had not forgotten the mood of their last meeting. When he saw her smile, he smiled back and his face was transformed, no longer harsh but alive with laughter. It revealed him suddenly for what he was, but she was undaunted, for she knew him of old. She saw no affection in him, nor concern for her, particularly, only a wild mirth, and an overwhelming liveliness that would be terrifying if she could not respond to it.

Oddny laughed in his face and ran past him, and he ran after her, their footprints weaving in a ragged pattern across the frozen slopes, one pair of bare footmarks running hard, interwoven with something even stranger, though perhaps more to be expected at this height and weather. Their tracks leapt another burn, then doubled back and recrossed it, running apart and together like an endless infinity sign spreading itself up and down the valley, crossing and recrossing the hill. The wind itself was caught between the hills and funnelled down the valley, with a high whistling that bore with it the thin echo of laughter.

She reached a flat marshy island in the burn and turned to face him amidst spiky hummocks of frosted grass that reached above her knees. He came up to her and was on her, rolling over and over among the grass tussocks. Oddny held on to him and turned her face to his. His hair was thick and cold and brushed her face with a touch like ice. She held him to her and felt the warmth of him against her, alive and damp and smelling of the deer. There was the coolness of snow under her back and over his shoulder she could see the stars, cold and piercing in a frozen sky.

"And now," said Oddny, her eyes on the cold pink glow in the east that presaged the dawn, "we have to talk."

He sat beside her, his feet, like hers, dabbling in the burn where it flowed brown and full between thin layers of ice that skimmed the water in the reeds. "If you wish." He spoke indifferently, as if everything important had already been said, although they had not exchanged two sentences in all the hours since they had met.

"No," said Oddny, "not by my wish. Do your deer sicken, or do they not?"

He turned to face her at that, his eyes bright and interested. "You know why? You did find out?"

"After you had gone," went on Oddny, as if he had not spoken, "I thought about your visit. Through all the years of decline and fearfulness I never saw you so touched before. You never listened or cared about what happened below the mountains. I knew none of our people had passed, or I would have heard of it. Your despair is nothing to do with me but if you had cause for it, it would be a cause that affects all. I can't help you because you haven't asked, but I do what I can to protect my own."

He didn't answer, but stared at the sky. The ridge above them was tinged with light, reflected from the brightening dawn.

Oddny waited a moment longer, and continued, "I have to do with the people as you do not. I went down to discover what I could. There is a reason for the sickness."

It was doubtful if he understood her explanation. The affairs of the people were of no interest to him and she was aware that he wasn't following very closely. Words had little power to move him, anyway, and words of alien matters, of which he could hardly begin to imagine, left him cold. Oddny told her story as if she were merely clarifying it for herself. Perhaps that is all, she thought, glancing at him sideways. He was still watching the dawn as if that were the only thing that life depended upon. It was growing fast; the sky had turned from pink to orange and the small clouds that scudded east were caught by the light and held fast, until they were tinged bright red, then swallowed up by the unseen sun.

She thought she had lost his attention altogether and was surprised when he looked at her again. His eyes were bright yellow in the daylight. He looked at her blankly, as though he had never seen her before. She was used to that too, so ignored it.

"Could you change it?" he asked at last.

She hadn't been expecting that, and it took her a while to answer. "I don't know."

"But if you were asked, you'd have to try, wouldn't you?"

He knew the answer to that, so she didn't bother to give it him.

"You would have to try until you had done what was asked."

"Or lost myself in the attempt," said Oddny lightly. He had her trapped, but she had no reason to protest. It was not in his nature to be considerate. Love, for him, was what he felt about the deer, and the mountain. He would always be true to that, and she would also be true to herself, until all things had their end.

"You would have no choice," he remarked, and bowed to the sun, as it swung clear above the mountain and fell in golden rays around their feet.

"I would like you to make a telephone call for me," said Oddny, "and after that I shall leave you alone."

"I'm not bothered about that. But are you sure about doing this? You don't know what it's like. It's no place for your sort, I can tell you that."

"Have you ever been there?"

"No," said the man in the Post Office. "But I know enough. It's too different from what you're used to. And you can't change anything. I don't think you realise how powerful these people are."

"I have no choice," said Oddny. "I have some small powers of my own, and I have to do what I can. I have to go to this place and see it for myself."

"Why do you?"

"Because I am the guardian of the well, and if any request help from such powers as water has, I have no choice but to give it, except to cease to be what I am."

"And you have been asked?"

"No," said Oddny with a sigh, "but I shall be."

It was raining hard when she set off home. The burn was loud with meltwater. The rain was cold, hard heavy drops interspersed with splashes of sleet. The wind blew the rain into her clothes until they were soaked through, clammy and heavy on her back. The snow had melted off the moor, and the grass in her corrie was brown and withered as it emerged again. Oddny took off her boots as soon as she left the people's road and began to hurry. When she got home the burn was deserted, the rowan trees sighing mournfully against the gale. The well had been visited, she was quite aware of that without even needing to look for the prints that had churned the boggy ground below the pool. She stripped off her sodden clothes almost fiercely. She stood for a moment on the rock that overhung the pool below the waterfall. The pool had risen since she left it this morning and the water foamed whiter. She smiled down at it with something approaching her old insouciance. Then she straightened up and dived like an arrow into the whirlpool.

She came up under the fall and let it flow over her. Then she let it carry her down, and take her to the bottom of the pool where brown water churned over the rocky bed. She opened her eyes to water shot with light and air, white and black and brown roaring round her, sweeping her in a circle past the curve of rock and up into daylight, the rain splashing on her head, beating down on the water and being instantly swallowed. She lay on her back and saw the rowans circling slowly, black branches etched against a moving sky. She rolled and dived again, coming up at the foot of the pool. She climbed ashore reluctantly, knowing what she had to face.

He had left gifts, as she had known he would. Precious stones from the heart of the mountain, gleaming in their bed of plaited reeds, and a small horn carved from the antler of a deer, chased with gold. She took them from the hollow rock above the well in an automatic gesture. She had taken so many gifts from there, both rich and poor, more than she could count over so great a time, but never one had she accepted with a heavier heart. Oddny held the treasures of the mountain in her cupped hands, and regarded them with indifference. In the people's terms they were so precious as to be beyond price, but to her they were of no help. She could hear his appeal, echoed in the voice of the fall, just as he had stood here and made it only an hour or two ago. She was the guardian of the water and she had no choice. For the first time in all those years she knew terror, and was sickened by its sour taste.

The shore where she landed was familiar to her, and still recognisable. It was not the same as she remembered it; that would have been too much to expect, but the waves still beat in their old rhythm against a long sandy beach with dunes at the top. The crossing had been easy, though more years had passed than she could reckon since she had put to sea. The wind still served her, responding to her words as it had always done, and the tide still aided her, respecting her frail craft as it had never failed to do. Cheered by this evidence that the world had not changed beyond recall, Oddny beached her coracle in the right place and found a place to hide it in a hollow among the dunes.

So far she had tried to ignore all evidence of human presence on her journey, although it was ubiquitous and never pleasant. To travel in the old way, she needed to fix her mind upon more ancient things and not to allow people to impinge upon her thoughts. Her voyage was done, however, and it was time for her to adjust to this new human world. She sat at the top of the beach for many hours, watching the waves break and the tide rise and fall again, until she was ready to face the thing that loomed behind her.

No one saw her when she finally turned inland. She crossed the railway unheeded, picking her way over the metal tracks. The railway was not particularly strange to her. A similar track had once been laid across the foothills of her own country and, for a brief space of years, she had watched the trains chugging to and fro like clattering slugs crawling across the hills. She had seen them come and watched them go; had looked down from the hills at men taking up the line that other men had laid so short a time before. The railway held no terrors for her and neither did the fence, which was similar to the deer fences that men sometimes raised across the hills. It would have infuriated the one who sent her here. He only saw deer fences through a red mist of anger, for he could not climb them, and too often they separated him from his own. But they presented no problems to Oddny. She climbed briskly over, avoiding the barbs, and found herself confronting the danger she had come to find.

It was vast, greater than anything she had allowed herself to imagine. When she faced it she felt the force of it for the first time and her impulse was to flee, to get back over the sea to her own hills, as far from this menace as it was possible to be. She had encountered evil before, but never on such a scale as this. The place emanated the distillation of all the horror that the people had brought into the world. She knew what people were capable of: the hills had seen suffering, betrayal, and bloodshed. Not even the people themselves could see what it was they were doing here. There was nothing to see at all except a vast ugliness. But it was possible for Oddny to feel, and she felt danger.

When she faced it, she felt reduced as if her bones had turned to liquid and her stomach churned. She turned her back; the sea was below her, glinting in the winter sun. She smelled salt. The waves broke against the sand in an erratic line of white. She watched them break nine times, and turned round.

She was better prepared this time. The thing loomed as huge as ever, but the fear of it could not pierce her as it had done before. She knew now she would not turn and flee. There was no going back, no safety in the hills anyway. She was here because the deer were sick. He thought they were sick from the short grass and lichen that they ate in winter.

The hills were poisoned, and the man from the Post Office had explained to her that the source of the poison lay here. Seeing the place, she knew in the depths of her being that he was right. She could not go back.

She made herself study the place calmly, walking slowly round it. There were towers, high-curved like the fortresses the people once built around the coast when danger threatened them from over the sea. But these towers were not for defence. They were made of concrete and curtains of water fell in a circle round their feet. The water should have made her feel more secure, but there seemed to be no life in it. It originally had come from the burns and the lochs in the mountains to the east but it held no memory of them, not in this place. If such water still had its guardians in the hills, they could not have dared to make their way in here.

There were other towers, high and straight, one scarred by fire. Oddny distrusted towers. In her experience, people who built towers had dangerous thoughts. Among the towers were great rectangular buildings, all made with straight lines that made her eyes ache. But towers and straight lines she had seen before, and the hills remained unconquered. The buildings were pregnant with some hidden threat; the thing her friend had explained to her. She needed to get inside to do what she had come for.

The place was confusing, being full of roadways and buildings. To find her way through it she had to think another way. An image rose in her mind: dunes thick with marram grass, behind them a sandy plain thick with gorse and heather. In spring the place was bright with gorse and the thick strong smell of it mingled with the salt breeze off the sea. She saw herself standing on the dunes looking inland to the mountains, seeing rounded hills white with snow. She knew the names they had been called by, and maybe still were: Whin Rigg, Sca Fell, Yewbarrow.

There had been settlements along this shore; small patches of cultivated land behind the dunes. They had not been her people but they had respected water. There were many streams of water then, flowing from the hills to the sea. The waters had been clean and alive, knowing where they came from and whither they must go. Oddny remembered the waters and the place became clear in her mind, so that in spite of the strange angles and concrete monstrosities, she found her way through.

Presently she came out at the main gateway, flitting past the policeman in his glass hut. If he saw a shadow flicker on the road, he perhaps thought it was a cloud drifting over the pale face of the sun. Oddny ducked under the gate and felt the current which would have made the alarm bell ring. But no bells rang for her.

She had made an effort to look as modern and respectable as possible, and was rewarded when she gave her name at the Visitor Centre. They didn't glance at her twice but suggested that she walk around the Exhibition Centre until her tour was ready to begin.

The important thing to remember now was her task. It would be like following a thread into a maze. So long as she felt the thread under her finger, she would know her way and be safe. If she lost it, her whole being would be threatened, for she had never been anywhere so alien in her life. There was nothing in the entire place that would reflect back to her the truth of her own existence. Deliberately she conjured up images of streams flowing among the dunes and gorse, and imprinted them on her memory like a talisman.

Meanwhile she studied the exhibits obediently, pressing all the buttons and watching the film. It was a curious way of representing reality. It interested her that people now had a concept of what they were made. One would think it would have made them more aware of their relationship to other kinds, but that was manifestly not the case, seeing what they were doing. She was familiar with the idea, of course, though this language was new to her. Sometimes when people bored her it amused her to half-shut her eyes and to refocus, so that she could see them dissolve into their component parts, a mass of atoms whirling through space with a pleasant view of

166

the sky through the gaps between. If she stared very hard at the atoms, it was intriguing to see the electrons circling round their nuclei, but hard to follow because they moved so fast. She had to speed up her mind, just as she had to slow it down to watch the stars doing the same thing. Interesting that people, who had such notoriously limited vision in every sense, should have followed these patterns in such detail; terrifying that they should know so much and emerge with less respect than ever. Oddny sat on the bench in front of the video screen, watching the infra-red rays and listening to the commentary. She felt alarmed and sobered by the implications of so much human knowledge.

She heard a name being called and recollected with a start that it was hers for the day. The tour was ready to begin. She picked up the thread of her mission. She was a spy, ready to subvert. The idea of it made her long for invisibility, but that would not be appropriate. A line of people, mostly keen young men, followed the guide into another room. Oddny hurried after them.

She didn't listen very hard to the talk that followed. It seemed to be a mixture of obvious facts and blatant lies. She watched the pupils of the guide's eyes contract and enlarge according to the accuracy of her statements. There was no direct evidence here of what she must do. No one mentioned the hills but some of them cared. There was more human emotion in the room than was comfortable for Oddny. She was glad when they all filed out, until she realised that they had to get into a bus. She had never yet ridden in a horseless carriage but today was unreal. She was penetrating another world because her own was threatened, and in pursuance of her ends she would have to endure whatever was required.

Twenty minutes later, still sick and dizzy, she stood on a metal platform five storeys up while the guide explained what lay beneath. Oddny needed no explanations: she could feel it. It was like standing on a battlefield, yet the people who stood beside her seemed neither to see nor to hear the signs. That gave the thing a deadly unreality. She could hear the matter of her world being torn apart, not just a little, as happens in the hills when the rocks fizz with strange energy, but hugely. The very stuff from which the earth was made was being torn apart only a few feet away from her and these people who, unlike her, were made of that same matter, ignored it as if their bodies felt nothing. Was it possible that they genuinely could not feel it? Oddny felt sick.

There was worse to come. She was shocked and dazed, so it was difficult to keep her bearings, but presently they entered a great white building and she made herself remember. She saw the plain, bright with gorse, yellow and orange, thick with butterflies, half of whom had left this land for ever, and the sun bringing out the scent of the heather which blew down from the hills and mixed with the pungent gorse. Oddny held that image before her like a shield and followed the guide.

There was neither air, nor light, nor silence, nothing real at all. A bleep like a heartbeat out of tune drowned out thought, obliterating the rhythm of her body so that the sun in the sky and the waves on the shore were truly hers only in memory. They had left the earth behind and all that dwelled within it. Life was no longer real, but only this dullness. White paint and endless staircases around huge sealed enclosures bombarded with the stuff of destruction.

She had never come so close to her own annihilation. Oddny was not matter. People might be destroyed in body, but if she were separated from the earth she would be nothing; she would be destroyed in essence.

I am nothing, thought Oddny, but the life that is born of living water; I am nothing but the sound of the burns that run for ever from the hills to the sea. I am nothing at all but the love of the people for their earth. I have no other name. If this is not the earth where I belong, I am nothing. I am becoming nothing.

Oddny leaned on a white metal railing, and felt herself grow insubstantial. If they had looked round at her then, they would have been shaken out of whatever world they inhabited, for they would have seen quite clearly the rail passing behind her body and the white treads of the staircase through the outline of her thin feet. There was a roaring in her ears which sounded like the sea, where all things have their end, but it was not the sea. It was like nothing on earth at all. Life was slipping away from her like a dream vanishing on waking.

She forced herself to remember what she had to do. There was still the thread to follow. She was here in answer to a supplicant who had come to the pool. She was an emissary with a task to perform. She remembered the gifts left beside the waterfall: precious stones from the mountain, the little horn encased in gold. She made herself imagine it as clearly as if it lay in the palm of her hand. She saw the chased pattern on the gold and remembered the coolness of horn and metal under her fingers. His deer were sick from eating the lichen that had been their winter food since the days when the hills were new to her. If there were no deer in the hills he would be gone, and the world would be drear and empty for the lack of him. She remembered what she had come to this place to do.

The people stood crowded around a screen. Through many thicknesses of material like glass she could see the poisonous stuff. This was the heart of the matter, the essence of the evil she had been sent here to confront. Metal arms guided it, stripped it of its covering, crushed it into a mass of concentrated death that would lie like a threat of doom in this place where the gorse should grow, until the sun grew cold and the world draw to its end. If it did not lie safe through all the centuries when the people would have gone as they had come, then life in the beauty she knew would have an end.

She clung to the image of the thread. They were in the heart of the maze now, and if she lost her track, she would be left to wander here like a disappointed ghost until the doom should fall. She had to keep her mission clear in her mind, clear as the yellow of the gorse in May, and seek for the moment when she should act. It must be very close now. A quiver ran through her, then, suddenly alert as she had not yet been amidst so much deadness, she followed the others.

Presently they all stood looking down on a great pool of blue water filled with metal containers that were lost in the depths. The hall was vast, edged with enormous pipes and walkways above the water. The water was sick and lifeless, not even aware of her presence. If death had power over water, it lay here. No such glimpse of death had ever touched Oddny before. She shuddered and drew back. The pool was making her weak and faint, a shadow of the thing she was. It was necessary to act at once, while some strength still lay in her.

It took all the power she had even to begin. But it was why she had come. She had never yet failed any who came to the well. He had come, not to her, but to the well, as a supplicant, in the proper form. She had to do what he demanded, and confront this thing, or renounce her place in the world. It was not fair of him to have demanded such strength from water, but the rules were inviolable. No supplicants who asked for what they had the right, had ever been refused.

She sat crosslegged on the metal floor. Far below, there was earth under her. She made her mind encompass it. There was water here on its way to the sea, diverted and imprisoned for an evil purpose. There was air trapped inside this place, forced down pipes and stripped of life, but still containing the vestiges of live air. There was fire, turned to an image of death. There was all matter, working in a way that belonged to the earth as much as the sun's rays upon her granite hills, magnified out of all proportion into a danger greater than any she had ever known.

Oddny summoned up the image of the land. She saw the gorse bent before the wind, westerly gales rolling in from the sea, the surf pounding on the shifting shore. She saw days and nights fading into eternity, the moon circling, the sun changing its pattern with the seasons. She saw the shore altering, dunes rising from the beach and being washed back to the sea; the mountains changing shape, worn by wind and rain, the burns turning to rivers, then back again to ice. She saw centuries of ice, water locked in the hills, the land sinking under the weight of it. She saw the same water flowing, the waves beating against the feet of the mountains, and the plain of gorse vanished for ever.

In the centre, where she sat, she saw the legacy of forgotten people, a danger that threatened the earth through a lifetime as long as hers, holding within it the possibility that consciousness should cease. She saw danger sealed here, while the land changed and the sea advanced and retreated, the rivers altered their courses in the slow washing of the hills to the sea. There was no guardian for such a power as that, nothing in life that could undertake the responsibility for such a thing; certainly not the people, for everyone but they knew they were as transitory as the summer's day. Her own powers were small in the face of such a thing, but what spells she had she would give to bind it, even if it left her without power for ever.

The danger was far stronger than she had realised. She was confronting it now. It loomed over her, aware of her. She experienced it as a series of images because that way she could make sense of it. It was the battle with the dragon, the serpent, the monster that dwells in the depths of the sea or below the waterfall. Yet it was not any of those, but they were the only symbols with which she could capture it. It shifted shape, and so did she, in a battle of energy that raged down all the centuries to come. A duel was fought that day across the plains of gorse, which left the place haunted throughout time, for those who had the power to feel. Again and again the new power threatened to overwhelm her, and each time she slipped out from under it and confronted it with new images: the snake, the bird, the tree, sometimes just words or notes, always elusive but never giving in.

But at last she felt her strength failing. The peril towered over her, about to sweep her down into oblivion. She would have fled, but the thread led straight into the heart of it. She followed, and held on.

171

It flinched. Then it struggled, changing its shape into further monstrous forms that terrified her, all armed and shielded against her. But she did not let go.

No power on earth prevails against water. In the face of direct attack she still yielded and gave way, but she never let go. Time had always been on her side, and she would not be hurried now.

She could not deflect it. Evil and danger lay there, and there they would remain. All she could hope to do was bind it, hoping it would be for long enough. She had the power to bind, but had never yet attempted to use it on a force so strong. She knew quite well it might turn and destroy her, which would mean that whatever she was, it would vanish for ever from the earth.

At last she gained the upper hand, and cast her spell. She almost felt it crack. She waited, quivering; to her joy it held. It was only partial, it only could be partial; but it held.

Oddny stood up and spoke to the gorse, the burns, and the waves that were still breaking on the shore.

"What was, will be," she told them. "All things change, but you will not die, nor cease to know yourselves. The people have betrayed their trust of consciousness. They may cease to be, but we will still know what we are, and they will never destroy us."

Oddny had taken very little time, of the sort measured by people, so no one had noticed her absence. The tour finished with a diagram of how the water was cleaned before being pumped into the sea. Oddny's head ached. She didn't use numbers in the same way that these people seemed to, so the explanation left her little the wiser. They left the last of the intrusive bleeping machines behind and were about to quit the building.

As they left they each had to step into a small booth, where a machine measured them for gross pollution. Oddny watched the procedure with a sinking heart. She was fairly sure of what would happen. Her turn came, and she stepped into the booth as instructed.

Nothing happened.

"Are you standing on the footrests?" called the guide.

"Yes."

"Put your hands right to the back of the slots."

Oddny obeyed, knowing it was useless. Her mind raced. She'd need to get out of here fast. She couldn't let them examine her. They'd learned too much in the last couple of centuries, and she didn't intend to upset the neat little system they'd constructed for themselves. She remembered the sickly blue water in that dreadful pool. The gods knew what they would do with her.

The guides were studying the machine. "It's very odd. It isn't registering that there's anyone in there at all."

"Shall we call the engineer?"

"Some sort of power failure, do you think?"

"Are you sure you're standing in the right place?"

"Yes," said Oddny wearily.

"Well, we'll have to wait until someone comes. I've never known this happen before. It isn't registering anything at all."

One of the waiting tour ventured a mild joke. "Perhaps it thinks you don't exist."

They all smiled perfunctorily.

There were footsteps in the corridor, and an engineer in white overalls appeared. "Now then, where's this lady who breaks our machines?" he remarked, looking over the tour, who stood like obedient sheep on the right side of the barrier.

"She's still in there, isn't she?"

"No."

"She must have gone back the other side."

"She's not round here."

"Look in the corridor, where the effluent diagram is."

"No, no, she didn't go back. I'd have seen her pass me."

"She must have gone through."

"She never came past me. We'd have seen her."

They looked at one another in consternation, while the engineer rolled his eyes upwards and muttered, "Women!"

173

Oddny scrambled lightly over the high, barbed fence, and ran for the beach. Her coracle was where she'd left it. She picked it up and hurried down to the waves. The coracle had left a small impression, round ribbed sides echoed in a pattern on the hollowed sand; then only faint bare footprints half running down to the breaking surf and the shifting surface of the sea, revealing nothing.

The snow had all melted now. She squatted on the rock above the pool. The moss was thick under her feet, soft between her toes. It rained steadily, drops of water trickling comfortably down her back and dripping off her. Her hair was wet and tangled. Water ran out of it, splashing into the moss which absorbed it silently. The daylight was almost gone, and the dark was comforting, blurring the shapes of things into the unseen unity of the night. A breeze came down off the hills. She could feel the nip of frost on her skin right down her left-hand side. The night was full of soft sounds, distinct over the falling water which she did not call a sound. Rain on grass, rain on rock, passing hooves muffled by turf, wind funnelling down into the corrie, bringing more rain.

"I thought I would never come back," said Oddny.

Her companion stirred. He had been sitting motionless on the other side of the pool, the outline of his antlers merging into the rowan branches. She felt him turn to look at her, though she could not see his eyes. "Even so," he said, as if following an earlier thought, "even if the thing is bound, it won't help the deer. Not now."

Something else had happened, then. She felt a flutter of panic, but said nothing. If he intended to tell her, she only had to wait.

It took him a while. He wasn't used to telling anybody anything, and the news he had was his own, not hers. "The people are driving the deer off the mountain," he said at last.

"I don't understand." She was alert now, straining to imagine what that meant. She had no concept of the mountain without the deer, or of the deer without the mountain, so

174

that what he was saying seemed quite impossible. It would be harder for him. He had no imagination at all: imagination was not part of what he was. He must be searching for words to explain this impossible thing that he had witnessed. Oddny waited patiently.

"They have driven the deer down inside fences, where I cannot reach them. The people are concerned about the sickness." He paused again. "I am afraid of what they will do."

Afraid he might well be, but he could not imagine. Oddny could, and her heart gave a queer lurch, and seemed to rise into her throat. "And you cannot follow? What will you do, then?"

She sensed him shrug. "My own kind are lost to me," he said at last, with no perceptible emotion. "The deer are doomed and so, therefore, am I."

"You'd abandon them, then?" she said, too quickly.

"Abandon?" he questioned, not knowing the word. "I am the guardian of the deer upon the mountain. There was a time when I was not, when there were no deer. I always knew that such a time must come again, for the world does not stay still. It should not have been done by the people; they were not born for that. They take on too much and will perish for it. But that's no business of mine. If the deer are gone from the mountain, I cannot stay, for I shall be nothing."

"So you're going?" Desolation welled inside her, but there was nothing to say. As he said, it was always going to happen. That was the way time worked, and there was nothing to be said.

"Out of the world," he finished for her. "Yes."

She thought of her struggle among the fields of gorse, which seemed now to be all in vain. "I did my best," she told him.

"There was nothing else you could do." He seemed to be struggling for words, and when he spoke again she understood why. The concept was new to him, and it was very difficult for him to express anything new. "You did very

175

well," he said. "If the thing is bound, then you have saved this world from a great danger. That is good, even if my own time has come. It is still good."

"Yes."

He was standing up now, and from where she crouched he seemed tall as the rowans themselves, a creature out of a dream etched against a dim starlit sky. A moment later he had turned and gone; only the faint thud of hoofbeats came down to her on the wind.

Oddny sat by the pool until the stars faded again and the dawn spread cold across the eastern sky. The world seemed empty. It was possible that she was the only one of her kind upon whom the sun still rose. She watched the water bubbling out of the earth, flowing towards the unseen sea. For the first time since the melting of the ice, when the spring burst out from the corrie floor, it gave her no solace. It was only water, and what was water? She would miss him, even if she stayed here until the end of time, and nothing that the earth brought forth would take his place for her.

A tear splashed down into the moss. She felt it hot on her cheek, and brushed her hand across her eyes. Then she crouched over the water, filling her cupped palms. The burn flowed over her hands and she realised for the first time that it was very cold.

An Apple from a Tree

You ask for the whole story, which seems a large return for the loan of a small towel, but since you helped me out when I needed it, I'll tell you what I think happened, which is, after all, as near to a whole story as anyone can get.

As with many significant changes, the story began in the Botanic Gardens. I have always enjoyed walking there, not only to commune with nature, such as it is, but also to watch people in the throes of conversations and encounters that are obviously about to change their lives. However, I always thought of myself as a mere observer. I thought I was as likely to become part of the drama as I was to start sprouting leaves in spring, or to receive a proposal under the lilac. Not only was I not expecting anything, I didn't want anything much either.

One day in early September, the gardens were almost deserted. It was a damp Monday evening and the place seemed separate and enclosed. After the weekend, the city had gone back to whatever it thought mattered, and a thick fog lay over it, obliterating the distinctive skyline. The muffled sound of traffic could have come from anywhere, and might as easily have been made by live creatures roaring in a wilderness of their own devising. Meanwhile in this oasis of calm, I wandered under the trees. The first leaves were beginning to come down. I wove to and fro across the grass, kicking as many leaves as I could, but they were still sparse. At least no one had attempted to rake them up. A balsam poplar grows just beside the gate, and when I reached it I scooped up a handful of leaves and held them to my face.

Damp and yellow, they smelt exotic and flower-like. I wandered on through the mist.

Twice I circled the lawn at the top, which is itself encircled by an ancient hedge of yew. Then I slipped in through a gap, and found myself under the great beech trees at the end. Perhaps their tops were above the mist. I couldn't tell, but there seemed to be a wind up there that spoke of cleaner air, sighing as it did among the branches, sending the first brown leaves scudding into the sky. I looked up and saw the mist clearing, the sky turning blue, like seeing the sea from an aeroplane when the cloud breaks apart. Hearing the sea up there made me nostalgic. It was autumn, and I had a whole winter to face in the city. The Firth hardly counted. It was brown and smelly, and when the tide went down it left a thick black scum, like the tideline from a diabolic bath.

I went to and fro under the beeches, as though by waiting long enough I could make something happen. That was foolish, of course, but the wind up there seemed so real and so near, I almost expected the waves of it to come lapping at my feet. I don't know what I was thinking of but, as the leaves came down, I jumped and tried to catch them. Seven years' good luck, we used to say. I don't know who taught me that. You don't catch luck falling off a tree; at least, I never supposed so.

Something came down hard that was not a leaf, falling straight towards me. I reacted instinctively, as though playing a celestial form of cricket. I cupped my hands together and caught it, letting my hands go with it so it didn't hurt me. It was round and solid, like nothing from a beech tree. I unfolded my hands slowly, and looked.

It was an apple.

Up I looked again, but there was nothing, only the beech trees tossing in a wind I could not feel. The last mist wreathed away like the tail of an unidentified creature whisking out of sight. Shadows that I had not known existed slid out of vision, and the leaves, both green and gold, were washed in sudden brightness.

I turned the apple over. It was not very big, greenish on one side, red on the other, hard and firm. There was a lack of emphasis about it I recognised as being old-fashioned. On a supermarket shelf it would have looked small and misshapen, and would probably have lain untouched until past its sell-by date. That gave me reason to suppose it might taste good. I smelled it cautiously. It smelled more like an apple than any apple I'd come across for years. It was more like the apple-scented bottles in the Body Shop. I'd forgotten that apple was astringent, sweet certainly, but almost as sharp as pine at the same time. I sniffed it again. Then, in spite of the fact that I'd no idea where it had been, I bit into it.

It seems tragic that a taste more subtle than anything we have come to know on earth should be wasted, but I hardly noticed it, for the very good reason that I was caught up in something that resembled, more closely than anything else I can think of, a Victorian steam roundabout. I once rode such a roundabout. I rode a great grey dapple horse with staring eyes and flaring nostrils; we tore up and down in strides like no horse ever made, faster and faster, with a wild music clinging to us that never dropped behind for all our speed.

This was not quite like that. There was no horse and no music. At least, I think there was not but, now I try to remember more carefully, I cannot say for sure. We did go round and round, in a spiral of leaves all caught up and rolled up, spun into a cone shape that whizzed over the lawn like a bobbin gone mad, until it fell apart in the long tall grass under the apple tree, flinging me down on knobbly ground that turned out to be wet soil strewn with windfalls. A painful landing, but I was too surprised to think about my bruises. I was still clutching my apple. I stood up, shakily, and realised that I was not alone.

The woman who stood watching me was quite naked. That was the first thing that I noticed about her. If that makes you think that I pay too much attention to trivia, you should read the regulations governing the conduct of visitors to the Botanics, and you will see at once why this should seem so startling. Also, it was September, and none too warm. She stood in thigh-high grass. Her dark hair fell right down her back, and was woven through with stems of bryony. She was brown, so evenly tanned that she might never have worn clothes at all, and quite slender, though not skinny. She seemed unmoved by my sudden appearance and stood regarding me without moving. It was a disconcerting gaze. Her eyes were so black they looked almost hollow.

"Hello," I said.

"Hello," she replied, so that it sounded like my own voice coming back at me. I thought she was mocking me and stiffened, but her gaze was not unfriendly. If she spoke English, I thought, it seemed all the odder that she should be naked. In case you think there is prejudice in that, let me remind you that it could mean only that she was able to read the regulations as well as I could. Assuming she could read, of course. I looked at her askance.

"Where have you come from?" she asked me next.

That flummoxed me. Surely she was taking the words from my mouth? "Me?" I said. "I was here all the time. Where have you come from?"

"I was here all the time."

I don't like being mimicked. She even had the same accent, but she seemed to be using it quite innocently. I held out the apple.

"I caught it," I said. "Does it belong to you?"

"It came off the tree." She pointed, and I looked.

The beech trees were gone, and the lawn, and the yew hedge. But it was still autumn and the leaves were still turning red and gold. This time they were apple leaves, for before me rose the hugest apple tree I ever saw, crowning the hill like a wreath of berries round an old man's head. The grass was long and unkempt, beginning to die back, but over it the apple-laden tree bent its branches low, so I could have reached up and picked and picked, though never got a tithe of all that lay beyond my reach. I never saw such a tree, nor so many apples, red and green and gold. I looked away, and saw

182

a line of craggy hills across the skyline, softened by the ranks of trees.

"Where is this? What is that tree?"

She looked at me, apparently puzzled. "This is the world," she said, "and that is an apple tree."

"Thank you," I said. I can be sardonic when I choose, but sarcasm seemed to wash over her like a summer breeze.

"That's all right," she said, and then she asked a question of her own. "What is wrong with you?"

"Me?" I was indignant. "Nothing. Why? What should be wrong?"

"You're all wrapped about. Even your feet."

I looked down at my feet. I was wearing trainers, somewhat damp and down at heel but perfectly respectable.

"My feet are fine, and so is the rest of me. I just happen to be wearing clothes. I'm surprised you managed to get here without, yourself."

There was no doubt about it then. She was laughing at me. I would have walked away with dignity, but I had the disadvantage of not being sure any more where anything was. In fact, I didn't know where I was myself except that I hadn't left the Botanics and was, presumably, still in them.

"Are you upset? Don't you like the apple?"

I had almost forgotten the apple. I looked at it a mite suspiciously, not being quite sure how far it was responsible. I had an idea and held it out to her. "Eat it yourself."

"I was going to, but then you caught it."

"Did you throw it?"

"No, he did."

"He?" I looked round nervously. "Who?"

"He," she repeated with emphasis. "Didn't you hear? I thought you said you'd been here all the time?"

"If I was, I wasn't listening." I looked at the apple as though it might bite me, rather than vice versa. "Why?" I asked, and failed to keep misgiving entirely out of my voice. "Perhaps you'd better tell me what happened."

"Nothing," she said. "After all that. I picked it, and I

183

offered it to him. And he said, 'I'm not hungry', and threw it. Then he went, and you came. That was all."

"Where's he gone?"

"I neither know nor care. He showed a lamentable want of curiosity. I don't think he's ever really interested in anything but sex. And food, of course. I'm not sure whether he never had any imagination, or whether nameless fears subsequently drove it out of his head. What sex are you, incidentally?"

"Me?" For the third time I was indignant. "I'm a woman, same as you. Can't you tell?"

"I thought so. It was the wrappings that confused me. What happened after you bit it?"

"I was here."

"Damn."

"I'm sorry?"

"I had hoped," she explained patiently, "that it might get one to somewhere else. Evidently not. Never mind. Shall we go now?"

"Go? Where?"

"Well, we can't stay here."

She was right. At any moment there would be voices crying out "Closing ti-ime" from one end of the gardens to the other. Such was the deception of the Botanics. Refuge seemed to be offered, a way out through the very heart of the city, then, just as the shadows lengthened and the truth seemed near at hand, policemen came shouting along the paths, expelling everybody, then closing the great iron gates behind them. I was never sure whether it was worse to leave before the expulsion began, or wait as long as possible, and be harried to the gates while the voices circled round me like sheepdogs driving an unwilling flock.

"Where do you live?" I asked her.

"In the world. Are you coming?"

If we passed through the gates, I never noticed. Once we left the apple tree behind, alone on the summit of the hill, we were down among the rest of the trees. The smell of balsam was still there, permeating the evening like a promise of

184

something new. But the trees seemed to crowd more thickly than usual, pressing together and lining our route, like people watching a procession. We hardly made a procession, she and I, and there was no other human being to be seen anywhere. The path wound this way and that until quite soon I had lost all bearings. Golden leaves were strewn underfoot. They rustled as we walked. Where there were gaps in the trees, the long evening light broke through, bright on the fading leaves above, then speckled further down, where the leaves interrupted its path.

Brambles grew beside the way, thick with berries. She picked and ate them as she passed, absent-mindedly, as though browsing were automatic and her mind far away. But it slowed her down, and I was glad of that. The trailing stems caught my jacket, and I had to keep stopping to disentangle them. It was warm and humid among so many trees. I felt the sweat gather under my shirt, and trickle down my back. It was quiet in the wood, but not silent. The squirrels were everywhere, up and down the trees and running across the path in front of us, stopping when they saw us, and regarding us with bright eyes from about a yard distant, perched on their hind legs, jaws chattering. I was pleased to see them; they helped me to grasp that I was in the Botanics, which is the only place I know where squirrels are that tame and numerous. But when we saw the deer, I began to wonder again. I know there is more wildlife in city parks than ever meets the eyes, but a herd of roe deer? The little group we saw bounded away through the trees as we approached, disappearing among the birch stems in a pattern of brown and silver.

Presently we crossed a burn. Luckily there hadn't been much rain lately; even so, we had to wade. A curtain of willow hung down over the water, stems trailing even in the diminished flow. She waited while I took my shoes and socks off, and rolled up my trousers. My clothes seemed to amuse her. To distract her from that, and because our brief halt renewed the chance for conversation, I tried to pin her down a little more.

"What is your name?" I asked her.

"Nosila."

I thought she might ask mine, but she didn't.

After that there was little opportunity for talk. We were ascending a steep hill, weaving our way through thick trunks and twining stems. The canopy was so dense here that the sun was quite blocked out. I would have said that it was getting darker, but it could not be less than an hour before sunset, for no one had called "Closing ti–ime". I wondered if I would wake up enough to hear them. I had had strange dreams in the Botanics before now, I told myself, and the police could surely be trusted not to ignore a sleeping body?

The hill hardly seemed to slow her down at all. I stopped even trying to think but stumbled after her, tripping over roots, and pulling myself uphill by thin stems. The forest badly needed clearing. No one had thinned out the young saplings, or cleared away the masses of fallen trunks and dead wood. Sometimes we climbed over these obstacles, sometimes we forced our way round, ducking under horizontal branches that were now pushing up new shoots from their sides, straight towards the sky. Even the sky shocked me; it was not pale, but a deep velvety blue, with one star showing. Even in the heart of the Botanics the dark could not look like that, even if one were allowed to stay and see. There had been times when I had circumnavigated the gardens at night, two sides of houses and two sides of endless iron railing, hoping for a glimmering of the night sky that might look down on the silent trees within. Shut out in an unremitting orange glow like tortured fire, I could only imagine it. The stars were lost to me. I could have clung to those railings and shaken them, hammered at the gates of the garden like a demented being, but I was afraid of the police, and of the danger of walking alone at night, so I walked quickly and never stopped.

Now there was no walking quickly, although the dusk filtered in soft and fast, swallowing up the tree tops, while the sky began to prick out stars, like the lighting of old-fashioned lamps. I could see better now. We were at the top of the hill and the slope below us stretched down to open ground. When I looked again I saw it was not ground but water. It was black in the half-light, uncannily calm, and on the far side it was lost in shadow where a great precipice towered over it. I found it weird, as though the place were full of hidden things I did not wish to think about.

"Where are we?"

"By the loch."

It occurred to me that she could not help being completely literal. Although she spoke as fluently as I did, perhaps her grasp of language did not go so far. If she sought for nuances in anything, it was clearly not in words.

"Where are we going?" I asked patiently.

"There is shelter. It will soon be night."

"I would rather go home."

She looked at me with concern. A slight breeze blew up, and I heard the water lap on the shore below, invisible in the thickening air. I identified a difference then, which had been present from the moment when I bit the apple. The trees smelled so sharp they overwhelmed me. The air was full of scents: leaves, water, soil, a tinge of salt on the breeze. Just as when I tasted the apple, I felt I had never known such richness. I sniffed again; and the breeze was damp and resinous, heavy with tree smells.

She answered just as I was about to speak again. The rhythm of her conversation was quite different from mine. She left long pauses for thought between each statement as though the fear of interruption was quite unknown to her.

"Are you tired?" she asked. "Are you hungry? You still have the apple."

I remembered, and took it out of my pocket. I was not sure what that apple was responsible for, and I distrusted it. "I'm not sure about it," I said. "You have it."

She took it. "You want to give it to me?"

She seemed to attach undue importance to my purpose. I

only wanted to be rid of the thing, and it hardly seemed such a momentous gift. After all, she could have picked as many as she liked.

"Yes," I said lightly. "Why not?"

Her eyes widened and she looked at it almost fearfully, as though I had challenged her to something. I was about to explain that nothing was further from my thoughts, and she need feel herself under no imaginary obligations, when she bit into it.

There was a roar like an approaching train from somewhere deep below us, and the ground seemed to quiver and to shake. I heard rushing water, like a great waterfall bursting its confines and engulfing the whole forest. We were flung together, and I felt her flesh under my hands as I clung to her, whirling downwards as the sky vanished from over us, until we landed hard on concrete, crashing in a heap amidst a tumble of wet leaves.

"Christ," I muttered, clutching my bruised head in my hands. There was an orange glow which hurt my eyes, and the roaring was still in my ears, with a stench like the pits of a furnace. I felt a clutching at my arm, which I gradually realised was becoming painful. I looked up.

We were sitting on the pavement at the foot of Waverley Bridge, and there were taxis turning in and out of the station. We must have just missed the iron railings that enclosed Princes Street Gardens behind us. It was dark in there, and silent, all locked away for the night. I found myself staring at a fat white airport bus, that ground towards us like a giant caterpillar.

Nosila screamed in my ear.

"Ow!" I tried to calm her, or myself, I wasn't sure which. "Now hold on. At least we know where we are." I turned and looked at her, and the appalling truth dawned on me: she was still stark naked.

I looked up and down the street in horror. There was no one on the pavement except an old wino huddled against the railings, and a shuffling woman weighed down with carrier bags. We were still unseen.

"Here," I said, struggling out of my jacket. "No, no, that won't do, it's too short. Oh Christ!" I thought desperately. "You'll have to take my jumper, You can hold it down at the ends." I tore it off.

"What are you doing?"

"Taking my clothes off," I snapped. "Here, put this on."

She stared at it as though it might shrivel her up. "Why? What is it?"

"It's a jumper." I realised, even in my desperate embarrassment, that more explanation was going to be necessary. "You have to wear it. Put it on. Like I did. You can't walk around here stark naked."

She looked round, her eyes dilating with fear. "What is naked?"

"I'll tell you when we get home. Now look, this is Edinburgh. Anywhere else, they'd probably take no notice. Put it on, for God's sake. Trust me."

Well, I got it on to her, and explained the necessity for holding the ends down so that they reached to her thighs. She was puzzled, but docile. I put my jacket on again.

"Come on, quick."

"Where are we going?"

"Home. It still looks most odd, though at least you're decent. But hurry."

She didn't seem to have any idea what the trouble was. In Princes Street the shops were shut, and the crowds had gone, but the evening groups of kids with nowhere to go were just starting to assemble. We had to pass a gang of boys with motor bikes as we scurried through the shadow of the Scott monument, and sure enough they stopped and stared, and muttered as we passed. I'd rather they'd shouted something lewd, it would have meant they didn't intend to do anything else, but they just looked after us in silence. Nosila's bare feet left marks on the pavement, still being wet from the leaves. I didn't look at her. I didn't want my worst fears confirmed. But I remembered the wreaths of bryony, and shuddered.

In Hanover Street there were people passing to and fro, and cafés open, as well as long queues at the bus stop. I hesitated, wondering if a bus would be easier, but then, I thought, there was no way I could allow Nosila to sit down, and it would be light inside. I grabbed her elbow and hurried her on.

That's when I thought of you. The idea of walking all the way home appalled me but your house was quite close. True, I didn't know you very well then but I thought you'd be willing to help, and that was the most important thing. As we hurried downhill I tried to think how to explain it to you. You hadn't struck me as being particularly quick on the uptake, when we met. Perhaps the less said, the better.

Nosila broke into the tail of my thoughts. We were just passing Queen Street Gardens when she pulled away from me. The next thing I knew, she was trying to climb the railings, abandoning every vestige of decency in the process. I grabbed her by the tail of her jersey.

"What are you doing, for God's sake? Not that way!"

I had to prise her hands away from the railings. I couldn't have done it if she had gone on resisting, but she seemed to give in suddenly and turned to face me. She looked wild-eyed and desperate, like a sheep that has been separated from the rest of the flock being brought in by dogs. I would have preferred her to cry. It would have made her seem less alien.

"What are you trying to do?"

"I want to go back where it's dark!"

"You can't. It's locked up. And it would be dangerous. Come on, I'll take you home."

"What is home?"

"Safe," I told her, and hurried her on before she got the chance to argue. We reached your street, I pressed your buzzer and thank God you were in. I thought for a moment, then decided to leave her at the foot of the stairs. I just couldn't see myself explaining everything.

"I'll be right back. Stand against the wall and don't move. No one can get in without a key. If they do, just stand back against the wall and don't say anything."

She stood at the bottom watching me. I tore up the five flights of stone steps as fast as I could, and found your door open at the top.

It would have been easier to explain if I hadn't been so out of breath, but I can't say you were helpful. The way you said, "Trousers?" as if I'd asked you for a time bomb, I could have hit you. That's why I gave up. You seemed to have a bee in your bonnet about lending a simple pair of trousers, as if I were about to go off and do something diabolical or humiliating with them. For Christ's sake, I thought, he thinks it's Rag Week or something. Anyway, that's why I ended up just asking for a towel, and that was hard enough. I never met anyone as suspicious as you seemed to be that night. And when you did produce a towel, it wasn't exactly generous, was it?

Anyway, it served to get us home. I tied it round her like a kilt, and tucked it in. She looked as though she'd been interrupted in the middle of a sauna, but no one accosted us. I realised when I got home that I was completely shattered, and so was she. I fried up herring and tatties for supper, and that made the world seem slightly more tenable again.

About halfway through the evening the phone rang. It was Kate. "Alison?" she said. "I was just phoning to see if you wanted a lift tomorrow."

"A lift to what?"

She was talking about that party at the gallery. I'd forgotten all about it. It was the last thing I felt like dealing with, but I can't afford to miss any possible opportunities, so I said I'd go.

I offered Nosila a bath, and that intrigued her. She seemed to think it was funny. I found her attitude slightly irritating, but at least amusement brought the colour back to her cheeks and restored her equanimity. After that I made a cup of tea and we sat down to discuss the situation. At least, that's what I'd planned to do. She didn't seem to know what a discussion was. She was more interested in my houseplants. I watched her wandering from one to another, apparently whispering sweet nothings into their leaves. It seemed like a caricature of myself going round with the Baby Bio, but I'd never behave like that if I were a guest in someone's house.

"Nosila, we have to talk about things."

She ran her fingers along the mantelpiece. She might have been testing for dust, but I understood by now she was only intrigued by the feel of paintwork. "You talk a lot," she remarked. "Does it make you happy?"

"I don't. In fact I'm remarkably anti-social. But we have a problem."

She looked round, but evidently saw nothing that might be thus defined.

"Do you think one of us is dreaming?" I asked her next.

She shook her head helplessly.

"How do you think you got here?"

"Like you," she said. Then she sighed. "Perhaps he was right to be content."

"I don't know what you mean. But think about this: if I bite the apple, we get where you were, and if you do, we get to where I was. Am. I mean we are."

"Yes," she said.

"But we can't either of us get back to where we were. Not both at once."

She seemed to be listening carefully. "Entwined," she said.

"I beg your pardon?"

"Hold out your hand."

I held out my right hand. She came round beside me and laid her own against it, palm to palm. Our hands were the same size, small but square and firm. Hers were more roughened than mine but there seemed to be no other difference. Moreover, her hand was quite real, flesh and blood. I could feel the warmth of it against mine. "That's touching," she said.

"I see it is."

"You want to let go?"

"I'm torn."

"Yes," she said. "We can't have two places at once."

"Then we have to find a way of separating."

"No."

"What do you mean, no?"

"It's all one."

I gave up then, and suggested that we went to bed.

The morning was sunny and hopeful. She was still there. I found her drifting naked round the kitchen, tasting the food from the jars.

"You can't eat raw flour. We'll have breakfast."

I was in a practical mood and, as the major problem seemed no nearer a solution, I applied myself to the more immediate task of acclimatising her to the world as it was. I took her shopping, and explained to her about traffic lights, and crossing roads. She kept bumping into people, and I taught her to say "Sorry" every time. I had cause to regret that, as it left very little opportunity for saying anything else. She just didn't seem to see people coming. There were other problems. She stopped and wept over the greengroceries displayed outside the shop on the corner and, when we passed a row of gardens, she kept trying to climb the low stone walls. By the end of the morning I was ready to try anything to be rid of her, even if I had to bite that wretched apple all over again.

In spite of it all, I decided to take her with me to the party that night. I didn't dare leave her alone in my flat and I didn't want to miss the party. I was too desperate for work to miss such an opportunity: it was the opening of a new exhibition. I knew the people vaguely and the more they saw my face the more likely they were to employ me.

I don't know what I'd have done if you hadn't been there. You hadn't distinguished yourself over the towel episode, but that evening you saved me from social disaster. I still don't know whether that was just a ploy but I suppose I had some idea what you were hoping for. Anyway, in my eyes you redeemed yourself.

I was trying to talk to the person I most needed to impress, but I could hear your conversation out of the corner of my ear. It made my own somewhat disjointed.

"A friend of Alison's," you were saying to her, "I thought you must be a relative."

"Yes," she said.

"Are you involved with art too?" you asked her.

"What is art?"

"Help," I heard you say, "I don't know that I'm in the mood for intelligent conversation. Are you a student?"

"No," she said. "I'm frightened already. I don't want more."

". . . And of course," the important person was saying to me, "you'll know the work of so and so and such and such."

"Well," I said cautiously, "naturally the names are familiar . . . Wasn't that . . .? Oh, yes, when would it be . . .?"

"1985."

"Of course," I said, "a breakthrough."

"You don't think that was mostly hype?"

"It's amazing what marketing can do," I said.

I had to concentrate for a bit. When I heard you and Nosila again, you were talking about the sex life of plants. She looked relaxed and happy, almost as I had seen her first. I took a deep breath, and turned back to my own conversation. "No," I said, "I haven't actually read it, but of course I saw the reviews . . ."

There was a hush, as the tape of soft music wound to an end, and for a moment conversation died with it.

Nosila's voice came loud and clear, "Why do they sway together so, like trees in a gale? Why do they express anger and sex at the same time? What are they trying to do to one another? Do you know?"

There was a silence.

"We must all have asked those questions," you replied easily. "A highly ambiguous work of art. Everyone thought so."

Nosila looked puzzled but I could have kissed you. A month later I did, of course, but by that time all was well.

"She must have seen the preview," murmured my companion. "It's booked out now, more or less until the millennium, I believe." She chortled at her own joke. "Luckily I was sent tickets."

"What is?" I said, and realised that I sounded like Nosila.

"The performance to which that girl referred. Surely you've come across it? It was reviewed everywhere."

"Oh yes," I said, subdued.

I had no idea what chivalrous impulse had prompted you but when I managed to get a word with you, just before I left, I said, "Thank you for taking care of my friend. She really isn't used to this."

"I admire her for it," you said, and left me feeling confused.

I was even more confused when you phoned me three weeks later to say you'd been meditating in a tent in the Cairngorms ever since, and you wanted me to come and live on an uninhabited island with you to grow potatoes and study the ancient philosophers. However, I was tempted. I'm glad we came to a more reasonable compromise than that, but that's not part of this story.

I woke next morning from a deep sleep and saw that the day was drear and grey. I pressed my face into the pillow, trying to recapture the dark. There seemed to be no greater gift than oblivion. Evading me, it hovered at the corners of my consciousness, tempting me onwards into a desire for something too close to nothingness for me to pursue with any courage. Reluctantly I sat up and faced the day.

It was raining. That upset all my plans. But then again, why not? At least the gardens would be deserted. I got up and surveyed Nosila. She was sleeping flat on her back, the covers flung away, her hair spread over the pillow like a black halo. To my jaundiced eyes, she looked like something out of Aubrey Beardsley. Irritated, I nudged her with one slippered foot. "It's morning," I said. "I'm going to make a cup of tea."

She was fully awake at once, jumping up eagerly to look through the window at the rain. It evidently moved her: she began to chant and then to dance around the room, thumping on the floor in a manner calculated to get the man downstairs balanced on a chair, thumping back on the ceiling with the end of a broom handle.

"Stop! You can't do that here."

"But it's raining."

"You can't do that even if it's Noah's flood. Here, borrow my dressing-gown."

She didn't want to get dressed that day. She kept murmuring that it was raining and what was the point? She seemed to be in a fever to get outside and, sure enough, once we were on the pavement she went leaping down the street, banging her fists against her chest and ululating at the sodden sky. The curtains of the flat below mine were seen to twitch and to remain poised half held, like a blocked-in question mark.

"Nosila, stop. You can't do that here."

Once we were on the path by the water, I let her go. She went dancing and leaping under the trees, her bare feet light as fallen leaves. I never did manage to make her wear anything on her feet, although otherwise I persuaded her to dress fairly normally. It was a relief when we finally turned in at the gates of the garden. I cast a doubtful glance at the policeman in his box as we passed, but he was reading the *Express* and didn't see us. Not that we were contravening anything, but Nosila certainly looked as if she might.

I felt I needed time to think, out of the rain, so I took her into the plant houses. Now, when I think of it, I am more satisfied about that than about any of the rest. I would like to think that she gained something from her experiences, and nothing else that I could provide seemed to make her any wiser or happier. But for her that place was enchanted. She touched everything, while I kept a wary eye out for patrols. She ran her hands up and down the stems of the palms, and poked her fingers gently inside the orchids. When she dabbled her hand in the pool, the carp came up and nibbled her fingers, and she laughed. The ferns astounded her. She stood in their house for a long time, as if she were listening. I was so near I could hear her breathing.

"But they are so old," she said at last. "Now there at last is a story worth the telling."

"What story?" But she was away, her hands moving up the vines.

By the time I got her out of there, the clouds had cleared a little. We walked up to the crown of the hill, and stood beneath the beech trees. The sound of water dripping from trees was cold and mournful. Dew clung to the grass, so that we left green footprints over a lawn that had been white. Nosila took the apple from her pocket. It was wrinkled now, and the two bite marks had gone quite brown.

"You try first," I said to her.

She bit, and screwed up her face. "It's sour now."

Nothing else happened.

"I was afraid of that," I said, and held out my hand. The apple looked thoroughly unappetising. I was aware of a pit of fear yawning inside me, and I think my hand was shaking.

"There's no other way," she said quietly. I sensed her desperation. I could refuse, I supposed, but then I'd feel responsible for her ever after. I hate responsibility, which left me no choice. I bit.

Since it was wet this time, it felt like being run through the rinse programme of an automatic washing-machine. We were caught up in a blur of spinning water, gyrating wildly. Sky, grass and trees melted away into rapids, all turning water-coloured. We were too entangled to keep our balance and when we fell we stayed entwined, like a four-legged monster gasping in its lair of thick grass, for the grass was long again. When we sat up we could see nothing but feathered seedheads bending before the breeze above our heads. The broken stems gave us a softer landing than before. Once we had reclaimed our respective limbs, we stood up cautiously.

The rain had gone. Sun dappled the grass, patterned by the shadows of the leaves. The air was heady with the smell of apples. All round us the forest was turning golden under the morning sun. The sky was pale blue, with a thumbnail moon rising high over the ridge to the south. This time I studied the horizon more closely. There were precipices over there, surrounding a craggy bluff topped by trees and, further east, a higher hill whose shape was more than familiar. The expanse of forest in between set it far beyond my reach. A line of grey cliff, surmounted by autumn gold, all still untrodden. I touched Nosila's shoulder. "Over there." I pointed. "You've been up there?"

She nodded, but her eyes searched the nearer woods restlessly and she hardly looked where I was pointing.

"What do you see from there?"

She glanced again. "From there? The sea, of course. Beaches."

"What colour is the sea?"

She laughed at that, as though it were a foolish question. "All colours," she said. "Like the sky, like the forest, like the loch. All those. Changing."

"I see."

She cried out then, throwing back her head and making a sound that must have echoed almost to the crags, a long, yodelling call that threw back an echo, then left the woods more silent than they had been before.

I stood trembling, not understanding. There was a movement in the trees, shadows passing, and the flick of branches pushed back. Then a man appeared, standing in the clear space that surrounded the apple tree, naked as the day he was born and brown as a naturist back from the Riviera. Nosila left my side and flung herself upon him.

I turned my back, and tried to steady my pulse by reciting all the regulations governing behaviour in the Botanics, from beginning to end. I had just reached the part about no sketching, painting or picnicking, for the third time, when various animal-like sounds behind me heralded the end of my ordeal. I counted to three hundred and turned round.

Nosila was on her feet again, watching me anxiously. "Are you ill?" she asked me.

"No," I said, "I don't know what I want."

"No?"

"I want both," I said, suddenly understanding, "but I don't know how."

"Let me think." She turned back to the man and began to talk to him in a low voice. I hardly listened. The apple was still in my hand. After the three bites we had already taken there was not much left. My time was running out. Was this my world, or hers? I only knew that I wanted to keep it, more than I had wanted anything in my life. I couldn't stay; I thought of you, without intending to. I wanted what Nosila had, but not here. I couldn't inhabit her whole world. There was no place for me in it. I glanced up at the apple tree.

There was my answer, staring me in the face.

"Nosila!"

She looked at me, still troubled. "What is it?"

"The apples," I said. "I'm going back now, but I want my apple."

She was puzzled for a moment, then she laughed, suddenly understanding. She pulled a branch down until it was level with my face. It was heavy with apples, two or three on every spur. I selected one, and twisted it off.

The man touched her on the shoulder, and muttered something. I wished he would stop hovering around, and leave us in peace.

"Why not?" said Nosila out loud. "She's free to do what she likes. Who's got the right to stop her?"

He shrugged.

My apple was smooth and sweet-smelling, red and gold and green. I put it carefully in my pocket.

She watched. "That's the first good reason I've seen for them."

"For what?"

"Clothes." She waved her hands in an effort to explain. "A way of carrying apples. That's all."

"Yes," I said, and hugged her.

"Are you ready?"

I nodded.

"Then give me the first apple."

The man said something incoherent, and she shook her head at him. "No, it's all right. We'll only be a few minutes."

He frowned.

"I promise," she said, and took the remains of our original apple from me.

I was elated, excited by my own cleverness. I could have both. I had an apple of my own, and so all the worlds I wanted were now open to me. I would go home and Nosila would be here, also at home. Separated, but entwined. I took her hand. She bit the apple.

The whirlwind that followed was nothing to the power I felt inside. I was drunk with it, my head still spinning like a top long after the rest of me had fallen with a thud upon the neat mown turf. I hardly noticed that Nosila had lost all her clothes, and here we were back in civilisation. It didn't matter. The familiar Botanic Gardens were all around me, and imprinted on my mind was the image of the wilderness they hid.

Nosila held my hand and we walked quietly down the hill. People stared at us, as well they might. We crossed a shrub bed. Luckily no uniformed official was in sight. There were railings in front of me. Eight-foot-high black railings and the road below. I felt the curve of the apple in my pocket and was reassured. I could see the Christian Science Church opposite, and the line of country to the south all blurred by rain.

"If I hold on tight," I said, "whatever happens, when it starts, you go. But I'll hold on. I think it'll work, if you hold the apple."

Her black eyes looked hollow again, as they had the first time I saw her. I would miss her physical presence, in spite of what I knew. I realised I was crying for the loss of it, although I knew it was illusory. She shed no tears. Perhaps she had none. I looked through the bars to the world outside.

She followed my gaze. "You belong there," she remarked. "Hold tight."

She held the apple to my lips.

I bit, and spat.

The world flung away from me. The bars bucketed like a boat in a storm. The apple was wrenched away, and something else, splitting away from my side like my heart being torn out, but I went on holding. I held so hard the iron bit into me, and I heard someone scream. It was I, and someone other, spinning away from me out of the world. Through the bars I saw a forest turning, leaves torn before a driving gale, and the sky circling below. Then slowly the grey road subsiding, the squat church, and a skyline of spires and defences. I sank to my knees, soaked, and exhausted.

When someone touched my shoulder I swung round, not knowing what to expect.

It was a policeman. Looking down, I saw his black polished shoes sinking into the newly dug soil. For a moment I was disorientated, then I felt the apple in my pocket, firm and real.

"You all right, hen?" he asked me.

I stood up slowly. "Yes," I said, without attempting to explain, and smiled at him, secure in my own knowledge.

A Life of Glory

1

Even in August it is cold at night in the Arizona desert. It is still and the stars are bright and clear. To a traveller from the other side of the world, they are foreign stars. To me, coming from wherever it was that I had been summoned, they were neither alien nor familiar. They were merely the beginning place and, consequently, engraved upon my being. I have never looked upon those stars with waking eyes, but I have no other measure of the sky, except how far it differs from that night.

The desert of Arizona is red. Perhaps there are other deserts of other colours, but my desert is red. The ground is red and bare, the rocks are red, twisted into fantastic stacks and shapes, as if some primaeval river should still be licking round their feet. For if it was not water that carved such shapes, I don't know what imagination could have conceived them. There are red cliffs which stretch for more than a hundred miles, and red arches over nothing at all, standing like triumphal monuments to some victory which never touched anything human. Apart from that, the land is flat. There are platforms of rock which extend for more miles than anyone could walk and between them are fissures and gullies and cracks in that dried-out land, all arid and empty.

Through the desert runs a green river, between red banks. It is held back by a great concrete dam, then runs again. The banks grow steeper, form a canyon, which excavates its own path ever deeper into that red earth, so that after thousands of years the canyon is nine miles across and deep beyond all history or measured time. If anyone ever believed the world was built on human scale, they should come here. It makes an apt beginning.

On the night of which I speak, two people camped out under the stars near the banks of the green river. Close by, the river had been dammed till it formed a great lake, warm to the touch. There was a small settlement upon the further bank but on this side there was nothing but a red airstrip scraped out of the rock and a wooden hut beside it. They had come by plane. The plane was tied down at the end of the runway, not fifty yards from the edge of the lake.

They had no tent with them, only a groundsheet and sleeping-bags. The mass of water flowed imperceptibly at their feet, towards the dam, the canyon and the sea. The stars slowly wheeled across the empty sky, as the world spun through the void which human beings ignore, except when they enter or depart. As a place to sleep, it was as close to the edge of the world as anyone can get, considering that the notion of an edge at all is at once fantastic and completely unavoidable.

There was little to impede communication. Only a few plants grew. There are cacti in the desert, and prickly pears, and small succulent plants that suddenly sprout magical flowers that bloom and vanish in a day, seeming like a mirage in that place where everything is red, and stone. Perhaps there were snakes, and lizards, and a few insects. I don't know. As far as I was concerned, life was represented by the two people who lay tangled together on top of their abandoned sleeping-bags, next to the river.

I find it hard to recapture the moment. I imagine looking down from a great height, and seeing the desert under the night: a thousand miles of empty land supporting nothing. That is to say, in human terms, nothing. I see the river below, as clear as if all this were yesterday, winding in slow curves, the water black with night, alien, hiding strange life that has nothing to do with me. I draw closer. Or perhaps I am drawn. I see quite clearly now: the two who lie together on the rumpled sleeping-bags are a woman and a man. Their bodies are pale, faintly visible under the stars. They think of nothing but one another and yet they are also caught in some magic of the night. We are very close to the edge of the world, and perhaps they know it.

And perhaps I do not know and all this is nothing. Possibly there was no moment when I looked down from some place between the rock and the stars and saw them as they were. Perhaps there was only silence and the utter blackness of unconscious night. I do not know what I am.

Some people are afraid of spiders and I think I understand that. It is the female who spins the web, drawing it out of herself like silk, a thread so delicate and beautiful that when the sun catches it, it shines like woven light in a pattern as inevitable as the spinning of life. Yet the thing is a trap, and reeks with sticky poison. When the fly is caught, it struggles till it dies, while she gloats and watches. Is there anything lovely in that? I don't know whether I agreed to this or not. Life is mostly pain, I believe, and there is only one way out of it, which we are all taught to dread. Perhaps our fear is so great because it is the only thing we long for. I don't know about that, either. I am robbed of memory. The stars are dimmed, and, until I am free, I would not know them if I saw them.

There was a moment in the Arizona desert which was an explosion of consciousness, a cataclysm more violent than anything which rocked the seas or blew the land apart. Something burst through, breaking its way in from beyond the edges of the world, and lodged itself, trapped itself, inside a grain of matter so small that those who made it were quite unconscious of their act. I have never been one to undervalue my own importance, and yet I have to acknowledge at this point that the decisive moment was purely subjective. No sound disturbed the peace of the night. The river never changed its course, nor did the stars diverge one iota from their ordained circuit. The two who lay entwined on the groundsheet never gave the event the beginnings of a thought.

Helen sat in the co-pilot's seat and watched. It was like being on another planet, especially arriving in this fashion. Nothing in her own country had even hinted that the earth could be like this. She had never before swum in a warm green lake, had never before lain on her back and watched the stars over the desert. Neither was she at all used to having no appetite for breakfast, but just at the moment food seemed irrelevant. She felt thirsty, and overcome by so much empty land. No one had ever made her realise before that the earth was mostly empty.

They passed over a dam, a long white strip of concrete holding a whole lake behind it. The river trickled out at its foot and slowly grew. It began to burrow down into the earth. The little plane traced its course. When Helen looked down to her left, she could see their shadow moving across the rock. The sun rose higher; the river delved deeper into the rock. There was a canyon below, strange red cliffs opening out in patterned strata, red and red and red. Helen watched, as though her eyes could tell her everything. It was impossible to imagine being down there. She remembered the heat by the lake, looked down into the gorge, and shuddered.

The pilot's hand touched hers. She looked round at him, half dazed. It took a moment to adjust to anything so near. He had caught the sun since yesterday and, in spite of his dark hair, he was coming out in more freckles. He might be American through and through, but to look at he was all Celt. Perhaps that was what she found disturbing; she didn't expect him to be foreign, until he said or did something indisputably alien. She should be growing used to it, as it happened about once in half an hour.

"Listen," he was saying. "I'm going down now. Just remember, I know what I'm doing. I'm not playing any fancy tricks, and I'm completely in control. Right?"

"Of course," she said, puzzled.

The plane dipped. Its shadow on the rock grew larger. It dropped to the level of the earth. Helen clung to the strap on the door beside her. The plane dropped below the earth, down into the canyon. She shut her eyes and slowly opened them again.

There was a wall of rock in front of her. Close to, the strata were not all red. Some were brown, some yellowish. The sun beat down on the cliff, burning every detail of it into her brain. The plane tilted and turned.

They faced the opposite wall. A fantastic pinnacle loomed up, a spire of rock the river had failed to wear away, sprouting from a ledge in the canyon. They swung again and passed it, a wing's length away.

Tilted, she could see the river down below, green and small. The scree was white with sunlight. Nothing grew. The plane righted itself, and began to turn again. Red cliffs curved past her like an arid dream.

"I had no idea," she told him, above the noise of the engine. "No one ever told me the earth was made like this."

He grinned at her, triumphant. After all, he had brought her here.

The canyon grew deeper. Looking up, she could see blue sky arched over the rock walls above. Another river joined them: the canyon forked. Helen gazed up the other tributary, unexplored, before it disappeared behind a wedge of rock. This was the desert, she could not hope to encompass it, only to look, then retreat. The plane curved and twisted. The rock walls drew close, receded, displayed strange twisted shapes, white against the sky. Time passed, slowly.

When the plane rose out of the earth at last, she saw the whole curve of the sky, and red rock fading to new horizons. There were mountains to the south now which had not been visible before. The ground was changing, rock slowly turning to scrub. The canyon widened, and on its shores the scrub grew thicker until it became a forest. Helen saw no tracks, only an occasional airstrip, which she would hardly have noticed if he hadn't nudged her, and asked her to watch out for each one.

The plane climbed a little, then they were over the Canyon itself. It was far larger than she had imagined. From where they skirted the cliff, the farther shore was hazy in the distance. The river ran green and sluggish. She knew – he had told her – the river was half a mile wide, complete with rapids, but looking at it from up here, it was difficult to believe. It was hard even to imagine water. She realised she was thirsty again, and reached for a bottle of lukewarm fruit juice.

He nudged her again, and handed her the map. He leaned over her and showed her the airstrip. It was much bigger than the others. They were coming back into inhabited country. Helen felt a twinge of disappointment. The last two days and the night had seemed like being out of the world. They had seen no one but each other, and the occasional voices on the radio had sounded remote, only adding to their isolation.

"We can take a car from there, and have a look at the Canyon. Walk down into it. There's tracks, see?"

She couldn't get used to the idea that he didn't have to keep his hands on the wheel. It made her nervous. Not as nervous as driving the thing herself, which he'd let her try yesterday. That really did scare her, though on the ground there was nothing foolish about her. Helen managed not to tell him to mind where they were going and concentrated on the threads of tracks below.

"All right," was all she said to him.

On the ground, she felt disorientated, hardly able to walk straight. It was painfully hot. The concrete apron beat heat back into their faces, and when they escaped into the air-conditioned buildings, there was a press of people which almost shocked her. In forty-eight hours she had forgotten what anyone looked like, except for one Celtic face which should have been close and subtle but instead flashed a disconcerting American smile, showing excellent teeth, when she least expected it.

However, he was very efficient. He hired a car with the ease of one who did it every week, and in a few minutes it rolled up to the door for them. Helen picked up her battered rucksack, which looked very stained and British, and got in.

"I could drive," she remarked. "I've got my licence."

"I thought of that. But it would cost a good deal more, and we're not going far."

"All right."

Perhaps I should have started by telling you his name. But what was a name to me? The crisis had come, and I was pitchforked out of everlasting space into – what?

I have tried to give you some idea of the beginning. I was lucky, I suppose, that my first impressions were not more confining. When I consider Helen, I realise that at that moment her gaze was fixed on far horizons. She was considering the vastness, and at the same time, the limitations, of this world. I had a view out, and that is more than most could say. If one must be reduced in a flash from transcendence to the confines of a cell, it is as well to be permeated by visions of rocks and water, sun and stars. It makes memory linger on more easily. Helen was stirred by undefined realisation, for no one had brought her to the boundaries of her world before.

I presume that was why she fell in love with him.

Did she fall in love that day? Or do I assume too much? A cell divides, unremarked, and divides again, second by second. Consciousness expands so fast, it bewilders me to think of it. The world is dark and infinite. I touch no boundary yet. I am filled with well-being. This universe can contain anything, and probably does. It grows larger by the minute under Helen's vigilant eyes. She was open to all of it; I can honestly say she hardly missed a thing. I had far more to miss, of course, but at that point I cannot say I knew it. We were content.

They stopped for brunch at a large restaurant on the lip of the Canyon. He had a rare steak with French fries. She had salad and brown bread, and a carton of mango juice which she had never tasted before.

"I knew you'd like it." He was exultant. It gave him so

much pleasure to give to her, because of the way she received, generously, holding nothing back. It was his country, and he had shown it to people before. But this woman was finding something he had not previously shown and, as he saw her discover it, he realised for the first time how much he knew himself.

"That's why I wrote and said you must come out west. I knew what you'd think. I knew you'd love it. It's my country and I wanted you to see it. I was raised in country like this."

She looked at him over her mango juice. "I can't imagine that."

"No?"

"Having the desert as normal. Your starting point, as it were. Didn't you feel very cramped in Europe?"

He shrugged. "Cramped? No. It was all new. Learning languages. Another culture. It seemed so rich to me. People warned me not to go, you know. People out here, they said it was madness to go that close to the Iron Curtain. Much safer in Arizona. You don't understand how far away Europe is in most people's consciousness. You might as well come from another planet."

"I don't think I'm European in outlook particularly. If you asked me where I came from . . ." She paused. "It would depend on where you asked me. Here, I'd say Scotland. In my own town, I'd say the street. You're something different depending on where you are. I've never been anywhere like this before, so I'm not sure who I am. You know?"

He grinned at her. "No. But go on. I like it."

"James, no. That's wasting words. They were meant to be thought about, not liked."

"I can like words if I like."

"It depends how. What you seem to mean is, I might as well grunt at you."

"Grunt away," said James. "Have you had enough to eat. Shall we walk?"

It was hot and the way down was thronged. A steady procession of people was moving downwards; sometimes

212

they walked alone and in single file, occasionally in huddled groups. They were not noisy, or, if they were, all sounds were absorbed by the flat white heat. Helen avoided tourists at home, but these didn't seem to her to be out of place. It was correct that there should be a procession, all trooping down.

There were a few people coming back, who passed them, looking hot and dusty. Most of them stopped to comment on what lay ahead, with the righteousness of those who had seen it all. Everyone talked, no one seemed to be a stranger. The path was dusty and adorned with mule droppings that stank in the heat. The way wound to and fro across the face of the cliffs, always descending through strata of red rock, turning to dust. As they went lower it grew hotter, waves of heat meeting them like a physical barrier. Helen felt sweat trickling down her back under her shirt. They stopped to fill their water bottles at a wayside fountain. Water had been piped all the way down this path and resting places were provided. Helen stopped to read one of the notices. It gave awful warnings about dehydration and sunstroke.

"As if you were all babies," she remarked to James. "Think of the warnings you could write all over the Cairngorms but nobody does."

"Take no notice. You're tough enough."

"I didn't have all the right things for breakfast," she said, reading the small print.

"I bet you survive, just the same."

They dropped lower, and the people thinned out. James walked beside her, and presently took her hand. "Like it?"

Helen frowned. A plant had forced its way out of the dust at her feet, bearing delicate pink flowers on spiky stems. It looked as frail as paper, but nothing else could grow there.

"I don't recognise anything. Things that grow. I'm used to knowing what they are."

"Do you mind?"

"I don't know. I'm having to judge things and I haven't any bearings."

"What do you have to judge?"

He spoke gently but the words weren't idle. Caution. Helen recognised it in a flash and retreated. Her eyes dropped and she shrugged. "I'm not sure," she said lightly. "Shall we go on?"

They came to an oasis, which the map told them had once been an Indian village. There were trees beside water that flowed out of the rock towards the hidden river. Helen gazed at the trees in astonishment. There were a few people sitting at picnic tables, obediently picnicking, and another notice warning of the dangers of the way back.

The path grew rough and stony. A long tongue of rock protruded, hiding the river, and the track wound its way over it, devoid of shelter. But there was a shadow. Helen looked up, and realised that shadows had grown all around them. The sun was dropping. Suddenly the rocks were no longer flat and white but red and vivid, full of curves and depths. Behind them the path was dipping into welcome shade, and even as she watched she felt a little coolness on her skin.

"Whatever the notices say, I don't think there's really anything to be afraid of."

He stopped and looked at her. "Are you afraid?"

"Not really." She added with sudden recklessness, "No, that's you."

"Me?"

"Yes. Oh, not of the flying, or the heat, or any of those things. But . . . would you not say you were very cautious?"

There was suspicion in his glance. "Cautious? In what way?"

Helen led the way ahead. "Oh, nothing. But I wouldn't want to have to test it. It's all right, I don't want anything."

Which was, of course, a lie.

Presently he spoke to her back. "You know what those are?"

"No, what?"

"Prickly pears. Useful to know, if you ever have to survive in this country. They're good to eat."

"What, those purple things?"

"No, no, don't touch them. I'll show you how to do it."

She waited obediently.

"Take a bit of grass, see, and brush off the prickles, otherwise you'll have them all in your fingers. There, now it's safe to pick it. Make sure you've rubbed off all the prickles. That's it. Quite smooth. Now taste it. Go on."

"It's good."

"I know." He was absurdly gratified, for about the twentieth time that day. He didn't stop to analyse it, but a vague warning flashed in the very back of his mind. There might be danger here, though there did not seem to be. He liked her very much. She was a friend, an extremely close friend, and he was glad of that. So why the warning? James pushed it away, and said, "Maybe we should turn back soon. It'll take twice as long going up."

She hesitated. "You reckon we can't reach the river?"

"Look at the map. We're not even halfway."

She sighed. "I'd like to have got to the river."

"It's a shame. We could easily have brought gear for the night and camped down there."

"But we didn't."

"No."

She looked ridiculously disappointed. It was only a river, after all.

"Next time," said James consolingly.

She glanced at him, unmistakably startled, but had more sense than to answer him. He was taken aback by his own words. But she was a friend, so she'd be back. Fair enough.

"Come another year," said James easily, "we might take a raft down the river. You'd like that. The rapids are really spectacular. You'd get a much better idea of it if we took a few days and went down it."

"You've done it?"

He nodded

"My God," said Helen, and for the first time that day there was a touch of bitterness in her voice. "You've done everything, haven't you?"

He looked puzzled. "Not quite. No, I mean not at all. Far from it, in fact."

She said very little going up. That was partly because she found it difficult to get her breath, whereas James seemed as fresh as when they started. She pointed this out, when they stopped for a rest.

"I was raised at a high altitude. You weren't. My lungs'll have a lot more capacity than yours."

"How unfair," said Helen flippantly. In fact, she minded. She was not accustomed to have to ask someone else's back if she could stop for a rest.

Also, she was thinking.

This relationship, if it were a relationship, seemed to be happening so fast, and in such an unfamiliar manner, that it took her breath away. Literally, she thought resentfully, struggling after him. It had been easy enough on her own ground. They had met at a friend's house in Edinburgh, when he had come over for the Festival. She was at home, although James never seemed to lack confidence, either at home or abroad. She was glad to think she had liked him in a strange country, travelling on his own two feet, with nothing particularly glamorous about him. They had had an argument about skiing, when she was being disdainful about the élitist rich, and he was full of the delights of speed and snow, and knowing how to do something well. It was much later, and only incidentally, that he mentioned that he flew as well.

"How curious that I should know you then," was all she had to say.

He was very pleasant to know. Easy on the eye, as her mother would say. Helen considered James's back. There were streaks of sweat down his red shirt, which stuck to him unattractively. He wore a battered straw hat, like Huckleberry Finn. He was tall and walked with an easy, loping stride, as though he had practised playing Indians when he was a little boy.

"Listen, James. Since my lungs lack capacity, suppose I

walk in front."

"Will that help?"

"Yes, because I won't have to keep asking you to stop. You'll have to, if I do."

"That's true. I should have thought of that."

Helen felt better in front, with a clear path ahead. It was a more familiar place to be.

So James, forced to walk more slowly, with a view of Helen's back, green shirt and white shorts, what was he thinking? There is no way of knowing but it is likely that he briefly considered the fact that European women often do not shave their legs. Helen at that time was thin and tall, perhaps too thin, but she appeared to advantage when being followed uphill, according to the kind of stereotypes that must have surrounded the developing James. Her hair was thick and fair, growing fairer every day in this climate, and somewhat coarse, so that it tended to stick straight up from her head. She had set out wearing a hat, obedient to the exhortive notices, but now the hat was shoved in her pocket. Hats didn't stay on her head. She looked better without it. Helen's idea of a sunhat was the white linen variety favoured by mothers taking their children to Berwickshire beaches in the early sixties. Apart from the offending hat, she wore her shabby clothes with indifference. The effect, James now realised, was completely uncalculated, but sometimes she looked like a model from an expensive magazine advertising pre-faded beachwear. Other times she merely looked like a tramp. Her sandals were thick with dust and down-at-heel. She wore a grubby canvas bag slung over one shoulder, in which she kept an apparently inexhaustible supply of fruit, and a purse stuffed with dollars. It seemed incredible to James that anyone should tour the States without either a credit card or a camera, but she seemed to manage. He liked that. She was easy company. Once more, James heard the faint clamour of warning bells at the back of his head and stopped in the middle of the path.

He had written to her very persuasively, encouraging her

to come this far. Her letter announcing her plans had been directed to his New York address, for since that week with her in Edinburgh, he had neglected to write, or to tell her of his move back west. In fact he had hardly thought of her again, but her letter arrived at a crucial time, and he had responded to it on an impulse. It went against his intentions. He had meant to keep women out of his life for a while and concentrate on work, which meant flying and taking photographs. He had moved here on those terms, and had taken a house in the mountains where he could live in peace and come to terms with himself.

Predictably, all the women he met had been fascinated by the whole set-up. He had ignored them, being somewhat stubborn when he put his mind to it, but he hadn't ignored Helen's letter. It was hard to say why. There had been a day that might account for it, when the Festival had been too much for both of them. He had had enough of crowds and bad theatre, and she had driven him in her car to North Berwick. They had eaten fish and chips sitting on the harbour wall, and then they had taken a boat out to the Bass Rock. She had told him some story about Robert Louis Stevenson, and about gannets, and, as far as he could remember, some sort of ghost story. It had been about a weaver in North Berwick, whose evil soul periodically left his body to go cavorting on the Bass Rock, until a heroic fisherman had pierced his ghostly heart with a rifle shot. An odd story, but he hadn't forgotten her face as she told it. He couldn't forget it, because he had taken her photograph. Her hair had been longer then, and he had caught her quite unconscious of the camera, facing into the wind with a heaving sea behind her. She was leaning against the side of the boat, hands stuck in her jacket pockets, looking away from him. No wonder he had remembered her as attractive. Then she had taken him to some castle. Ruined, of course. They usually were in Scotland. James followed Helen up to the top of the Canyon, and struggled to remember.

"Helen?"

She turned. "Yes?"

"What was the name of that castle? Where we watched that sunset, after we'd been to the Bass Rock? That ruin we climbed to the top of?"

She grinned at him. "Tantallon," she said, and went on walking.

Tantallon. He rolled the name over in his mind, and wondered what he wanted. He had done his very best to persuade her to come out west and, without any difficulty, he had succeeded. He had made love to her in the middle of the Arizona desert, which was not calculated. He had never planned to make it happen but he had had to admit, when she had asked him, that he was not completely unprepared. Just as well, because she hadn't brought anything. The last thing he needed to do just now was get a woman pregnant.

"James?"

"Yes?"

"When we get to the top of here, are we allowed to have tea?"

"Allowed? You can have whatever you like."

"Not tea, I often find."

James looked at his watch. "It's more like dinner time, I'd say."

"Suits me. I could begin to imagine how you could eat a steak."

"You mean you will?"

"Not bloody likely."

They were very separate, these two. Perhaps if they had needed to discuss the day to day details of life, the intensity would have faded. They did not talk much when they were together, because they were very active. They walked in the mountains, they went flying, they swam, they made love and they went out for meals in different places every night. Occasionally they did start to talk and did not stop until far into the night. Such discussions seldom come in adult life. Each found in the other the excitement of discovery, which can only happen when life is still fluid and a person is on fire

219

with change. No one can live like that for long. They both
knew it. Neither had any plans. Physically, they were in love,
whatever that means. To touch was electric, even to look at
one another was vibrant with excitement. There was danger
in it; they had both lived long enough to know that if a river
runs swift and full it makes perilous rapids in rocky places.

Cells divide and divide again, matter forming at a rate that
seems unbelievable. A blob of life, growing. There is no
turning back. Change is possible but the river cannot flow
uphill, nor the stars change in their courses. No one is fully
prepared to accept responsibility. Perhaps it is the ones with
no forethought who are the most resilient. I know which of
the two of them I would trust. Luckily, for I had no choice in
the matter, my fate was bound up with the right one.

James wanted to know himself. Helen wanted to see
America. They ended up having dinner in another restaurant
overlooking a different part of the Canyon. They sat eating
slowly, sharing a bottle of wine. From their table they could
watch the shadows reclaim the Canyon. They did not drift in
gently like the Scottish twilight, but divided the land fiercely
into light and dark. There was only the one thing or the
other. The sky had lost its blaze and had turned a strange
metallic blue. Helen studied the menu.

"I know I'll get twice as much as I want. Will you share a
pudding with me?"

"Pudding?"

"Sweet. Dessert. I call this food substantial but unexciting,
don't you think?"

"You preferred last night?"

"What? Old sandwiches and apples?"

"I mean the night before."

"Oh that. Dead sophisticated, that was. D'you think I'd
look good in a ten-gallon hat?"

"Are you laughing at the natives?" asked James, mock
indignant.

"Of course not. I just worry you all eat too much. You
don't think you'll grow fat?"

"Me?" enquired James in astonishment, looking down at his neat leather belt.

They slept out under the stars again but in a campsite this time, which lacked the solitary abandonment of the previous night. Perhaps it was as well. Peace is necessary for growing, and when growing happens at such a rate, there is no knowing how disturbance may be felt. It is hard to recapture those moments of acute sensitivity. Never again did energy course through my body at such a rate. It was like falling into a river, plunging instantly into the rapids, evading dangers which would have been terrifying if they had not been gone before they were apprehended. Rocks pierced the torrent like teeth, but I never knew of them, not until I was swept past them, down and further down, spiralling into the world on a flood of expanding life.

Helen lay on her back, quite apart from the huddled body next to her, and stared at those alien stars. There were pine trees surrounding the place where they lay; she could dimly make out feathery outlines against the sky. There was no moon. The sky at this latitude seemed so open, as though the atmosphere were transparent not only to the eye but also to some unidentified sense that was seldom awakened. The stars had never seemed so close. Helen was conscious of her own body, the steady beating of her heart. Regarding the sky arched over her, she found the problems of scale too bewildering. What was size to me at that moment? If there were a universe which had no imaginable end, that night I encompassed it all.

She, of course, was not thinking about that. She was sensible enough not to think much at all. She had been lifted out of her own confines and was able to regard her place from outside, but not clearly. She was not sure enough of where she had landed to be very precise. This was not the moment to work it out. This was the time to experience and to that she abandoned herself, deliberately.

It would have been easier to think about the person if he had not presented her with the place. It was the place that overwhelmed her. This country of his: did he even know the vastness of what he offered? In the west the earth was raw. It reassured her: whatever anyone did, the red desert would remain. There are some things, thought Helen, that do remain. At this moment the waves are breaking on Scottish beaches, with the same rhythm that I feel now. Perhaps I hear its echo. It is the rhythm that I was born to and for me this is a foreign country. Perhaps the rhythm is the only thing that I can recognise.

The most incalculable factor in all this is James. Perhaps, thought Helen sleepily, if there is an equation to be made, and no one ever said there was, we could call James "X". I am not quite sure what we are doing together. I know that this is not ordinary life. If it were, I would have to be able to fly the plane myself. Only visitors can stay passive. Perhaps it would be fairer to say receptive.

It occurred to her that she might indeed fly a plane. She had all the faculties required. James had told her a story earlier that day about meeting a woman in her seventies who had learned to fly. James had been quite gentle and condescending towards this old lady, until she happened to let drop that she had flown the Atlantic solo, twice. James didn't mind telling stories against himself. He didn't try too hard to maintain his image but then he hardly needed to, did he? But I couldn't fly a plane, thought Helen, it's far too expensive.

If I really wanted to, I would find the money.

James grunted in his sleep, muttered something, and rolled over. Helen shifted away from him. I could learn to stop being afraid. It's going down I don't like. It's too much like falling. I don't like falling. Is there really anything to stop me flying? It might be the one thing I most need to do in the world. If I did it, I would certainly know if it was the man I wanted, or the flying.

Triangles of velocity.

She groaned faintly. She'd watched him doing calculations this very morning, and even then it had reminded her of school. There was no way she could take that on. No, in that case she would remain upon the ground and only ascend the heights by invitation. Except, of course, in dreams.

So do I, or do I not, love James?

Helen looked at Orion, and recognised it as something well known but tilted at the wrong angle, in the wrong place. The question seemed crass and irrelevant, like being brought to the gates of Eldorado and asking for a guidebook. She would keep it for later. It would go suitably with doing her accounts afterwards, and finding out how much all this had cost. She had a brief vision of herself sitting at her kitchen table writing out columns of income and expenditure. The significance of James would do for then. Just now, she could make the most of him. Life would not always be like this.

They spent the morning driving slowly along the lip of the Canyon, stopping at various promontories to look down. It was impossible to take in the scale at ground level. The Spaniards had thought the river was six feet wide. The Canyon had defeated them the first time; after surveying what they could, they had retraced their steps south. It seemed extraordinary that they should have penetrated this far in the first place.

"It makes me wonder what right I have to be here," said Helen.

They discussed Western imperialism desultorily, for it was growing very hot. At midday they turned back, having toured the excavations of an Indian settlement. They had to be home by sunset, James explained, or the airport would be shut. Helen felt a flicker of anxiety. She felt more comfortable when there were no deadlines.

That afternoon they flew a different way. The desert changed. The trees faded, the land stretched red and arid and began to throw up freakish shapes; strange stacks and monuments, and jagged changes of level, where vast cliffs scored the empty rock. The plane dipped and began to fly among the outcrops, like an inquisitive insect buzzing among statues in a museum. Helen watched until her eyes ached. The columns

223

and arches of rock were like some half-formed attempt at life, as if someone had once begun to carve giant creatures out of the living rock but had abandoned the scheme halfway to look for something better. There should have been some animation in them, some hint of consciousness, but in all the sun-dried miles below them there was nothing. Perhaps those endless cliffs should have been damp with spray, facing a living sea, but at their feet the rock was the same, merely empty. It was like a stage set for life, with the play abandoned. If ever there had been a script, it had returned to dust long ago.

"It makes you think," said Helen over the noise of the engine. "It wouldn't be surprising to see a dinosaur round the next stack, would it?"

"It would surprise me."

If dinosaurs would have seemed logical, the settlement, when they came to it, was completely bizarre. They landed on a hot red strip that ended abruptly at the foot of a cliff. The heat met them painfully. Helen recoiled, and searched in her pocket for the sunhat, but it was lost beyond recall, somewhere in the last thousand miles.

The settlement was a Navajo village, with two close ranks of new houses, built almost windowless against the desert sun. At first sight it was as full of life as an Edinburgh close on a wet Sunday. Too much weather drives anyone indoors, thought Helen, trying to shake off a growing apprehension. There was something too alien about the situation. Not the village, since that belonged here. It must be herself. She had never felt so foreign in her life.

When they found some people she was disproportionately relieved. Some teenage boys were playing with a pinball machine in the shade cast by the porch of the general store. There were more people in the shop. James bought fruit, while Helen studied the notice board. There was a hugely blown-up photo of John Wayne. She recognised the stone outcrops behind him and realised that the picture had been taken just by the airstrip. She read the other notices. There was a tupperware party the following Friday and some regulations about Navajo trading stamps.

There seemed no reason at all why she should be here. Helen bought two postcards, as if that made her presence logical, then she and James went out again, and the heat hit them.

"There's a restaurant up there. It's supposed to be good. All the film stars stay there."

"Film stars?"

"Westerns. That's the main source of employment. Didn't you see the photos?"

Helen wandered back, although it was an effort to take six steps uphill, and studied the photos in the porch. There was one of a cavalry charge and close-ups of cowboys in white hats. Their faces were vaguely familiar.

"It's too confusing," said Helen, and in spite of the heat she shuddered. "It's creepy. I don't understand it. Can we go on?"

"I'll be happier leaving than landing, certainly. I never saw an airstrip like it."

Helen regarded the usual red strip below her. "Why, what's wrong with it?"

"That cliff at the end. No one ever builds a strip with only one exit. It's dangerous. Suppose I'd miscalculated the landing? Usually if that happens you ascend and start again. Not here. If you missed the strip you'd be straight into the cliff. Splat!"

That time her shudder touched me, it was so strong. A wave of cold swept me. Did I recognise it? It is possible to believe that until that moment the bitterness of fear had never reached me. What can the world have been like, for those glorious hours? Red, I imagine it. Red with daring, confidence, courage, high hopes. Red is a brave colour. It warms the heart of being.

But so short! Yet in those hours a concept was formed, and I never lost hold of it entirely. It comes to me in glimpses.

225

There are moments – there were two or three moments, perhaps, in the length of my life, when I felt it. Oh yes, I have been fearless. I would like you to know that about me. It is the most triumphant statement I have yet made.

I began without fear. When it came, I started to drown. Life was in full flood; the river took me, down and down, but I was not afraid, until that moment.

Splat!

When I think how carelessly he said it, I want to murder him. It infuriates me that he should be so brutal to one so young and frail, and of his own creation. Should I forgive him on the grounds of unconsciousness? If I do that, I must forgive the whole world, including myself. The issue seems too complicated. Suffice it to say that, when James said that to Helen, she shuddered, and I was choked with the chill of it, and I have never recovered myself again, not perfectly.

James put his arm round Helen's shoulder. "It's all right. Going out, there's no problem. We've got the whole sky in front of us. Anyway, I wouldn't have miscalculated."

"Anyway," said Helen, withdrawing, "you didn't."

After that, they flew home.

To James's home, that is. James didn't live in the desert but in the mountains. They flew north-west, and the evening followed them, overtaking them, so that they were caught in its light, a tiny speck of white hovering over mountains whose shapes were incredible. They were so sharp and new, never subdued by ice, still raw in the passage of time. She watched valleys open up and disappear behind them, faintly covered by scrub at first, then thick with vegetation. The plane rose higher, and snow-capped peaks glinted in the sunset.

"I never thought anything on earth could be like this."

Helen was not at ease in the air. A Taurean creature, she felt at home on land. She was also used to being completely in control of what she did. Up here, she had surrendered her safety to James, who exulted in the command of air. It made

226

her uneasy, and I think that in some corner of her brain she was aware all the time of death. It sharpened her perception of the landscape. Mortality is an excellent indication of scale. She would not have seen those mountains with the same eyes if she had not deliberately decided to ignore incipient terror.

I realised that my condition was inspiring but lethal. Never in my existence – and who can say how long that had lasted? – had I been in a situation of such acute danger. Possibilities stretched ahead of me, incomprehensible questions on a map I had no power to read. But I began to feel the peril. It would be no smooth path, this one. Those mountains were forced out of turmoil. I have never seen beauty that was calm. I think of what is tranquil: the sea on a still night, when the waves have ceased to break, and I know, because knowledge comes from memory, that I recognise peace because I was present in the storm. I was filled with wonder, but somewhere in the maelstrom, among the dance of cells, the shadow came.

"The shadows are so beautiful. Look at the shape of that mountain, against the other slope. It makes you see how deep it is, I mean how high."

"It was the right moment to come back," agreed James. "What's the time?"

"Ten past seven."

"Perfect."

When they finally got home, it was dark and very cold. It took a long time to put the plane to bed. Helen had experienced the same problem with boats. The people that loved them seemed to enjoy the hours of fiddling around as much as the voyaging. She did not love either. The plane had been a means to an end. She was moderately grateful to it but she was far more grateful to James.

Perhaps that was irrational. James could not fly.

"It must be very pleasant knowing you can fly."

"It must. Not bad knowing you can fly a plane either."

James had a penchant for choosing good restaurants. Tonight's was in a shack, apparently miles from anywhere, and crowded to the door. There was just one free table, and somehow James got it in front of the queue. Helen made her way after him, round the packed tables and chairs. The food was excellent.

"What do you eat when you're on your own?"

"Beans mostly. No, no, not your British sort. Real beans. But that's only when I'm working. They don't do for company. If I go out, I eat out first, so I don't fart."

"How practical."

"Well – it's only considerate. We can stay at home and eat beans tomorrow, if you like."

"As long as we both do it, I suppose it's no problem."

Helen slept well that night. She would have liked to make love to James again but she was exhausted and, when she looked at him, it was clear that he was too. His eyes had turned bloodshot from being fixed upon the blazing sky and the red land, and a two days' beard was growing dark on his cheeks.

In two nights life can double and double again, like the grains of corn on the Arabian's chessboard, until it is a million times more substantial than it was at the beginning. In two nights a woman's heart beats – how many times? For ever, in my view. It was all the rhythm in the world: thudTHUD thudTHUD thudTHUD. I had no heart of my own, no nerves, no spine. So what was I, speaking in terms of this world? A growth, an amorphous thing seeking a body, and finding – well, hardly that, I suppose. A blob of matter, invisible, floating in dark space. Did I say I was confined? Perhaps I was wrong; the whole of space was still open to me. I was attached to nothing, drifting without boundaries. Only the rhythm was beginning to impinge. thudTHUD thudTHUD thudTHUD. That is all the world is made of.

"So it's your last day."

"Yes," said Helen, chopping apple over her muesli. Tomorrow she would be gone, flying back east. Nothing had been said about any future. Perhaps there was none.

"Coffee?" asked James.

"No, thank you."

"Of course not. I forgot."

They ate in silence. Helen spooned up muesli and stared out of the window. James ate muffins and bilberry jam, and stared at Helen.

James's house was hardly more than a shack. It was made of prefabricated wooden boards and sat upon the mountain-side as if it had been lowered there by helicopter. There had been no attempt to root it to the earth in any symbolic way; the stout wires that pinned it down were severely functional. It sat upon a jutting ledge, among prickly bushes and white stony soil. It was strange soil to find at seven thousand feet, a thousand miles from the sea. It was all shells. If one scraped away a handful of earth it was gritty and, among it, spread upon one's palm, would be at least three perfect shells. It was like walking along a beach, as though the mountain had only risen from the water yesterday. Helen had sat on the bare hill sifting shells through her fingers. It seemed a mockery of time and that excited her. It was appropriate that outworn gods should be mocked. In the old world to which she belonged it would not have been possible.

"Why don't you make a garden?" she had asked James. "You could grow alpines. Not many people ever have such an opportunity."

"What for? Anyway, I don't know how long I'll be here."

So far from making a garden, he had hardly unpacked inside. Most of his belongings were stored in cardboard boxes, some of which were turned on their sides to make impromptu bookshelves. His books were mostly about flying and photography. There were a few about sex and relationships. Helen had glanced at these and even read a chapter here and there. She wasn't really very interested. It was a pity

229

he didn't have a flower book, or a bird book, which was what she was looking for. For want of better bedtime reading she had studied one of his manuals of aeronautics. It was heavily annotated, and fell open at important passages. Helen read his notes, as if they might tell her what it was she was missing. His handwriting was messy and unformed, like a young boy's. Men often wrote like that, in her experience.

"Seeing it's our last day, what do you most want to do?"

She dragged her eyes from the mountains outside the window. Perhaps he was right not to try to plant anything. There was no need. Sheer peaks rose opposite, across a valley thick with aspen trees, leaves dancing brilliant shades of green in the early breeze. The mountains rose out of the trees to towering cliffs. In a crevice far above, snow shone in the morning sun, an arm of white reaching down between the rocks towards the sunlit trees. The horizon was fantastic, like mountains in a child's drawing, zigzag strokes drawn boldly across the sky from one edge of the paper, or window, to the other.

"I don't know how I knew," said Helen, not answering, "but I remember drawing mountains just like that, right across the page, and yet I never saw anything of the kind. Why is that, do you suppose?"

"I didn't know you drew."

"All children draw. To do? I don't know what I want to do. What haven't we done?"

"Almost everything. But that doesn't matter. We can carry on next time from where we leave off."

Next time? She didn't query him aloud. "I don't know when I'll come back, unless I inherit a fortune. I'd like to go up, that's what, as high as possible. On the ground, I mean. How high can we get into the mountains?"

"Good idea. I had it in mind myself. There's a place we can drive to. A pass. Twelve thousand feet, then walk, if you like, into the snow."

"Yes, please. I can't imagine snow just now."

"But you can see it." James waved his arm to include all

that lay outside the window.

"Seeing isn't imagining."

"Well, bring a sweater, and some pants. It might be cold."

It wasn't precisely cold. They reached the snowline at about noon and the sun beat down upon them. Helen stood with her feet in the snow, feeling it ooze and melt on her bare skin through her sandals. She squinted up at the sun. It seemed very high up in the sky, high and cold, as if it had overstretched itself. The sky had darkened; wisps of cloud tore over their heads, rolling and breaking apart. She had never seen the sky so vivid. It was darker than it should be, yet transparent. It had turned thin, and the cloud was unpredictable, twisting and disintegrating like a speeded-up film. The air was strange to her, neither hot nor cold, until she breathed it in. It felt chill then, and rare, with an edge to it like wine.

"See those clouds? There haven't been clouds all day."

James looked. "Stormy. It often is around midday. It could even rain, but not for long. There'll be some turbulence up there."

"Rain?" repeated Helen, and looked around. Nothing, to her eyes, spoke of rain. The sun shimmered on the snow. She picked up a handful of snow and pressed it into a snowball. Cold burned her hands, not unpleasantly. The heat of the sun pierced her shirt, and sweat trickled down between her shoulder blades. It had been a steep climb. Helen dropped the snowball.

"It's unreal."

"No, just different. Do you want to go on?"

They traversed a ridge where half the mountain had broken off, rocks tumbled into the valley far below. It could have been last week, thought Helen, but no doubt it was several thousand years ago. Up here it seemed to make very little difference. They could now see down into another valley, silent in the sun and thick with aspens. Cliffs sparkled, perhaps with water, perhaps minerals. It was hazy and she couldn't tell. Two birds soared over the empty land below them. Eagles, maybe. She shielded her eyes, watching them. They were merely outlines, black against the sky, catching the air as it eddied up over the cliffs.

She looked back at James, feeling slightly dizzy. He was watching her. She was growing used to that. He had said very little since they had landed yesterday, but whenever he had the chance he had hardly taken his eyes off her. Perhaps it was a private farewell. She had no idea.

On the way back she asked if she could drive. It wasn't the first time. He had lent her his car before, one day when he had work to do. She had driven into the next valley, half frightened, half exhilarated. She discovered she liked driving a pick-up truck. She enjoyed driving on a road that crossed sheer hillsides, zigzagging through mountains with an impossible drop below her, and huge boulders on the other side, where the road had been hewn out of the rock. It had been a huge relief to be alone again, and in charge of something, even if it were only a borrowed truck. At the back of her mind had lurked the question of what to do if she got a puncture. She should have looked to see if there were tools for changing a wheel but, with James waving goodbye to her, it had never occurred to her.

She had not had a puncture and she had returned much refreshed. Driving now, with James sitting next to her, was another thing, but also pleasant.

"Thanks for letting me," she said to him. "I don't make a very good passenger. At least, not all the time."

"Next time I'll teach you how to fly the plane."

Next time. Twice he had said that, in one morning. Ought she to ask him to be clear, or should she just stay in the present? No future could rival this present. It was a gift of the gods, or of James. Helen changed gear and negotiated another bend. They were descending now, down from twelve thousand feet into a strange valley. There were no aspens here, but cleared land thick with flowers. They drove closer.

"Lupins."

"What?"

"Those flowers." Helen drew up beside the road. "Lupins. Wow!" She turned off the ignition. "It beats every herbaceous border I ever saw. No one told me they were supposed to be like this."

"What's a herbaceous border?"

She ignored him. The lupins were all blue. That made sense. Lupins did revert to blue. The whole valley was covered with them. There were trails winding among them, and log cabins dotted here and there. Log cabins?

"What is this place?"

"It's a deserted mining settlement. They've done it up as a sort of museum place, I believe. Do you want to walk around?"

The cabins were crudely but strongly built. Helen examined each one, frowning. The only sign of life was one lizard, which slithered away from a stone doorstep as their shadows fell across it. The interiors were all deserted, but in one house there was a stand with postcards for sale, and a money box. Helen bought two postcards, one of the lupins, and one of assorted alpine flowers.

They wandered down to the river, which rushed between boulders like a Scottish burn. They sat on a large flat stone and dabbled their feet in icy water. This was their last day together, and nothing said.

"I'd like to see you again," remarked Helen, her eyes on the water that eddied round a jagged rock in midstream.

James was weeding seelings absent-mindedly from a crack in the rock, but at that he looked up. Helen felt his eyes on her again but she didn't look round.

"Of course you'll see me again," said James, "won't you?"

"Well, I'd like to. That's what I said. But I live halfway round the world, so I don't know when."

"No, no more do I. Does it matter?"

"Probably not. I have my life to get back to."

There was a pause.

"Tell me the truth," said James. "I hope you don't mind me asking . . . Have you ever thought about coming out here?

To stay I mean. For longer."

She felt the blood rising to her cheeks. Of course she had. It was inevitable really and nothing to be ashamed of. For all that, she had no intention of telling him so.

"One day, maybe. I've always meant to live abroad one day. Not yet. Like I say, I've got my life at home."

"I just wondered."

His turn. "Do you think you'll always live here?" she asked.

James shrugged. "I've no idea. No, of course I don't. I'm not thinking about settling down anywhere. I could be off any day. Next month, maybe. Maybe not. I might go back to Central America. I certainly haven't given up the idea."

Helen was silent. He wasn't just not attached to anyone, but he didn't feel he belonged anywhere either. Maybe it was his work that mattered to him. He said very little about it. She had a copy of his book, and had studied it. It consisted of photographs taken in various countries in Central and South America. It had been a bestseller in a particular arty, left-wing market. She might feel cynical about that, but not about James. She suspected that, besides being an artist, he was also drawn to danger. That she did not understand. It was not for compassionate purposes, though he would say his reasons were political. There were aspects of his life that scared her. She would never have gone with him, not that he would ever invite her. His work excluded people. That might seem odd for a man who had won prizes for taking sensitive portraits, but Helen knew that it was true.

"I don't know what I shall do," she said aloud. "In a way it'll be a relief to get home."

"I can understand."

"At home I know things. Like what grows, what lives where, what sort of weather to expect. If I was an indoor sort of person, I suppose it wouldn't matter so much. If I ever wanted to work over here, I'd have to learn everything again. I'm not sure I'd want to. And I wouldn't have a green card."

"No."

There was only one other way to get permission to work in the States. Helen wondered if he had thought of it and whether he would think that she was thinking of it. She ordered herself not to be paranoid. He was probably only thinking about lunch.

"What about lunch?" said James.

That evening he took her to a hot spring. At first sight it was disappointing, more like an outdoor swimming-pool than a convulsion of nature. There was a complex of changing-rooms, strictly segregated, with lockers, a paved area full of wet people of astonishing shapes and sizes, and a murky pool that steamed gently in the evening sun.

Helen waited for James to reappear out of the door marked MEN. He did so, dripping from a shower. Was one supposed to have a shower? She hadn't, anyway.

"Try the hot pool first."

They sat on the steps, up to their necks in very hot, soft water. The heat was just going out of the sun and the water felt magical. Helen sat with her eyes shut, and felt with all her might.

"This is true comfort. I never experienced anything like it, not since I was born, I imagine. Why don't you spend all day in here? I would."

"You should come when it's snowing. You sit in a hundred and four degrees, while it snows on your head. Come back in winter, and we'll do that."

Helen sighed. "One day, maybe. Oh yes, one day."

James stretched himself out in the water and contemplated his toes. "When you get home, do you think you'll stay on your own? I mean, is that what you intend?"

It was too hot to bother what she said. "I don't know. I like a little comfort in my life but I don't always know how to get it. I suppose I shall be on my own, because there isn't very likely to be anyone else."

"I don't see why not."

"Why should there be?"

"How do I know? I'm asking you. You didn't have anyone last summer when we met. I thought you maybe meant to keep it that way."

"I don't have any intentions. One day I'd like to fall in love, I think."

"Odds on," said James, grinning. "If that's what you want. You'd have no trouble getting anyone to fall in love with you."

"Is that what you think?"

"I know it. I guess if you mean to fall in love, you will do before the year is out. Want to bet?"

"No thank you."

That night they did make love again. They had only the one night and they seized it passionately. No other time would do, because there would be no other time. That in itself was magical, with an edge of pain to it that neither dared examine. To grab hold of the moment and try to keep it, fossilised in some bell jar of the mind, would be to kill it. Content is something that grows with the years, like moss that creeps and softens stone, hiding its shape but never changing it. Neither Helen nor James knew anything about content, but the present was theirs.

It left me untouched. I was no more disturbed by it than the flowers on the mountain are disturbed by the turmoil of the clouds above them at midday, when no rain falls. The universe was mine, so what had human love to do with me? I clung to nothing, needed nobody. I had never heard of warmth or sustenance. No chains yet bound me. The taste of freedom was known, and lost again, before I had so much as a bone in my body. They were drowned in sex; I floated, free even of the concept of breathing. Impossible to touch me. Yet he had already bequeathed to me a part in this. Was it his gift to me? Could one say that? Curious to think that one's place in the world is formed by a chance as arbitrary as the throw of a die. Whichever way chance fell, I was caught up in this act of theirs, as inevitably as all the rest. Sex meant nothing to me, yet the choice was made, and either the one part was mine, or the other.

What would I say to him? I see him as if it were now, and I had eyes. He lies sleeping, flat on his back, one arm outflung, his mouth a little open. His other arm is round Helen, who lies, almost face down, her face turned against his shoulder. His dark hair is damp with sweat, pushed off his forehead so it stands almost straight up. His lashes are black against his cheeks. They give him a curious look of innocence, almost child-like. But his face is not a child's at all. His nose is slightly crooked, and his profile is angular; even in sleep he looks arrogant. His cheeks are smooth, but no longer rounded, and his beard, which grows fast, is beginning to darken the line of his jaw. He is very tanned, down to a V shape that comes just below his collar bone. Below that, his chest is white, with a few dark curling hairs. His body looks younger than his face. Against his white skin Helen's hair is tangled, reddish in the growing dawn. Her face is hidden. Her arm lies across his chest. The skin on her forearm is darker than his chest, and is covered with a soft down of fair hair, and is sprinkled with freckles. She is surprisingly muscular for a woman. Even lying across him like that, her body looks capable and tough. Her back is tanned a pale golden colour. Her shoulders are thickly freckled.

What would I say to him? Looking at him like that, I see very clearly what he gave me. Perhaps I feel some sort of kinship. I would like to see into his eyes, but he is asleep. I am not sure that there is anything he could tell me.

It was a small airport, serving a town dominated by the film industry on holiday, so that everyone waiting in the airport lounge looked casually rich. They might seem ostentatious to a Scottish eye but, to an American, it was possible that they merely looked exceptionally clean and healthy.

Helen and James sat at a table in the corner of the cafeteria, looking out on the runway on which they had landed from their own particular flight two days ago. Helen had a tumbler

237

of juice in front of her but she had given up attempting to drink it. Her baggage was checked. In five minutes her flight would be called. She swallowed. Her throat was dry and constricted. Everything was still left unsaid and now there was no more time. The words would never be spoken now. Perhaps there were no words. The present was turning into the past, sand in a glass, trickling. There was a chilly void in her stomach. She held her hands together, clasped on the table in front of her. No doubt she would see him again. No doubt.

James stirred and stirred his coffee, but did not drink. Sometimes he watched the spoon turning in the cup, sometimes his eyes were on Helen. When she looked at him, he looked down. Then her eyes caught his and held them.

"I love you," said Helen, inconsequently.

She had told him that before. When aroused, she sometimes told him again and again. He remembered it with a pang he had not expected to feel. He had never answered her in kind and, more remarkable, she had never seemed to expect him to answer. Outside sex, she never referred to love, and seemed to forget afterwards that she had ever mentioned it. She had never spoken of it before dispassionately, across a table, like this. James was shaken, and that startled him.

He reached out and laid his hand over her clasped ones. Her hands were taut and cold, clinging together. Otherwise she seemed the same as ever, calm and cheerful, with an appearance of being willing to be amused. It was what he had liked about her. She had been a very restful companion.

"It was a good trip," said James.

"Yes, it was."

He pulled her hands apart, and held one of them.

"Thank you for taking me," said Helen. "It . . ." She seemed to search for words. "It changed my world, somewhat, seeing your country. Like seeing the world through someone else's eyes. I have to thank you for that."

"It was . . ." He had been going to say a pleasure, but the word seemed too weak. "It was a joy to take you."

"I'm glad about that," she said absently.

238

She was studying his face as if trying to learn him by heart. James stared back, and felt a twinge of something like alarm. Of course, she had no camera, only memories. There was nothing to take back, no part of him at all, only a picture in her mind, which would fade, and change, and perhaps turn into something else that was not him at all.

"I'll see you again. I'll be in Europe again, some day. When I am, I'll come and see you. Definitely. I . . ."

Her flight was called.

Helen leaped to her feet grabbing her canvas bag. She looked really frightened now. That was new to him. He came round the table and caught her in his arms, and held her to him, hard.

"That was my flight! I have to go."

"A minute. You have a minute."

She was stiff and tense. She liked to be early for everything and hated to hurry.

Suddenly he felt safe. She was going and had made no attempt to tie him. She had asked him for nothing, nothing at all. In five minutes he would be alone again. God knew when he would see her again. She had never even asked. James shed his fears like an old coat, and saw for one moment what it was they shielded.

"I love you," said James into her hair. "Helen, I love you too."

She looked up and kissed him, reassuringly, perhaps, but also as if half her mind were elsewhere. "I have to go, James. They're all going." She almost pulled herself out of his embrace and turned to the gateway. A steward reached for her boarding pass. She was about to give it to him, then turned back suddenly.

"Goodbye, James. Thank you. I love you. Thank you very much."

Then she was gone before he had time to think about it, cramming her boarding pass into the man's hand and fairly running on to the tarmac.

He didn't stay to watch the plane leave. She wouldn't be

able to see him anyway. She knew that quite well, so she didn't even bother to look. Her window faced the other way, out on to the towering slopes of the mountains. It was strange to be a mere passenger again, among rows of others. Strange to sit at one small window, waiting for the voice on the intercom. It was not flying as she had experienced it. It was not like flying at all.

2

The steps of New York's Metropolitan Museum are truly monumental. Even to enter the place is daunting. How can anyone take in all that human culture? With what faculty are they supposed to do it? Helen had wandered round and stared, at Persian carpets, Attic red figure pottery, Art Nouveau stained glass, reconstruction colonial interiors, and Renaissance sculpture. By some process of staring, and occasionally consulting the catalogue, the whole of human history and endeavour was supposed to become internalised. She felt dazed. The sky outside was the colour of Persian tiles that had lain underground for twenty centuries. Helen blinked up at it, and saw the curve of a jet trail. A woman was selling pizzas from a trolley at the foot of the steps. Helen bought one, with a can of juice, then she chose a place about halfway up and ate slowly, watching the people passing up and down.

She found it easy to be foreign in New York: naturally, for it could hardly be more unlike home, but there was no sting in it, because no one else had so classified her. Foreign-ness was something she identified in herself, not a definition forced upon her. She relished it. It was unusual for her to eat junk food. The pizza was bland and a little soggy, but under that sky it was merely part of how things were. Helen felt her being expand and warm itself in the heat that beat upwards from the stone steps. There was a vast freedom in this place, where she was not expected to be anything to anybody. Something unfroze inside her, and she began to realise how she felt.

Tears rose slowly to her eyes. She followed their progress with mild astonishment. One spilled over, and trickled down her cheek. She felt it very clearly. Then another. The first tear tickled her chin, then dropped on to her shirt. A tide of tears rose gently within her. She sniffed reluctantly, and brushed her hand across her eyes. Thank God this was New York, where no one would take a blind bit of notice.

Helen rolled up the pizza paper, and stuffed it in her bag. She sat, elbows on knees, chin cupped in her hands, and wept silently. Usually too much crying hurt her chest, not that she did it very often. This did not hurt. Her tears were running down her hands, down her arms, dripping into her shirt. The people passed up and down, singly, in couples, in groups. Their babble was louder than the traffic in Fifth Avenue, but came to her subdued, like the cooing of pigeons. She had never sat on the steps of a museum in brilliant sunshine before, weeping. It was an entirely new sensation. There seemed to be two of her: the one who mourned, and the one who experienced the weeping, the city and the sun.

James.

He appeared inside her mind like an apparition, unsummoned. She had not meant to think of him. As far as she was aware, she had not been thinking of him all morning. She was not sure if she had been thinking of anything. Her journey through the museum had induced a state of receptivity. It was not possible to think about everything in that place at once, or what it all meant. She had only looked around, and trusted herself enough not to demand a reaction.

So why James?

James had been left behind in Colorado. Now she was in New York, which demanded all her presence of mind. She had come to travel in the States, not to see James. There was a fountain flowing in the court of a Persian house, reconstructed from an excavation and housed on the first floor of the museum. The fountain had played in a real house, for real people, in about 500 BC.

She had come to America to see that. That, and many other

things, and James. She could see him so clearly in her mind's eye that he seemed to be superimposed against the background of crowded steps. A party of Japanese tourists passed her, speaking so quickly it was hard to imagine they were making words at all. James. Dark hair, falling a little forward, fair Celtic skin that flushed easily. A touch of freckles, slightly crooked nose, his smile a degree lopsided. In James she was always seeing two things at once: both the foreigner and the man of her own blood. No wonder he had such power to disconcert her.

But I love both, thought Helen, and almost sobbed.

Rubbish, she told herself severely. How maudlin can you get? Of course you love him. Why not? But now there is a continent between us, as you always intended that there should be. So that's that. Where am I going next?

She did not reach immediately for her street map. To sit and weep in the sunshine, among the moving crowd of indifferent people, was a novel luxury. She realised that she quite enjoyed the presence of so many people, when no one required her to participate. She didn't even have to stop crying, and that was excellent.

Nothing can last for ever. Presently Helen got up slowly, and drifted back into Central Park. It was hot and dusty on the path but the trees cast a pleasant shade. Squirrels ran to and fro across the grass in front of her. She dragged her feet, trailing across the grass without purpose. Skyscrapers framed the horizon, and the roar of traffic lulled her. Consciousness begins with a far-off roaring in the blood. Perhaps that is why cities can reassure us, in spite of all that we have done.

There was a baseball game going on ahead of her. Helen picked up the thread of a purpose, and made her slow way towards it. She sat on one of the tiered benches, a few feet along from a group of little boys, and two young women whose boyfriends were quite obviously in the winning team.

Helen didn't really watch the game. She wasn't quite sure what the object of it was, anyway. No one questioned her presence there. She might be from anywhere in the world, but she was free to sit in Central Park and watch a baseball game. Freedom is an extraordinary thing, thought Helen.

> "A, fredom is a noble thing
> It makyth man to have lyking."

Too right. So, given the choice, this is where I happen to be. Considering all the options possible, my presence here is remarkable. In fact, it goes beyond the bounds of any conceivable probability. Why are they cheering? That black man has obviously scored something. A goal, or a round, or whatever it is they do score. So, given the choice, which I undoubtedly am, I choose to sit in the sun weeping about James. Whatever for? I find it very hard to understand myself.

Thinking of myself, I echo her thought. Of course, the first limitation we impose upon ourselves is so tremendous in its implications that it hardly bears thinking about. Was I aware that I had imprisoned myself? Or would I have described it as an opportunity? I have to acknowledge that the powers of judgment or description were not available to me. No, I am not sure whether I do acknowledge that. I look at Helen, sitting watching the baseball game in Central Park. I think I envy her. She didn't know precisely why she was there, or what process of free will had brought her to that point. But at least she knew that she was there. She knew where she was. She had a street map in her canvas bag and a mental map of the globe inside her head. She knew where she was in relation to several fixed points that were already familiar to her. Lucky, lucky woman.

I turn my mind to a pinprick of matter, without form but potent with purpose, still drifting in the void which could, for all the difference it seemed to make, have been deep space. Nothing pulses. No blood flows. No waves, no current, no consciousness. No? The question demoralises me. If I were truly unconscious, then what is this thing I remember?

The baseball game grew more exciting. The spectators

were sitting upright on the benches, waiting for the decisive moment. Helen never noticed. In her head it was all memories. The sun beat down on her bare head, and warmed her back through her shirt. She saw the running men, the trees behind, and the skyscrapers like a cardboard cutout across the horizon. And she saw James. James showing her how to pick prickly pears; James flying his plane, relaxed, gazing down on an endless desert of red rock which he called home. James sleeping, black lashes soft on his cheeks, still flushed from loving her. If she had realised what she was thinking about she would have stopped herself. It was not part of the bargain she had made with herself. But she was off guard, and the part of her mind which was supposed to be vigilant was lulled to sleep by a fountain that had not sparkled in the sunlight for two thousand years.

I, of course, do not share the import of these memories. At that point I was still completely detached. Not exactly an onlooker – no, I don't think I could possibly say that. In some subtle sense I was not quite there. The process had been initiated, whether or not I had given my consent, but I was still not truly present. I look down on those amoeba-like cells, dividing and dividing, and I repudiate them. I never sank so low. No, some part of me was floating free, above the Manhattan skyline, watching the slow rivers part and meet around that extraordinary island. I was attached to that freckled woman in a white shirt, sitting in the park, as a kite is threaded to the one who flies it, but that was all. I was tied by the touch of a thread. Perhaps I still believed that I was free.

Not true. It is wrong not to respect the amoeba. The die was cast. I had set my stake on life and won. There is nothing on this planet that I dare despise. Very well, I accept it. No consciousness. Only the rhythm of life, flowing fast. And more. The potential in this blob is infinite. Each part in it has a dramatic piece to play, and the script is already written upon each atom. The whole is beyond limit. If you don't believe me, go and look in the Metropolitan Museum of Art, New York.

On the sixth day there was a change. Helen was flying again, for the last time in this history. She had half slept through the night and felt sticky and exhausted. She had curled up in a heap in two aircraft seats, which were not enough. In the small hours she would have given all she possessed to be able to stretch out properly. Luckily no one had made her such an offer, for in the dawn she would have regretted it. She was woken by a stewardess bearing a tray of hot face flannels, one of which she offered to Helen with a pair of tongs. Helen stared at it suspiciously, then realised it was not more preheated food. It was surprisingly refreshing. She sat up painfully, and looked out of the window.

"It's Goat Fell," said Helen aloud, in her surprise.

The dawn was breaking over Arran. The ridge of mountains was tinged with pink. The mountains were not particularly high but they rose out of the sea dramatically. Waves washed their feet, a line of white rising and falling all round the island. She saw the beach at Sannox, and the grey line of houses at Brodick, lining the sea. The hills were plain in the sun below her. She knew them well, but had never seen them whole, like this. The force that shaped them was revealed quite clearly, in the shaved and broken rock, the corries and the curved valleys tunnelling down to the sea. Ice. It was the touch of long-gone ice that made this world familiar. These were hills as they were meant to be. They were lit now from the east, sun streaming up Glen Sannox where the red deer grazed. There were trees down there, beeches, she remembered, though she could not see. The slopes were thick with bracken, turning to woodland where the burn flowed out.

Then Arran was gone and the low line of the Ayrshire coast stretched ahead, a haze of pollution settled grimly along its length. Helen leaned back in her seat. It was strange to be in a plane still. Planes belonged to foreign places, not to the islands. The world had settled back into its own shape and still her feet were not upon the ground.

The stewardess spoke over the intercom, giving directions for landing. Helen groped for her seat belt.

It was the sixth day, and I found her.

The universe is all one for a creature that floats in the dark, knowing nothing. If the boundaries are inconceivable, centimetres or light years are all the same. Freedom is blankness. I could not see beyond it, because there was nothing to see.

No longer alone, no longer floating free. The thread had become a vice, holding me, sustaining me. I was embedded in softness, and I surrendered. Not only matter, but dependent. Yet without surroundings, I had been nothing. Identity is a small price to pay for life, perhaps. Anyway, I paid it, unknowing.

And so I proceed, into the radiance and the pain. This part takes place in a city. Here, Helen was no longer a visitor: she belonged. She was made here, and eventually born here. The idea of belonging became real to her, in a manner it had never done before, when she walked across the town on a September Sunday, shortly after her return. Absence makes familiarity seem all the stranger, for never having been noticed before. Also, she was perhaps more sensitive than usual, for, although still unaware of my presence, I cannot have failed to influence her.

She was climbing up towards the castle, having wandered into the gardens and crossed the railway bridge. Here, she had waited idly while two trains passed. As a child, this had been the highlight of the morning's walk, to stand, hands clutching cold iron, staring down into the cutting, hearing the rumble and clatter underground, then watching the train burst out from the tunnel into the sunshine. Engines with great names, thundering beneath and enveloping her in a cloud of dirty steam, while she peered down through the criss-crossed metal bars. Now, she could look right over the top of the parapet and there were no steam trains, only the smell of exhaust fumes and plastic litter on the verges. Helen left the railway, and began to climb up patiently.

It was so unlike that other climb, down into the Canyon. The sun shone so thinly here, but more bright and piercing,

247

and the cold came with it, a touch of future frost. No haze over red cliffs, but a sharp blue distance. Nearly at the top, she turned round to look, and there beyond the city was the sea, blue beyond grey, and the hills of Fife green and distant, like another country. Down below, Princes Street was almost empty, shops barred against Saturday night, caught out in the indifferent light of morning. Helen stepped back and broken glass crackled under her feet. She glanced down, and saw half a green bottle, a smatter of glass, and a red stain on the muddy gravel. She drew back her foot, but there was blood on her shoe. She wiped it on the wet grass. The mud made everywhere sticky, for the green cover was sparse, and it had rained in the night. Trickles of eroding soil had made small deltas on the path, a few feet from the broken glass and blood. An empty cardboard cup lay in a drift of wet leaves and, beyond, the spires and streets of a glorious city fell away to the glistening shore. Helen turned away suddenly, and scrambled up to the gate as fast as she could.

The gate into the castle esplanade was locked and through it two young sentries stared at her, guns slung over their shoulders, while she peered through the bars. She could have climbed over quite easily but, being observed, she slipped away, and half slid down the sodden grass, avoiding the path. When she reached the level below, she slumped down on an empty bench, as if all motivation had left her at the locked gate.

The pain was terrible. I hardly know how to describe it. I was aware of it where I lay embedded. It was concentrated above me, a heavy load under her ribs, where there should have been movement, and softness. With the locked gate, it had consolidated itself again, resettling itself in her stomach, refusing to budge. There had been moments through the last two weeks when it had lifted and almost gone. It was like mist lying in a valley, and I, caught under it with nowhere to go, lay watching and enduring. I watched so closely it was hard to know any more what was real. There seemed to be movement. Sometimes the fog would lift a little, sometimes the heights above were nearly illumined, sometimes I was merely conscious that they were there. With each lifting came a little easement, then the blanket of cold fog dropped again, engulfing us.

She had not thought about it all the time. She was back at work again, and that was a distraction. But the distraction was only like a dream. Helen went through the motions of waking life, but the only thing she truly felt was the pain under her ribs, a dead weight that had to be secret. I am not sure whether she thought it shameful, but she did feel it must be hidden. She had told one or two close friends a little, but to no one had she communicated the pain. They could not have felt it, anyway. Each one has her own burden and, although Helen's fate was for that short period shared, only I knew of that, and I knew nothing of the world and could do nothing. I almost find myself saying I was nothing, but that cannot be true for I remember the feelings, and therefore must have felt it all.

There was no one about. Helen allowed herself to rock to and fro, sitting on the bench, her hands clasped tight over the place where it hurt. She was quite skinny and had not eaten properly for two weeks. She could feel the edge of her rib cage sharply and the hollow underneath where her stomach was swallowed up in this tortuous knot of agony. No, I am not able to say exactly how it felt. No one feels any pain but their own. You do not have to know.

I have let myself love him, thought Helen. He lives on the other side of the world and I shall never see him again.

From the vantage point of that clear sky, poised high over the castle, looking down and seeing so clearly that stubborn lump of volcanic rock that had resisted everything the ice could do, so that now a trail of débris drifted down from it like a tadpole's tail, with a few hundred years of human history piled on top . . . From there, looking at the firth widening into the arms of the sea, and the Ochils, the Lomonds, the Pentlands, the Moorfoot and the Lammer-moors, seeing the marks of great convulsions left upon the scarred and battered earth, the causes of her agony seemed so trivial as to be ridiculous. There is nothing that has not been suffered. Why did she think she deserved anything different? One does not have to cross half a planet to experience love, or pain. So why did she do it? If it had not happened, they would not have made me. And if that were so, who would have looked down on this corner of earth, and seen the only thing that mattered, a woman sitting on a park bench above the railway, just below the Mound, in Princes Street Gardens.

I would much rather not have returned to her but the attachment was strengthening. A red cord of blood now bound me to her and, day and night, it pulsated with the change. I raged against it. I wanted no blood or sustenance. I wanted nothing she had to give, and certainly I did not want her pain. Here in this city where she belonged, I was becoming sensate in a new way. I had as yet no senses of my own, nor thoughts. The first sensation I could truly call physical was Helen's pain. Beyond that lay the vision of where I actually was, untouched. I longed to retain it but slowly it became harder to reach out, and harder still to see. That day I looked down on the city glinting in the sun and saw the bare bones of the land cloaked by a broken pall of human art and misery. That was the last time that I knew anything clearly until the day that I became free.

A week later I had become so accustomed to imprisonment I had forgotten everything but the dark and the damp, soft movements and muffled sounds. My true sense was eluding me, and what makes a human being sentient was not yet developed in me. In a state of dream-like confusion, I was brought up short by the concept of incarnation and found that it appalled me.

She was nervous. There were several women in the waiting-room, each sitting pale and separate, eyes avoiding one another. Helen picked up a magazine and read the letters and the problems page without comprehending either. The solid lump of pain had dissolved unpleasantly into a jittery molten chaos that invaded her body, pumping itself down her arms and legs, making her scarcely able to keep still. Her hands were cold and sweating and I could feel her shivering. Panic in the gut, churning me out of my security like a storm at sea, waves breaking into hidden geos and gullies, routing out such craft as sought a fragile shelter. When waves grow wild and steep, they start breaking further back, so that the hidden rock shows like teeth between the breakers, in a flurry of white water and torn seaweed. Such terror as this can expose everything. I rode my mooring, fastened by a bloody cord to this pain I did not want, and trying to look up and see the stars.

Helen's name was called, and she made her way into the surgery.

"Sit down please. And what can I do for you?"

A woman in a white coat, with gold-rimmed glasses, sitting at her desk with a pen poised over a prescription pad. In front of her, the clock on the wall jerked out the seconds with an electric hand.

"I think I might be pregnant," said Helen baldly, and turned white.

I see the surgery, with a high couch lined with paper, bright lights, a calendar on the wall, all spinning madly round, up and down, like horses on a merry-go-round. Diabolic music, bells and pipes, a sleigh ride through the freezing pine woods. An old man's laughter sinister and dangerous, bringing gifts and terror, forcing his way in by chimneys and keyholes, spinning round and round, a planet spinning, tilting, the snow melts and the ice retreats, and the woman in the white coat is standing over Helen and forcing her head down between her knees.

"All right now? Do you feel faint?"

"I never faint," muttered Helen, but there was no stopping her dizziness. She could smell her own sweat, drenching her, dripping down her neck, prickling the backs of her knees. Cold, stone cold, and the terrible pain under her ribs turning to ice.

251

She never fainted and she did not faint now. The doctor, surrounded by drugs and machinery and notebooks, gave her a glass of cold water to sip, and asked her questions.

"Seven weeks," said Helen. "I know. I was in San Francisco, and it was hot. It started the day I went to see the redwood trees. It was inconvenient, so I remembered."

"The date?"

Helen looked at a note she had written on the back of an envelope, and gave it. "I can tell you when I must have conceived too," she offered. "If I did. Five weeks ago. There's no other time it could have been."

The doctor made another cursory note. "I can examine you. By now I might get some idea. But we'll need to take a sample and do a proper test. Then you can phone in for the result." She glanced appraisingly at Helen. "If it's positive, you'll need to make another appointment."

There was no indication at all as to what that appointment might signify. Helen was trying too hard to hold herself together to let the words have any effect. To me, it was all immaterial. The question of incarnation, if it had ever presented itself to me, was meaningless. I suppose I still resented my imprisonment, but that too was becoming a vague memory. To become rational, one must first become sentient, and to be sentient, one must first take on matter. I never accepted that. Matter was engulfing me, swallowing me up, dragging me out of the world and into the dream, but I had not grasped it yet. Whether becoming is a moment or a process, I have no idea, but to know oneself is not the work of a moment. If I had known of the comparison, I suppose I would have felt that I was dying, but no human being knows that, so I can hardly say.

Helen did not need the result of the test to tell her the truth. I try to think now how she did find out, but during that week so much eluded me. I was growing so fast. My own heart beat so much faster than hers, by which all time had been regulated from the moment that time began. Heart, lungs, limbs, senses, and the mind that makes sense of them all. There were times then when I seemed to be nothing but a blob of matter, a catalyst of growth, cells dividing and dividing again, detonating into silent life. The flesh had hold of me then, but its grasp was uncertain and the essence slippery. There were chinks still in the bars of the cage. Before that doctor came poking in at me, rough fingers feeling, discerning signs, external physical signs that something new existed; until then there was no evidence. I had made no mark in the physical world. There was no need to believe that I was caught up in it.

But Helen had thought it out already. Perhaps I slept at the time. I imagine her now – but it is imagination, not memory – sitting at her desk, looking out into the neon-lit evening, frowning and chewing the end of a pen. She writes numbers and dates on the back of an envelope, consults her diary, subtracts days from days, dividing experience into a biological time scheme that is beginning to betray her. I don't know what warned her. She was not one to calculate the days of her cycle precisely. She knew where she was by how she felt and that served her well enough. Very often she had no idea of the date anyway. The days of the weeks mattered, because of work, and weekends were a different colour from ordinary days. Her trip abroad was now in another world and incalculable. It was strange to her to incorporate it all into a scheme as exact as the phases of the moon and the changing of the tides. On the whole she accepted that such movements might affect her subliminally, but she didn't try to think too hard about them. Life is livable without being reduced to pure mathematics, which is where any genuine attempts to arrive at the truth seem, so often, to take a person. Helen had no time for that. The sums she had to do were hard enough and she didn't even possess a calendar.

No, it would not have been the date that alerted her but the state of her own body, although she was not particularly sensitive to that. Being alone, she thought very little about her physical self. Since she had spent too much money on her trip, she was now trying to economise by not turning the heating on for as long as possible. This made her even less familiar with her changing body, as getting dressed and undressed had to be done hastily, and in some discomfort. She had grown used to warmer weather. To think of herself sexually was too agonising, because of James. She neither looked at herself nor touched herself. She felt nauseous but then she had not eaten properly for weeks. Her stomach was tied up with pain, and to this she attributed its sudden unreliability. Her breasts felt sore and heavy, but only occasionally, and she soon forgot.

It was nothing particular that made her realise, just a slow combination of circumstances. It was seven weeks since she had left San Francisco and she felt sick. These two facts converged in her mind one evening while she sat at her desk and contemplated the frost-tinged geraniums in her window box, their leaves mud-brown in the light of the street lamps. So she painstakingly made her calculations and went to the doctor after work next day.

It was not until she sat in the surgery that she stopped being numb and realised what was going on. Probably the numbness cushioned me, so that I drifted on, still mostly in that world which was turning from actuality to memory. But when she knew, I had to know too. I shared her consternation, but the cause was different. I did not want to fall. I had stood on the shores of that river, watching the souls being sucked down, but never a drop had touched me. Now I too was under the water and in my mind I struggled like a drowning child. Never a flicker of movement, only growing, and the silent chaining of my mind. That pain she felt, thinking about James – he hardly deserved it. Perhaps it was only the echo of what I was feeling now.

When the result came through, it said nothing that was new to her. Helen put the phone down and sat on the floor, and pressed her hands to her eyes. She wasn't crying. There was nothing to cry about, for around her there was only the void of having no idea what to do. It was like reaching the end of a road and finding there was nowhere to go, and no turning back. There was just nowhere to be next. Nothing.

She must have sat like that for twenty minutes. Then she realised she was cold and switched on the electric fire, both bars at once. She did not know what to do after that. It was almost worse than the pain. Existing is nothing but a liability, when you have no idea at all what to do next.

Helen tried to think. She could get up. Make a cup of tea. She was cold, and shaky. She could make a hot water bottle and go to bed. Then she would have to lie, and exist. No good. She could go out. Take a walk. Go to the park. She was cold. She might faint. It was no good. A cup of tea. It would not hurt to put the kettle on. She imagined herself doing that. Stand up. Go to the kitchen. Turn on the tap. Fill the kettle. And then . . . what? Was she thirsty? Helen shivered. She did not know if she was thirsty. She could lie down. On the sofa, or in her bed. There was no need to lie down. She was not ill. No need for anything. Only for time to pass. But that was too slow. Nothing would happen. If only she were not alone.

Then there were tears, pouring down her cheeks very steadily, splashing down. More tears than she would have thought possible, her face and hands soaked with them. The lump of pain shaken by them, churned about but not dissolving, or only a little at the very edges. She could cry or not cry. She did not know what to do, so it hardly mattered. It would be better to sleep, but impossible.

An idea. She seized it, never thought about it. Anything was welcome, and it was something. The telephone again. Realising she didn't know what to dial. Phone Directory Enquiries. Asking. How do I get through to the United States? Yes, I have a number. An internal number. What do I dial first? Write it down. The back of an envelope again. Yes, yes, I have it. Dial the number. I know the rest.

The phone ringing. On the other side of the world. Ringing, in an empty room perhaps, perhaps not. Her hand clasping the phone, so hard it hurt, gripped to her ear, pressed against her head. Ringing on and on. Stopping. A silence. A voice.

"Hello?" said James, sleepily, in Colorado.

Helen slammed the phone down, rolled face down on the floor and sobbed hysterically.

She had a short time to make a decision. Meanwhile I was growing, wanted or unwanted. As I was, I could not grasp the question. It seemed irrelevant, frivolous. I was not sure what she was asking. One day we took the bus out to Cramond, with her friend. They sat in front, on the top, and talked in low voices. Wanted, or unwanted? People got on at every stop and others got off. Does it matter which stop, or how long you stay? Whatever the length of your journey you have to pay for it. I was not interested in that, being engulfed by the experience itself.

At Cramond there is an island, and a causeway which can be crossed at low tide. Helen and her friend walked down from the bus stop to find the way over just uncovered. They didn't stop, but scrambled down the beach over the tideline and began to make their way over in single file, stepping from boulder to boulder, while the tide rolled away from them on either side, and slowly the bare mud emerged into the pale sunshine. It had rained recently, and might rain again. Patches of cloud chased one another down the Forth, coming in from the west, over the bridges, then drifting on towards the open sea. There was a shower just as we reached the island and we sheltered in one of the ruined cottages, surrounded by dripping trees and sodden bramble. Someone had lit a fire here. The ashes were black and sticky with rain. Charred ends of wood were scattered over the grass.

When the cloud passed, Helen and her companion began to circumnavigate the island slowly. Presently they reached a green knoll, commanding a view out into the estuary, and tacitly they sat down on the turf, just above a Second World War gun emplacement. Helen sat on her anorak to keep the wet from coming through and frowned at a couple of shags that were flying low over the sea, black wings beating.

"So you haven't really decided after all?"

"No. I know what I ought to do. Of course I do. I can't do anything else. I'm not going to be a single parent. I've got my life. I don't want to change it. Well, I told you all that."

"So what's different?"

There was a pause. The two birds disappeared from sight in a shifting pattern of ripples. "Fantasies," said Helen abruptly, without looking round.

"You mean you want his baby?"

"James? He doesn't want a baby. I wouldn't even tell him."

"That's not what I asked."

"No."

Another dark cloud came down before the wind, and the air turned damp and drear. There was a hint of drizzle, but no rain fell.

"I won't ask you anything if you don't want. I thought it might help."

"OK," said Helen. "Yes, I want it. I imagine it. This year, next year, sometime, never. All that rubbish. Dark or fair. Boy or girl. My child. It stinks, doesn't it?"

"No."

"I start to think about who it is. Sometimes I talk to it."

That was true. I don't know that her words made any sense to me, or on what frequency I received them. Intuition seemed to be draining away from me so fast and in its place came a kind of meshing together, my whole being with hers, as if the two of us were becoming so close we were almost the same. She talked to me about simple things, like what we should eat, whether we should have a bath, go for a walk, phone a friend. Nothing to do with me, any of that. There were moments when I didn't want to know about her. I didn't want all this interference. I was just myself before that. As I resented her, so she resented me. Sometimes all this closeness made me sick.

"I've heard about women doing that. I suppose it's natural."

Helen made a disgusted noise in her throat. In a way I agreed with her. We had been in the British Home Stores the day before, and she had caught herself dreamily examining little socks, striped, and plain-coloured, the foot hardly the length of her thumb. Socks? I didn't even have toes yet. She had been horrified at herself and in terror I retreated to the innermost depths of my being. But I couldn't get out any more. When I tell you about the Forth, and the bridges, it is not because I saw them, not that day. I was confined, blinded and silenced by an alien flesh. It sickens me to think of it now.

"So when's your appointment?"

"The day after tomorrow."

"But you might not go?"

Helen didn't reply for almost a minute. Her friend watched her anxiously, but Helen never met her eyes. She was looking out to sea in the wake of the departed birds. "I might go," she said at last. "I might check in, and undress, and get into bed. They might take my temperature. I might let them give me that injection, whatever they give you first. I might lie there until it was time to get wheeled away. And then I might get up and dress and run outside and escape and never go back. How do I know what I'll do? I don't know."

"If you do that, you'll still be pregnant, won't you?"

"Jesus. I never really believed in it. I never really believed my body would do it. Not really. I just didn't believe it."

"Didn't ever want it?"

"Oh God yes, I want it. Except that I don't. What would you do, if you were me?"

"Get an abortion. It's not for ever."

"What? Oh, I see what you mean. But as far as this one's concerned, it's for ever."

"But it's not as though you knew it yet."

"It? Him? Her? I don't know what I know."

Wanted, or unwanted. I'm glad she had a friend to talk to. I ceased to follow their conversation properly. It concerned me, I suppose, but then I could hardly conceive of anything in this universe that did not. I had not arrived anywhere, so any talk of my departure hardly made sense to me. Besides, I had new problems of my own. I was not comfortable. It was not pain like Helen's, which I knew all too well. Merely a kind of chill, a separation, a thinness in the blood, which suggested that materially all was not as it should be. I looked down on this phenomenon from far off, but from where I cannot tell, for the old vision was going. The earth was shrouded in a grey mist that had nothing to do with the day. Perhaps it was not mist, but water. In the end, perhaps, we are all drowned. Drowned, or dying, there is a cold that strikes one, but muted, like drifting into sleep. I do not care.

They sat there for a long time, until they grew chilly. Then they walked on briskly. As they rounded the island, they saw the tide far out, still not turning, and the sun dropping behind the hills to the west, the sky suddenly red and gold. Helen broke into a run, her friend following. She was tough and a fast runner. She ran right round the rest of the island, in and out, following the indentations of the black-rimmed coast, up and down over mounds, round clumps of shrubs and concrete gun turrets, then back down to the stepping stones. She did not stop there, but ran, jumping from one to another, gasping for breath but not stopping, her friend trying to catch up with her, until just before she reached the further shore she was forced to halt. She stood bent over, hands at the stitch in her side, red-cheeked and dripping with sweat, the haunted look almost gone.

They stopped in the village and ate a large tea of scones and cakes in a café. It was the most Helen had eaten all at once since she got home and she, who never ate anything unhealthy, gorged on China tea and chocolate cake, while she watched the sun set over the flooding tide. I think she must have decided what to do, for her mind felt more settled. I don't know. In a few hours the tide would ebb again and my blood was growing thin.

That night Helen slept heavily. She dreamed, at least, I think the dream was hers. To me, it was a way out. In the dream I saw the stars, big and clear, emblazoned over a red desert. I heard the rushing of the river, black between shadowy banks, full and silent. Around me in the darkness was red rock, sand beaten into rock, rock worn down by water, strange petrified shapes, canyons going thousands of years down into the red earth. In the heart of the desert I saw a sea, grey and icy, with black clouds blowing over it. The clouds parted. The stars were cold and far away, and beneath them was a city, clinging to the stubborn rock that ice could never wear away, a road winding down the dragon's tail towards a palace, the whole hill drenched in blood and history. The sky was cold and clear as death. I saw the earth turning, one side and then the other coming face to face with me.

Helen stirred in her sleep and moaned a little. It was pain again that was bringing her awake. Physical pain this time, not a knot under her heart, but engulfing pain like waves, forcing a way into consciousness. I heard her groan, and turn over.

She was awake then and switching on the light. Hands down between her legs, then held up to the light. Blood.

I am back in the river, dragged down, water over my head, pulled down into what they say is life, drowning, drowning.

She is out of bed, in the bathroom now, crouched down, trying to stop the blood, which does not stop.

I am choked by the darkness, falling, fainting. The cord of blood is breaking and, for a moment of panic, I try to cling on to her, as if I really wished to die.

I realise that although she had decided, she had never been sure. Wanted. What else can anyone do but look two ways at once? Perhaps every decision means a lifetime of regret, if only we knew but mercifully we forget. She was crying, for loss and relief all at once and, at the same time, doing what needed to be done. It never crossed her mind to ask for help. It was the middle of the night and she was used to looking after herself. She never thought she might be in danger. There was probably none. I know that she was thinking about me.

The cord breaks and I am alone again. The river takes me. Washed on a river of blood, going down, torn away, the gates broken and the flood let loose. I am going down and the dark is receding.

Helen is still squatting on the bathroom floor, tears still flowing. She ignores them. There is something in the hollow of her hand. She will treat it with reverence, I think, but I cannot stay to see.

The world is opening up behind me, and at last I turn. Rushing towards me, I feel the desert stars.